Written by Cricket Erling in *Wee Me*,
Jeremy Erling's baby memory book:

<u>Saturday, April 5</u>

Jeremy doesn't have a daddy. His father left us
before Jeremy was born. But today Jeremy said
"Dada" for the first time. To Tim Vogel. Tim lives
upstairs in the big old house we share.

Jeremy was having his picture taken, and he didn't
like the photographer. The photographer asked
Tim to make that funny face he likes to make, and
it made Jeremy laugh. I laughed, too. After Jeremy
called Tim "Dada," the photographer thought that
the three of us were a family.

Tim didn't seem to mind. When I apologized for
not setting the photographer straight, Tim said,
"It's only natural that people should mistake us
for a family group. Heck, sometimes *I* mistake us
for a family."

Now, what did he mean by that?

Please address questions and book requests to: Harlequin Reader Service
U.S.: 3010 Walden Ave., P.O. Box 1325, Buffalo, NY 14269
CAN.: P.O. Box 609, Fort Erie, Ont. L2A 5X3

Born in the USA
WISCONSIN

PAMELA BROWNING

Fly Away

Harlequin Books

TORONTO • NEW YORK • LONDON
AMSTERDAM • PARIS • SYDNEY • HAMBURG
STOCKHOLM • ATHENS • TOKYO • MILAN
MADRID • WARSAW • BUDAPEST • AUCKLAND

HARLEQUIN BOOKS
225 Duncan Mill Road, Don Mills,
Ontario, Canada M3B 3K9

ISBN 0-373-47199-8

FLY AWAY

Copyright © 1988 by Pamela Browning

Dear Reader,

Manitou, Wisconsin, is a fictionalized version of the town where my great-grandfather Jaeger opened a bakery after immigrating to the United States. My grandfather and my mother were born there. I still remember visiting that oh-so-fragrant bakery when I was a child and being allowed to choose anything I wanted from the assortment of pastries so beautifully arranged in that big display case.

I suppose it's only natural that when my hero, Tim Vogel, needed comfort, he flew away to Manitou. And when he met Cricket and her baby, Jeremy, of course he wanted to stay. But would he?

When I started writing this book, which was originally published as the second book of the Heartland Trilogy, even I didn't know the answer. Now I do. And so will you after you read Tim and Cricket's love story.

Enjoy!

Love,

Pamela Browning

I wish I were a little swallow,
Or a lonesome turtledove,
I'd fly away from grief and sorrow
And light upon some land of love.

—American folk song

A Bitter Harvest

"At first, when we were told of these treeless lands, I imagined that it was a country ravaged by fire, where the soil was
so poor that it could produce nothing. But we have certainly
observed the contrary; and no better soil can be found, either
for corn, or for vines, or for any fruit whatever."

Louis Jolliet
American Explorer, 1645-1700

The vast American Heartland, settled by hardy pioneer men
and women, responded to their hard work and ingenuity by pro-
ducing a wealth of food, not only for Americans, but for the
world. By one estimate, the produce of two out of every five acres
of farmland in the United States is sold abroad.

But now our farmers no longer can count on selling their
bounty in other countries. The poorest countries cannot afford to
import food. Other countries, former customers, have increased
their own food production so that they are self-sufficient.

Government policy has helped to price our exports out of the
remaining market. Farm subsidies and authorized annual increases
in crop loans encourage farmers to grow bigger crops than our
home markets can absorb.

If the government knocked out price supports, farmers would
then be forced to grow no more than could be sold. This, however,
would result in foreclosures and bankruptcies unlike our country
has ever seen. And there have already been enough of those.

Cruelly caught in the middle of this ongoing dilemma, rural
Americans who work the land struggle to understand what is hap-

pening to them. They see a way of life disappearing—and they mourn that way of life. Many of them have already lost the land that their families have farmed for generations.

The loss of the land is painful, especially when a man's hopes and dreams have been nurtured by its promise. Whole families find themselves torn apart during bankruptcy proceedings. They want to blame someone—anyone—for the tragedy, and sometimes they end up blaming one another.

After the bitterest of harvests, winter comes. The winter can be cold and bleak while it lasts. But then, in the never-ending cycle of renewal, comes spring.

Spring, wafting in on a warm wind of hope....

Chapter One

Tim Vogel stared at the television screen in his shabby rented room and ignored the persistent buzz of a fly that kept dive-bombing the televised image of ABC newsman Peter Jennings. Tim couldn't keep his eyes away from the screen. He simply couldn't make himself get up from his chair, walk to the television set and turn it off.

He was watching a news special about the current farm crisis, and Tim knew all about the farm crisis. Too much, really. He and a couple million other viewers on this night were about to see his family's farm in Curtisville, Kansas, being sold at auction.

Of course, the deed had already been done. The Vogel farm, their family home for generations, had fallen to the auctioneer's gavel five months ago. Tim hadn't been there. Couldn't have stayed to watch the sickening reality of it for the life of him, which is why he had left Curtisville with no explanation last August. He'd simply left in the middle of the night like his older sister Norrie had, years ago before he was born. Well, at least he had written a few days later to let his parents know he was all right. At least he had done that, which was more than Norrie had done.

Tim batted the fly away from his face and concentrated on Peter Jennings. The reporter wore a Levi's jacket and somehow managed to look suave and urbane in spite of it. He stood in front of Curtisville's own prairie cathedral, one of the gleaming white grain elevators rising at the edge of every podunk of a town on the Kansas prairie.

And then the image on the screen changed, and Tim saw them.

The impact of seeing his mother, Mina, and his father, Frank, bigger than life on this flyspecked TV screen in Belle Glade, Florida, hit him so hard that he uttered a soft indeterminate syllable and fell back against the sticky plastic upholstery of the armchair.

Frank was grim and tight-lipped. Mina, wearing a scarf over her graying hair, appeared calm and accepting, although tears trickled forlornly down her lined face. The sweetness of her expression was what really got to him.

How could she be so calm? Tim wanted to bash in the television screen, wanted to silence the loudmouthed auctioneer's strident, unintelligible singsong, wanted to beg his father who had always been able to fix anything, "Do something, Pa, can't you *do* something?"

But there was nothing to be done. The farm had been sold.

Instead of living in the comfortable farmhouse where Tim remembered so many good times, Mina and Frank subsisted now in a small, used mobile home on the outskirts of Curtisville. Mina wrote that their new home was comfortable and insisted that she actually liked not having to clean a big old house anymore. Reading between the lines, Tim knew that Mina was characteristically trying to make the best of a bad situation. She was doing her best to cope with what life demanded of her.

Embarrassed for all of them, Tim had answered none of his mother's letters, and his mother had been the only one who wrote. If he didn't write to her, if he never actually penned their new address on paper, he wouldn't have to think about his parents' reduced circumstances. Tim could no more imagine his mother and father living in a two-bedroom trailer than he could accept the fact that his home was now this rented room. Tim was in search of a new life for himself. He would have it, though he wasn't sure how. He knew only that there had to be something better somewhere. At the age of twenty-eight he was still trying to figure out what it was.

The camera panned the Vogel farm as it looked on the day of the auction. Just thinking about all they had lost, Tim felt a lump growing in his throat. The commodious farmhouse, big and built of limestone, with green shingles peeling off the roof because there had been no money to repair it. The surrounding windbreak of leafless trees, their branches whipping back and forth in a fierce prairie wind. The barn, the newest tractor sitting idle inside. The land, stretching out acre after acre. The land. Vogel land.

After all these months, seeing the old home place on the TV screen only made him feel worse because he knew it was gone. The pain of his family's humiliation and loss pressed down on Tim. He was drowning in sorrow.

The camera lingered too long on Mina's face. Helplessly Tim watched his mother's brave smile crumple before she hid her face in the sleeve of his father's windbreaker. Then the camera mercilessly sought his brothers, Bernie and Leonard. Stunned, Tim watched as tears welled up in Leonard's eyes. He couldn't ever remember seeing his brother cry before, not even the time he cut his hand in a nasty combine accident when he was in his teens.

Tim closed his eyes. A harsh metallic taste cleaved his tongue to the roof of his mouth. He should have been there. He shouldn't have run away and made his family face this awful ordeal without him. There was strength in numbers.

But, no, as always in the face of an emotion he couldn't handle, Tim had run away. Flown away, actually, in a King Air propjet with a stranger, a pilot who'd stopped at the tiny Curtisville airport to refuel. Tim had hitched airplane rides all the way to Florida with pilots flying alone and eager for company and a copilot. Tim, after all, was a pilot himself. And so here he was, far away from home, while his family in Curtisville painfully picked up the pieces of their broken lives.

Back to Peter Jennings again. Jennings explained what had caused the Vogels and people like them to lose their farms. High interest payments, he said. Overproduction. Falling crop prices. Inefficient management.

Tim's father's face filled the television screen, pathetic in its woe. "I never dreamed," Frank Vogel said, his voice cracking, "that it could happen to us." And then, after swinging his big head from side to side in puzzled dismay, he stared blankly into the eye of the camera, a very private man baring his soul for the world to see. The camera was relentless. It didn't blink. It was Frank Vogel who turned away first, and his eyes shone damp with tears.

Tim's fist crashed down hard on the arm of the chair, splitting the plastic the way he would have liked to split somebody's head. If he had been at the auction, *he* wouldn't have quietly slunk off the family farm, his tail tucked meekly between his legs. *He*, Tim, would have told Peter Jennings and the camera, and indeed the whole rotten world, what he thought of it. He wouldn't have left the land until he had screamed out what a dirty deal the farmer was getting from the government and from the banks and from anyone else he could think of to blame. And he wouldn't have said it nicely, either. They'd have had to bleep out every other word.

Tim lurched heavily out of the chair and slammed the power button on the TV so hard that it fell off. Then he scooped up a flyswatter and went to kill that fly. He finished off the fly in one murderous blow and steamed around the room a couple of times, trying to figure out what to do next. In his present mental condition, if he stayed in this cheap little room, he'd go bananas for sure. Tim's clenched fist was itching to drive a hole in the wall, an action which, after last week's party, certainly wouldn't help his relationship with the landlord.

He stormed outside into a night calm with the fresh scent of green, growing things. He'd been staying in Belle Glade for the past six weeks. The crops lay lush in the fields now, in January, while Kansas fields slumbered through the long prairie winter. The crops were the reason that Tim Vogel was in Belle Glade. The farmers needed him to spray the crops. Tim was an aerial applicator, which was the professional name crop dusters gave themselves these days.

That was in the daytime. The nights were his to do what he wanted. And on this night he wanted to find a bar. He wanted to drink himself into oblivion. Maybe he'd find a woman, too.

He rocketed off down U.S. 441 toward West Palm Beach. His headlights careened off the chrome of oncoming cars, as he negotiated the two-lane highway known as a killer. He didn't care how fast he took the curves with their deadly dark canals on either side. He didn't care about anything.

A small voice inside him told him that his present wayward route wasn't the way to happiness. He'd held one job after another since he'd left Curtisville, working his way south as a crop-dusting "gypsy." A drifter, that's what he was, with no clear idea of where he wanted to be or what he wanted to do. He knew he should settle down somewhere, but in his present state of mind that was impossible. He felt rootless, friendless and alone.

He'd been raised with good old-fashioned values. What had happened to them, anyway? *Gone,* he told himself. *Everything's gone. The farm, my family and even the guy I was.* If indeed he had ever been the person he thought he was. Would he ever be that person again?

Tim zoomed full speed ahead past the neon-bright honky-tonks on the way into town. He headed for a glitzy watering hole where he knew he could count on pretty women, ready booze and a rock beat to numb his senses in case the women and the booze didn't.

Tim was in the process of demolishing his double Scotch at the Trifles Lounge of the Canfield Hotel when he caught the eye of a blonde with great legs and golden earrings so long that they swung against her shoulders. Fascinated, he let his gaze linger. He hardly blinked when she stood up from the table where she sat with two female friends and sidled onto the bar stool next to his.

"Hi, stranger," she said. She wore a strapless dress in a vibrant shade of pink.

"Hi," he said.

"I've missed you."

Intrigued and distracted, he said, "You have?" He didn't know what game she was playing, but he might as well play along.

"I thought I'd see you at the beach again, but—" She lifted one bare, tanned shoulder and let it fall.

"Well, you know how it goes," he replied noncommittally.

"Usually it doesn't go so quickly, if you know what I mean. After you came to my place that night, I thought you'd at least call."

"Why'd you think that?"

"Oh, *you* know," she said, her green eyes sparkling, and then she leaned toward him, cupped her hand around his ear so that there would be no mistake about what she was saying and whispered an extremely intimate suggestion.

The Scotch was beginning to get to him, and he reeled back.

"Well, don't you think that's a good idea?" she said archly. Her hair bounced around her shoulders.

"Since I don't even know your name, it probably isn't," he said. He motioned for another drink and treated himself to a long swallow of it. When he looked up from concentrating on setting his glass down precisely in the middle of the damp circle on the bar, the blonde was pouting.

"Mark Sherrod, if I didn't know you better, I'd think you'd lost your mind. On the last occasion when we were together, you whispered my name over and over and said it was the most beautiful name you'd ever heard. 'A real jewel of a name for a jewel of a woman,' that's exactly what you said."

"Pearl?" Tim said hopefully. "Ruby?"

"Ruby!" Spots of color spread across both cheeks, and she started to stalk away indignantly. Tim caught her by the wrist.

"Hey," he said, surprised at the way his own voice buzzed in his ears. "Don't run out on me! What *is* your name, anyway?"

She stopped and looked deep into his eyes. She was only a few inches away, and he could hear her breathing. She studied him with growing awareness, then took a small deliberate step away from him. He released her wrist.

"You really don't know, do you?" she said with an air of total bewilderment.

"No," he said slowly. "I really don't. I've never seen you before in my life."

"My name is Amethyst Marlowe, and you're supposed to be Mark Sherrod. But—but I can see that I've made a mistake." She regarded him in wide-eyed amazement.

"Maybe not so much of a mistake," Tim said, feeling expansive.

"You're not Mark, are you?" she asked, narrowing her eyes.

"No. People have called me a lot of names in my day, but never Mark. Tim Vogel's my name. From Curtisville, Kansas." He held out his hand in exaggerated friendliness. She ignored his hand and frowned.

"Well, Tim, you could pass for Mark Sherrod any day. You sure had me fooled. Sorry, but I think I'll go back to my friends."

"Say, uh, Amethyst, don't do that. Have a drink with me instead."

"I don't think you need another drink," she said pointedly, looking at his almost-empty glass.

"No drink, then. Just talk to me. We could sit at that table over there." He gestured with his head.

"You certainly do look like Mark Sherrod," she said. "I just can't get over it. You could be identical twins."

He vaguely remembered somebody saying something similar several years ago when he was still in the air force. Maybe he just had an ordinary face.

"Tell me about it," he said, smoothly leading her over to the secluded corner table. To his surprise, she followed without objecting.

The music wasn't so loud here, and she began to tell him how she had met his look-alike, this Mark, at the beach one day. "He had the same wavy dark blond hair, the same electric blue eyes. He even had the same way of quirking one side of his mouth up when he smiled," she said, studying him intently. "Only somehow I think it was the right side of his mouth. Yours quirks up on the left."

Tim encouraged her to talk, not because he wanted to know about her former boyfriend, but because he needed someone to sit across from him and carry on a conversation. Maybe that would dull the pain.

Before he knew it, Tim was telling her about his family's problems. He poured out the story of the bankruptcy proceedings and the subsequent loss of the farm. She'd seen the Peter Jennings ABC special before she'd left home that night, and the plight of the American farmer had made a deep impression on her.

Amethyst listened sympathetically, which was exactly what Tim needed. He told her how guilty he felt that he had run out on his whole family when they needed all the emotional support they could get. He felt like a traitor to all he held dear. When Amethyst smiled and reassured him, he felt a warm glow of gratitude toward her, but the feeling refused to blossom into anything more.

Later they danced beneath the tinsel above the tiny dance floor. For a moment while they were dancing, Tim desperately wanted to want her, but as much as he wished to, he felt no stirring of desire. He hadn't wanted to be close to a woman since he'd left Curtisville. He was normal and healthy. He simply didn't need the emptiness of a dead-end relationship right now.

Amethyst must have recognized the lack of chemistry between them, too.

"I've got to go to work tomorrow," she said with a wide yawn when it was only eleven-thirty.

Acting on an impulse, Tim walked her to the parking lot. He

sensed a forlorn sadness in her goodbye and in the way she studied his features, as though bidding him farewell for the last time. He had the sense to know that it wasn't Tim Vogel she was thinking of, but the other guy.

"I hope you find this Mark Sherrod," he said, meaning it. "Especially if he's important to you."

She shrugged and laughed. "He's the kind of fellow who comes along once in a lifetime," she said quietly. "I don't know where he's gone, but he won't be back."

"I'm sorry," Tim said.

"So am I. I hope everything will be all right with you, Tim. And with your family." Her eyes, illuminated in the yellow light from the street lamp, searched his.

"Come on, Amethyst," her girlfriend called impatiently, and with an apologetic smile and a flick of blond curls, Amethyst slid into the back seat of her friend's Toyota.

Tim decided to call it a night. He didn't feel like bashing anyone now. In fact, he was beginning to feel the seed of a monumental headache growing behind his eyes. He should have known better than to drink two doubles in rapid succession.

He got back into his car and drove to Belle Glade between farm fields green with the promise of the upcoming winter harvest. The night was sultry and humid, and the air smelled of wet, black earth. By the time he reached his room, his headache was worse. He hardly slept all night.

The next day he attempted a too-fast turn of the Cessna Ag-Truck he was flying. He stalled in the turn at the end of a bean field and plowed into an adjoining field of soft Everglades muck. The plane sustained extensive damage to its wings and body, and Tim suffered cuts and bruises and five broken ribs. He was lucky, everyone said, that he hadn't been killed.

What wasn't so lucky was that he lost his prospects for working until he was completely healed. Tim was at loose ends, and he wondered what he should do next. He most certainly couldn't go back to Curtisville and face his family.

On the day he was released from the hospital, he was throwing his few belongings into his old air force duffel bag when a nurse sauntered into his room distributing mail.

"Something for me?" he said, turning over the envelope with its Wisconsin postmark. He couldn't figure out at first who could have sent it. His family didn't know about the accident, and he knew only a few local people.

He grinned when he read the card inside. It was from Haggerty, good old Haggerty, the crusty owner of a charter flight and crop-dusting service in Manitou, Wisconsin. Haggerty had read about his accident in a bulletin of the Aerial Applicators Association, the safety-minded organization of professional crop dusters.

"You've always got a job with me," Haggerty had scribbled beneath his signature.

Caesar Augustus Haggerty had been almost like a father to Tim when Tim had shown up in Wisconsin last June to help him spray the crops. Haggerty and his wife had treated Tim to some wonderful home-cooked meals, and Tim had shown Haggerty's grandson how to make a kite, even going so far as to explain the aerodynamics of it. Haggerty had been so nice to him that Tim had hated to leave Manitou to go back home to Curtisville.

"Haggerty," Tim muttered under his breath. "I'll go see Haggerty."

That day Tim sold his car to pay his bills. A few days later, at the end of January, Tim Vogel air-hitchhiked north to Manitou, Wisconsin, with the leftover cash from the sale of his car in his pocket and the vague hope of healing not only the wounds of his body, but also of finding a safe haven where his soul could mend, too.

Chapter Two

In her first-floor apartment in a big drafty old house in downtown Manitou, Cricket O'Malley Erling was sudsing her infant son's round stomach and singing her own particular off-key version of "Row, Row, Row Your Boat," which was the only song she could think of to accompany a baby's bath time.

Jeremy blew gleeful bubbles, especially at the point when Cricket supplied her own version of the ending. Instead of "Life is but a dream" in the final line, Cricket often sang, "Life goes down the drain." It was a mistake she'd first made when she learned the song at the age of three, but the words seemed even more appropriate now that she was a worldly-wise single mother of twenty-six.

She settled a sweet-smelling Jeremy in his crib, sipped a cup of hot tea while she waited for him to stop babbling to himself and heaved a sigh of relief when he subsided into sleep. Then she pulled her thick psychology textbook out of the bookcase and settled down at the kitchen table for what she hoped would be a long study session for her last final exam before semester break at the local Manitou College.

A knock at the back door scuttled her hopes of that. Cricket saw that her visitor was Trudy Johnson, smiling through the macramé screen Cricket had made for the small, square window in the door.

"I just popped in with a quick question," Trudy said, shaking her blond Dutch bob free of its scarf.

"Good," Cricket said. She was happy to see Trudy, in spite

of all the studying she had to do for her exam on Monday. ''Hey, aren't you supposed to be at work?''

''Yes, but I hurried home to let my brother in the house. I didn't expect him to get here until tonight, but you know Talbot. He found somebody to take over his afternoon classes at the university, got an early start from the campus in La Crosse and guess what.''

''He won a million dollars in a lottery, and he wants to share it with us.''

''No, you nut. Talbot brought one of his fellow assistant professors from the University of Wisconsin with him, and the three of us are planning to go out tonight. Talbot's looking for a date for himself. I suggested you, and Talbot said, 'I thought she was married,' and I said, 'She isn't married anymore,' and Talbot said, 'Great! I always did like redheads. Fix it up, will you?' and that's why I'm here. Come with us, Cricket. We're going to Eau Claire for dinner and maybe some dancing.''

''You're *positive* that Talbot didn't win a million dollars in a lottery?'' Cricket said, stalling for time. She liked Talbot, sure, but she didn't think she could handle a date with him. Or with anyone, for that matter.

''No, although on his salary he'd probably like to. Oh, come on, Cricket. It's about time you had a little fun. It's been a year and a half since Old Stoneface left.''

''My ex-husband's name is Hugh, Trudy.'' She said it even though she knew Trudy would never call him that. Trudy had coined unflattering nicknames for all of her own ex-boyfriends, and she refused to refer to them by their proper names when the affairs were over. Cricket could hardly expect Hugh to be exempt.

''Hugh Erling will always be Old Stoneface to me. What'll I tell Talbot?''

''Tell him that I'm flattered, tell him to come over and see the baby and tell him that I'm still adjusting to motherhood and I'm not ready to date anyone yet.''

''Cricket, that kid is eight months old already! How long does it take to adjust to motherhood, anyhow?''

''When you don't have a husband, and when you're taking almost a full load of college courses and slapping together sandwiches every night until thirteen or fourteen o'clock and delivering them at dawn, it takes a long, long time to adjust to motherhood.''

"Well, just don't make a lifetime occupation of it. There are a lot of other things in the world to see and do, and I don't want you to forget it.''

Cricket sighed. "I won't forget it. I just want to bypass it for the time being. Thanks anyhow, Trudy. It was nice of you to ask.''

"Who am I going to get for Talbot? I can't leave him home alone. And you should see his friend. His name is Walt, and he's got the saddest brown eyes I ever saw. He thinks I have gorgeous skin and the electricity is there, believe me!''

"Call Mary Sue for Talbot. She's always liked him. And watch out for the electrical sparks from Walt. You might get burned again.''

"Don't even talk about it! I have high hopes. Would my loving brother bring some geek to spend the whole semester break with his sister? Sorry you won't be with us, Cricket. I'll see you later!'' With a flurry of scarf and a swirl of skirt, Trudy was gone.

Cricket pensively refilled her teacup as she watched Trudy march across the backyard to her own apartment in the house behind the hedge dividing the two properties. Trudy was part of a fast-paced singles life that Cricket couldn't even begin to imagine these days. At the age of thirty-five, Trudy was the veteran of several ill-fated romances, but her conversation sparkled with the eternal hope of an attractive woman who had never married but who fervently wished that she eventually would.

The next guy Trudy met was always going to be the one, the dream man, the prince who was going to rescue her from loneliness, depression and anxiety about the future. Only something always happened. Either the man didn't want to commit himself to a serious relationship, or he ran around with other women while ardently declaring his love for Trudy, or he wanted to borrow money from Trudy's meager supply, or his kids from his former marriage hated her with a passion.

Well, maybe it would be different with Walt. Cricket hoped so for Trudy's sake.

Outside, a light drizzle began to fall. Cricket managed an hour and a half of study before Jeremy awoke. She heard him cooing in his crib and decided to let him stay there as long as he was happy. When he wailed, she rushed in to discover that he was ready for a diaper change.

She had just finished changing him and was tickling him to make him laugh when the front doorbell rang.

"Let's go see who it is," she said to Jeremy who settled himself comfortably on her hip as Cricket hurried to the door.

She opened it, her eyes widening when she saw that her visitor was a man hunched over and seeking shelter from the rain. He wore a tan jacket lined with plaid flannel where the neck gapped open, and there was a navy-blue toboggan cap pulled low over his forehead. Bright blue eyes gleamed above the three-days' stubble of beard.

"I'm Tim Vogel," he said in response to her startled greeting. "The landlord, Mr. Riordan, sent me over. Didn't he call you?"

Cricket shook her head, and then the telephone rang. "Wait a minute," she called over her shoulder as she rushed into the living room to catch the phone, and then, because he looked so forlorn standing on the porch, she said, "That's probably Mr. Riordan now. Come on in."

The phone caller was indeed Dennis Riordan, and he hurriedly told Cricket that he'd sent Tim over, and that, according to Haggerty at the airport, Tim was a fine young man, and that it would be safe to let him in.

"I already have," Cricket informed him. Tim was standing in the foyer, staring down at the place in front of the door where the varnish was scuffed off the hardwood floor.

"Let him have the key to the upstairs apartment. I was in a hurry when Haggerty sent him to see me, and I didn't have time to bring him over myself. He can move in tonight if he wants to."

Mr. Riordan had always been agreeable whenever Cricket asked for an extension on paying the rent, and she was happy to do him a favor now.

"I guess you can show yourself the apartment," she said to Tim when she had hung up. She dug around one-handedly in the drawer of the desk where the telephone sat, but she couldn't find the key.

Cricket straightened and shifted the baby to the other hip. The baby stared at Tim, his eyes wide. He was drooling all over Cricket's sweatshirt.

"Now where did I put it?" she mused out loud. Then she remembered. The key was on her dresser where she had tossed it weeks ago after the previous tenant had handed it to her on the way out the door. She walked rapidly back to the foyer and headed for her bedroom on the other side.

"Here, you hold Jeremy," she said on her way past, and with that she plunked the baby into Tim's arms and disappeared into an adjoining room. The baby oozed a dollop of warm saliva onto his hands, and Tim winced. He didn't know what to do, though, except to keep holding the baby, which he did awkwardly. Jeremy continued to stare up at him, and then he puckered his face and hollered. *Now* what was Tim supposed to do?

Cricket reappeared, dangling a key on a string. "Here," she said, but he couldn't take it and hang on to the baby, too. He wasn't used to holding kids. Did they always feel as though they were going to flop this way and that if you didn't grasp them with an iron grip?

Cricket, seeing what the problem was, stuck her hand into Tim's coat pocket, leaving the key there. The baby leaned toward her and more or less fell into her arms.

"I'll just go up and take a look," Tim said as he surreptitiously wiped his hands on the back of his coat and steered clear of the baby's clutching little hands. He practically ran up the stairs, which were surmounted by a door.

The upstairs apartment was nothing special, and in fact, it was about what Tim had expected. There were four rooms, three of which were former bedrooms. What had once served as a roomy closet had been transformed into a cramped kitchen and was furnished with a combination sink, stove and refrigerator unit. The fridge was miniscule, but that was okay because he wouldn't be keeping much food around.

To eat, he'd have to carry his food into the room across the hall, which was furnished with an age-blackened dining room table and a matching breakfront, both of which looked as though they might have been used by Queen Victoria in her salad days.

The bedroom was so-so, with a comfortable bed and a bright red bedspread. Overall the place was homey and had big windows, and he liked the cheerful colors of the hand-crocheted afghan draped over the back of the couch.

He loped downstairs. The baby was still wailing. He tried calling Cricket, but she didn't hear him. Feeling like a trespasser, he walked through the living room and found her in the kitchen on her hands and knees. The baby was in some kind of sitting contraption with wheels on it and was screaming at the top of his lungs. A tide of water advanced menacingly from the cabinet beneath the kitchen sink.

"Hey!" Tim said. "What's going on?"

"I dunno, looks like a pipe broke or something." Cricket peered doubtfully under the sink.

"Do you have a flashlight? And some rags?" He had to shout to be heard over the baby's yells.

"Sure."

While Cricket was gone, Tim wiped up some of the water with paper towels. He got down on his back to inspect the J-joint in the drain beneath the kitchen sink. When he touched it, his finger poked through the rusty metal.

Cricket came back and edged carefully around his outspread legs. He took the flashlight when Cricket offered it. The baby stopped crying and hiccuped a few times after she picked him up, but she gave him a bottle of juice and set him in a high chair, where he sat noisily sucking on the bottle. Cricket began to mop up the rest of the water on the floor.

"You need to replace this joint," Tim said. "I don't see anything else wrong. It's a fairly simple job."

"I'd better call Mr. Riordan," Cricket replied, heading for the phone. Tim lifted his head up and eyed her from beneath the sink. Her pink-gold hair was the exact shade of new pennies. With those wide-set gray-green eyes and the freckles colliding into star bursts on the bridge of her nose, she couldn't exactly be called a classic beauty. But still there was something fascinating about her, about the way she moved.

"Hey, it won't do any good to call Dennis Riordan," Tim called after her. "He's gone to Kansas City for the weekend. That's why he sent me over to see the apartment alone instead of coming with me."

"Uhh," Cricket said, flitting back into the kitchen, and then, as though the breath had gone out of her, she sank onto a kitchen chair.

She looked so tired and downhearted that he said helpfully, "Your husband could fix it for you."

"I don't have one of those," she said.

In confusion, Tim glanced at Jeremy and back at her.

"My husband and I were very recently divorced," Cricket explained.

"I see," Tim said carefully.

Suddenly Cricket buried her face in her hands.

Tim watched her uneasily. He thought she might be crying.

But she wasn't. When her hands fell away from her face, he realized that it had been a gesture of weariness. Her skin was bleached out in the wan winter light from the window. She looked exhausted and in no shape to handle the difficult matter of finding a plumber late on a Friday afternoon.

"If you don't mind, I could probably fix this for you," he offered, surprised at himself.

Cricket's expression softened. "Oh, that would be too much to ask. Really too much."

"No," he said. "I'd like to, I honestly would." There was something immensely appealing about her.

She seemed to take heart. "I guess if you're going to fix the plumbing, I ought to at least introduce myself. I should have done it earlier. I'm Cricket Erling, and my son's name is Jeremy."

He smiled. "Well, Cricket, where's the nearest hardware store? I hope it's within walking distance, because I don't have a car yet."

"There's a hardware store around the corner, and Cal Munsen knows me. He'll put the cost of supplies on Mr. Riordan's bill if you tell him who you're buying them for."

Tim left her to mop up the rest of the water while he walked to the hardware store on Main Street and bought a J-joint. When Tim told him whose plumbing needed fixing, Cal Munsen even let him borrow the necessary wrench.

"Are you going to take the apartment?" Cricket asked suddenly when Tim was once again lying on his back in front of her sink trying to get the pipe to go on right. His ribs, still taped after the accident, hurt. He tried not to show it.

"What?"

"I said, are you going to take the apartment?"

"Oh, sure. It seems comfortable."

"Are you a college student?"

"No. I've got a job working for Caesar Haggerty at the airport."

"No kidding! Doesn't he do crop dusting? There can't be any crops to dust in the middle of winter around here."

Tim felt himself growing short of breath. It was hard to breathe in this position, with his head angled so he could work on the plumbing.

"Oh, Haggerty has work to do year-round. They're minor things, but I can help him with them," Tim said. He gave the wrench a mighty tug. That should finish the job, he thought.

He sat up. His ribs hurt like the dickens. Maybe he shouldn't have been doing this.

"Are you all right, Tim?" Cricket asked anxiously. His hair had fallen back, and she saw a large yellowing bruise on his forehead.

"Yeah," he said.

"But that bruise!" She was sure that if Tim was working for Haggerty, he was a pilot. "You haven't been in some kind of accident, have you?" she asked.

Tim stood up. He felt suddenly dizzy. He slumped onto a chair.

"Your face is positively white. Something's wrong, isn't it?" Full of concern, Cricket sat down on the chair beside his.

"I *have* been in a little accident. Crop dusting. Down in Florida. It wasn't much." Funny, but the air seemed so thick. He was having trouble drawing it into his lungs.

"Is there anything I can do to help?" Seeing him in distress aroused all of Cricket's protective mothering instincts.

"Just let me sit here a minute," said Tim.

Cricket regarded him with alarm. He looked as though he was going to pass out right here in her kitchen. When he stopped breathing so heavily, she said gently, "When was the last time you ate?"

"A pack of cheese crackers from the vending machine at the airport for lunch."

"I'll fix you a hamburger. Could you eat it now, or do you want to wait?"

"I can't impose—" he began, but saw it was useless to argue.

"You and I are going to be sharing this house, and you were kind enough to repair the plumbing. Let me pay back the favor in the best way I know how. I wouldn't have had the slightest idea what to do about the J-joint with Mr. Riordan out of town.'' She laughed a little. ''I didn't even know what a J-joint was. I'm glad *you* did.''

He watched her as she bustled around the kitchen, alternately darting anxious looks at him as she tended a hamburger patty sizzling in a frying pan, and talking to the baby, who was gnawing on a rubber teething ring. Cricket looked as though she was afraid Tim might keel over. Well, he wouldn't. He was just tired, that's all. And hungry.

She was certainly a tiny little thing: slim, fine-boned and full of energy. Cricket had to be one of the liveliest women he'd ever seen. Was she ever still? He doubted it. He enjoyed watching her as she exploded in one direction or the other all over the kitchen, like popcorn popping out of control.

Cricket set the plate down in front of him, and before he even took a bite, Tim's mouth was watering. She turned on the overhead light, which cast a mellow glow over the big room. The kitchen was painted yellow, and a philodendron spread glossy green leaves over the windowsill above the sink. The sugar bowl on the table looked familiar, and Tim recognized that it was the same blue cornflower design as the one that had sat on the kitchen table at his mother's house. Somehow this gave him a familiar, homey feeling.

Cricket spooned baby food into Jeremy while Tim wolfed his hamburger, and even though watching a baby eat wasn't the most appetizing sight in the world, Tim enjoyed his meal very much.

''Aren't you going to have some supper, too?'' he asked her when she had finished feeding Jeremy.

''Oh, I ate this afternoon. I'm not hungry now.''

''That was a delicious hamburger, Cricket. Really first-rate.'' It had been thick and juicy, just the way he liked it.

She smiled. ''I'm glad it was okay.''

He stood up. He was glad when the room didn't whirl around him. Evidently he was over his previous dizzy spell. He must have been hungrier than he'd thought.

''I guess I'll go get my stuff,'' he said.

''Do you need any help?''

''No, I only have one duffel bag. I left it on the front porch.''

''You should have brought it inside.''

''I didn't know I'd be staying.'' His grin caught her by surprise.

Jeremy, beginning to grow impatient in his high chair, beat his teething ring clamorously on the metal tray.

"Thanks for the hamburger. And everything," Tim shouted over the din.

"You're welcome. And thank you, too." She tried to ignore the persistent growling of her stomach, and she was glad that Jeremy was making so much noise that Tim couldn't hear it.

"See you. You too, fella," he said as he ruffled a finger across the sparse brown hair on Jeremy's head.

Her stomach rumbled again, and she went to the refrigerator and poured herself a glass of milk. It was all she had left in the house to eat or drink, other than Jeremy's baby food and the makings of the sandwiches she sold to convenience stores. She hoped Tim would never find out that she'd fed him the hamburger that was supposed to be her dinner.

Tim called from the foyer, "Hey, is it okay if this cat comes in? He acts as though he lives here."

"Sure. That's Mungo."

She heard the front door close as Mungo, a huge Maine coon cat, bounded into the kitchen and peered hopefully into his dish. Cricket doled out a ration of Cat Chow, and Mungo commenced eating.

Upstairs, Tim stowed his little bit of gear in one of the closets and peered at his image in the bathroom mirror. He fingered the stubble on his chin. He had to admit that he looked a little rough.

He heard a timid knock on the door. When he opened it, there stood Cricket. She was a short little thing. Her head barely reached the top of his shoulder.

"Cricket," he said. "Come on in."

"Oh, I can't. But I wondered—do you have sheets? Towels?"

"I never thought to look," he admitted.

"The college girl who lived here before brought hers from home. I don't think this place is equipped with linens. So if you don't have any, feel free to borrow some."

He lifted his hands helplessly. He was tired, he hurt, and he'd never thought about sheets or towels.

She read the exhaustion in his expression. "Come on down and take a look at my linen closet," she urged.

He followed her downstairs. She wore a black Manitou College sweatshirt which effectively hid the curves of her breasts, and her faded jeans hung loosely on slim hips. Her hair glowed bright above the black of her shirt, and he thought how pretty her hair was. She wore it feathered in the front and sides and hanging in a curving mass behind. Her earlobes were tiny and pink.

She threw open a door next to the downstairs bathroom. "Here's the linen closet. Take your pick."

Tim was faced with an array of sheets and blankets in all colors. There were plaids and prints. There were white eyelet ruffles. He was too tired to choose one over the other.

"Where'd you get so many?" he said stupidly. His eyelids felt heavy; and his tongue felt thick.

"I had a linen shower before I was married. Anyway, I got all these sheets and towels and things, and they've outlasted the marriage."

"I don't have any idea what I need," he said.

Cricket took charge. "You'll need sheets for a double bed. Here, take the blue plaid, they'll look nice with that red bedspread up there. And here's another set, gray with tiny black dots." She piled the sheets into his arms.

"Now, towels," she said, picking those out, too. He was grateful for her help. He wouldn't have had any idea what he needed. Sheets and towels were always something that appeared miraculously on schedule in his mother's home, in the air force and at the motels and boarding houses where he'd lived since last August.

"That should take care of that. You *do* know how to make a bed, don't you?" She cocked her head at him curiously.

"My mother taught me when I was a kid," he said.

"Fine," Cricket said.

He turned to go.

"A couple more things," she said to his retreating back. He stopped.

"The way the house is laid out, the downstairs is divided by the foyer. I sleep in the bedroom on one side of the foyer, and Jeremy's room is in the former sun porch on the other side of the foyer off the living room. You and I share the foyer. That's the only way for you to get up to your apartment. But I have to leave the doors on either side of it open so I can hear Jeremy if he cries at night. So every time you come in, you more or less have to walk through my home. I just wanted you to know that I won't mind."

"Oh," he said, trying to make sense of a monologue that seemed to describe an architect's nightmare. He turned around to face her. It struck him as impolite to let Cricket go on talking to his back.

"My cat is allowed to go in and out at will, so feel free to let him. Also, if you hear noise very early in the morning, it's just me and Jeremy getting up to run my route. We're usually back by eight-thirty, and then we go to class at the college. I hope we won't wake you." She looked worried.

"Right."

"I guess that's all. See you later."

"Thanks, Cricket. I mean, thanks a lot." He attempted a smile.

"Anything else I can do, let me know."

"Sure."

He made it up to his apartment without her saying anything more, and in a fog of fatigue he tossed the sheets over the mattress pad and wrapped himself up in them. His mother wouldn't approve of his innovative method of bed making, but then maybe she'd never find out.

His last thoughts were of Cricket. What a nice person she was. What kind of route did she drive in the morning, anyway? And did the baby go to class with her, or what?

He was sound asleep before he could even speculate about the answers.

DOWNSTAIRS, CRICKET PUT Jeremy to bed with a bottle. She had recently cut down on the number of times a day she breastfed him, and now she customarily nursed him only once a day, in the morning. She smoothed the blanket over his small form and tiptoed out of the room. She studied for her exam for a while before going into the kitchen and pulling out her sandwich-making supplies.

Ham on cheese, mustard on bread. Chicken salad on white, chicken salad on rye. Bologna on wheat, bologna on white.

Assembling over two hundred sandwiches every night was downright monotonous when she really thought about it, which she tried not to do very often. But it was a way to make a living, albeit a skimpy one.

Tuna on white, tuna on wheat. And she was almost out of mayonnaise.

Liverwurst on rye, liverwurst on wheat, liverwurst on white. It was all she could do not to eat any of it, hungry as she was.

But it wouldn't hurt to skip a meal. She'd skipped plenty of them before. These sandwiches would bring in money, and she and Jeremy needed every penny they could get.

Peanut butter on white with grape jelly. This kind wasn't too popular, but she always sold a few.

Swiss cheese on rye, swiss cheese on wheat.

Finally Cricket couldn't resist it. She built herself a sandwich of monumental proportions and set it aside to eat while she watched the late news on the television set in her room.

She put everything away in the refrigerator, ready for tomorrow's early-morning run, and wiped off the countertop with a damp sponge. She was finally ready for bed.

Chapter Three

It was the following Tuesday, the beginning of Manitou College's semester break, before Cricket saw Tim again.

Cricket was hiking down Main Street with Jeremy slung against her front in his blue baby sling when she thought she spied Tim on the other side of the street. But he disappeared into the bank, and she shrugged and walked on.

It was a beautiful winter's day, the sky milk-white and windswept. A few dry leaves rattled in the gutter and others, more lively, swirled across the wide brick street. With the college closed for the semester break, the Manitou population of fourteen thousand had been depleted by the exodus of the eight hundred or so students who had gone home until classes resumed next week.

Cricket had taken advantage of her freedom from classes and of the bright, warm day with highs predicted in the fifties to walk the several blocks from her apartment to Main Street. Walking not only saved on gas for her aging Volkswagen camper, it was also refreshing exercise after being cooped up inside during the harsh January weather. They'd suffered a period of ten days in a row when the temperature never rose above zero.

The hands on the clock on the spire of the college bell tower at the end of Manitou's newly refurbished main street were positioned at exactly one o'clock, and Cricket speeded up her step. It was almost time to put Jeremy down for his nap, and he'd get fussy if she didn't get him home soon. Trudy's Gift and Card Boutique was the spiffiest shop on the block. Cricket opened the

red-painted door and was immediately greeted by an effervescent
Trudy.

"Cricket! What brings you in here? I'm so glad to see you!
Here, let me hold Jeremy. There, there, come to Aunt Trudy.
That's a good boy." Trudy jounced Jeremy expertly in her arms.

"I just stopped in to say hello," said Cricket. "Jeremy and I
have been enjoying the nice weather."

"I have some exciting things to tell you." From the way
Trudy's eyes sparkled at her over Jeremy's peaked hood, Cricket
knew that what Trudy had to tell was something about a man,
probably the friend who had shown up with Trudy's brother.
Cricket had seen Trudy in this ebullient mood before.

"This wonderful news must have to do with—what's his
name? The friend your brother brought here to spend semester
break with you."

"Walt. Oh, he's wonderful, Cricket. I think this is the real
thing."

"You're *not* in love with him, are you, Trudy? You've known
him less than a week!"

"Yes, but it's as though I've known him forever! Do you
know, he's the most tender, compassionate man I've ever met.
He's wonderful, Cricket. I can't wait for you to meet him."

"Neither can I, if he's that terrific. I'm glad you're hitting it
off so well. He sounds like he's all pluses. Aren't there any mi-
nuses?"

"Well," Trudy said, looking uncomfortable.

"Well?"

"He's been with a woman named Rona for a couple of years.
He doesn't know how to break it off. He doesn't want to hurt
her, you see."

A clamor of warning bells sounded in Cricket's head. She wondered why Trudy didn't hear them, too.

"But he *is* going to break it off?"

"Oh, yes. As soon as his job situation settles down. That's one
reason Walt's here. He's checking out the possibilities at Manitou
College. He's only been teaching at the University of Wisconsin
at La Crosse for one semester, but he doesn't like it. If he gets a
job here, that would be the perfect time for him to tell Rona it's
over."

"Mmm," said Cricket, wondering where Walt had moved from

when he'd moved to the university. If he and Rona had been together for a couple of years, then Rona must have accompanied him. Why wouldn't he have broken off with Rona then?

"He's not attracted to Rona anymore, he says. But he feels sorry for her, and she has two kids who are emotionally attached to him. It's a tough situation, and I feel sorry for him. He's talked to me about it for hours, Cricket, poured his heart out. He needs someone to talk to."

Cricket wanted to say, *Trudy, be careful.* She wanted to say, *Trudy, this sounds like a repeat of the last time you were hurt.* But it was as though her tongue had calcified. Cricket simply found herself unable, in the face of Trudy's glowing happiness, to say anything the least bit negative about Walt.

Cricket was saved from having to say anything at all by the tinkle of the bell on the door. The new customer was Tim Vogel.

Tim nodded at Cricket. "How're you doing, Cricket?"

"Fine, Tim. Tim, this is Trudy. She's our neighbor."

In response to Trudy's puzzled look, Cricket explained rapidly, "I haven't had a chance to tell you, but Tim's renting the upstairs apartment."

"How nice," Trudy said with a speculative look.

"I stopped in to buy a card," Tim said uneasily. He had the idea that the two women were sure to discuss him as soon as he left.

But Trudy became her professionally helpful self. "What kind of card?"

"Oh, I'm not sure. Not a birthday or anniversary card. Maybe something more in the line of an I've Been Thinking About You card."

Trudy handed Jeremy back to his mother. "We have a wonderful line of friendship greetings," she said, hurrying toward the back of the store. She showed Tim where the cards were, and then hurried back to Cricket.

"Anyway," she said, keeping her voice low, "when can you meet Walt?"

"Oh, I don't know, Trudy," Cricket said, purposely being vague. "I'm so busy, trying to get caught up with the housework during my college break and everything."

"But Walt wants to meet *you*," Trudy said.

"How about if I give you a call?" Cricket hedged.

At that point, Tim Vogel emerged from the racks of cards.

"Didn't you find what you were looking for?" Trudy asked.

"No, not today," Tim replied. He had been looking for something to send his mother to let her know about his change of address. An I've Moved card seemed too cold to send his parents, and the Thinking of You cards didn't express the emotions he felt.

"Well, come back again," said Trudy.

Cricket gathered up Jeremy. "Wait, Tim," she said. "I'll walk with you, if you don't mind." Anything to get away from Trudy's effusive descriptions of Walt, and Trudy would be pleased to think that Cricket was leaving with Tim.

"I'll talk to you soon," Trudy called as Cricket escaped.

Tim swung into step beside Cricket on the sidewalk. Strange as it might seem, she hadn't seen Tim since that Friday four days ago when he'd moved in. Their schedules hadn't meshed, and she'd wondered how he was getting along.

"So what have you been doing?" she asked. He was clean-shaven now. He looked rested.

Tim smiled down at her. It was a lopsided smile, higher on one side than on the other. It gave him an intriguing little-boy look.

"Today I bought a car," he said happily. "We don't have to walk home."

Cricket's eyebrows swooped upward. "You've bought a car?"

"I certainly have. Not a big car, but nice. I signed the papers at the bank today. Come try it out with me."

"I can't joyride. I have to go home. Jeremy's ready for his nap. I'll walk."

"No, let me drive you. It's this little black Mustang here."

"Oh, it *is* nice," she said, running a hand admiringly over its sleek finish.

"Go ahead," urged Tim. "Get in."

She slid in on the passenger side, and Tim got in behind the wheel.

"I needed something to get me back and forth to work," he said.

"You're going to be flying for Haggerty?"

"Not until I'm feeling better. Then I'll probably fly a few charter flights. Haggerty's getting old, and he's tired. I'm going to keep the accounts for his business, order some of the supplies, that kind of thing.''

"Good for you! Do you think you'll get back to crop dusting later?''

"Oh, undoubtedly.''

"Even after your accident?''

"The accident was my fault. I shouldn't have been flying that day.'' Tim decided that it was time for a change of subject. "Are you sure you can't take a ride with me? Just a short one?'' He smiled at her appealingly.

She glanced down at Jeremy. He looked good-tempered and wide-awake enough as he reached for one of the shiny knobs on the dash.

"A quick spin around town wouldn't take long,'' insisted Tim.

Cricket smiled up at him. Tim was so eager to share his pleasure in the new car with someone. "Okay,'' she agreed. "A quick ride around town would be fun.''

As they drove past Munsen's Hardware Cricket waved at someone she knew from one of her classes.

"I guess you know a lot of people in town,'' said Tim.

"I've lived in Manitou all my life,'' Cricket told him. "My parents owned a little restaurant here when I was growing up. After they died, I lived here with my grandmother.'' They were passing the new shopping mall, and she pointed it out to Tim. He should, after all, know where to go to buy things.

"Ojibwa Mall is nice inside,'' she told him. "It's giving the downtown businesses a little too much competition, but I like to shop here protected from the weather. There's a J. C. Penney store that does most of its business through mail order, and there's a shoe repair place and a music store, and even a trendy restaurant—well, as trendy as you'll find in Manitou.''

"I'm from a small town myself,'' he told her. "A little place called Curtisville, Kansas. Have you ever heard of it?''

Cricket shook her head. "No, I'm afraid not. You're a long way from home, aren't you?''

"It's a day's drive. If I wanted to drive it,'' he said, and from the expression in Tim's voice, Cricket got the distinct impression that he didn't want to.

"Let's cut through the college campus,'' suggested Cricket

suddenly as they were about to pass the red-brick gates. "I'll give you a guided tour."

"How long have you been a student here?" Tim asked with interest as he headed the car through gates that said, Manitou College Founded 1903.

"I've been a student for three and a half years, off and on. I'll graduate in June with a degree in psychology. Oh look, they've put up a new notice on the marquee outside the Performing Arts Building. Let's see what it says."

Tim slowed down in front of the sign. "Manuel Susurro," he read. "Performing Next Week. Wonder who he is."

"He's a classical guitarist," Cricket informed him. "I read about him in the college newspaper. He's supposed to be pretty good. The successor to Andrés Segovia."

"No kidding," said Tim. "How can I get to see him?"

"I could probably get you a ticket that someone isn't going to use. That is, if you really want to go."

"I learned to play the guitar when I was in the service. The experience left me with a solid appreciation for those who are good at it. Yes, I'd like to get a ticket if I could. How much will it cost?" After buying the car, he was a little short on cash. He hadn't received his first paycheck from Haggerty yet.

"I'll find you a free ticket. The students each get a free one, anyway. I'm sure I know someone who can't go."

"If it's a lot of trouble—" he began.

"It won't be. I promise."

He looked down at her. Her mouth was slightly parted. He'd never really noticed her mouth before. It was nicely shaped, with full lips. Altogether, he considered it a perfect mouth. He forced himself to pull his eyes away and concentrate on his driving.

The campus wasn't far from their house, and as they drew up in front of the curb, Tim was wishing that it had been a longer drive. He would have liked to spend more time with Cricket.

"I'm not coming in the house," he told her when her eyes inquired about the fact that he didn't turn off the car engine. "I think I'll run out to the airport and see if Haggerty's there. I'd like to show him the car."

Cricket slid out, taking Jeremy with her. "Thanks for the ride, Tim," she said. "And I like your car." A gentle breeze fluttered the reddish-gold tendrils around her face. Her eyes were a complex dazzle of green and gray. She slammed the car door and turned to go, but then Tim reached across the front seat and opened the door on the passenger side again.

Cricket had almost reached the porch when he called out to her. She turned halfway around to see what he wanted.

"About that trendy restaurant," he said. "The one in the new shopping mall?"

"Nickelodeon's. Yes?"

"Is there any chance that you'd like to go there with me sometime?"

"Well, uh," she said, totally taken by surprise. Jeremy grabbed at her hair, and she tried not to wince when he yanked it.

"Any night after Friday," he amended. "That's payday."

"I—I suppose so," she said, her mind racing. She'd have to get a sitter for Jeremy, and that wasn't always easy.

"If you really don't want to, it's okay," he said, watching her. "But I don't know any people in Manitou who are anywhere near my age, and I liked being with you this afternoon. How about it?"

Put that way, how could she turn him down?

"I'd like to," she said.

"What night?"

"Oh, Friday?"

"You've got a date, lady. And thanks. Thanks a lot." He grinned at her, and she realized that she was grinning back. He slammed the car door, and with a chipper wave, he drove off.

Cricket let herself inside the house and settled Jeremy in bed for his nap. Tim's last words to her lingered on.

He'd said, "You've got a date, lady." How long had it been since she'd had a date? Oh, a long time. Since she and Hugh had first separated, before their temporary reconciliation that had resulted in the birth of Jeremy.

Maybe it wasn't really a date. Maybe she shouldn't think of it as such. Tim just needed someone to show him around town, to introduce him to Manitou's recreational resources. But the words had opened her mind to a new world of possibilities. Maybe soon she'd be ready to date again, the way Trudy had been urging her to do. Perhaps it was time.

ON FRIDAY MORNING, Tim came bounding downstairs, whistling a happy tune. He knocked at the open double doors leading from the foyer he shared with Cricket.

"We're in the kitchen," called Cricket.

He found Cricket layering lunch meat in big Tupperware containers. Jeremy sat in a playpen, stolidly playing with a Busy Box. Jeremy smiled when he saw Tim.

"You're an industrious soul, aren't you, Cricket?" Tim said. "It's only nine-thirty."

Cricket laughed. "My day starts early," she told him, setting aside a square box filled with salami slices.

"What kind of a route do you run, anyway?" he asked her.

"It's a sandwich route. I make sandwiches and sell them to convenience stores and gas stations in little towns for miles around. They stock them in their refrigerator cases and sell them to truck drivers, workmen and passing motorists who are in too much of a hurry to stop at a restaurant for lunch."

"How long have you been doing this?"

"Ever since Jeremy was born. I'd been working as a hostess at a nice restaurant in Eau Claire when I was married, but I couldn't do that once I decided to take a full load of classes at Manitou and had Jeremy to think about."

Tim had wondered how Cricket managed. He leaned against the doorjamb and said, "Go on."

"I had to figure out some way to bring money in, so I took Jeremy and went around to all the convenience stores that looked like they sold cold drinks, asked them to put my sandwiches in the refrigerator case next to the drinks, and they went for it. Maybe they took pity on me because I made it clear that I had to support a baby on the money I'd make. Anyway, it worked." Cricket separated the slices of ham she had bought that morning from the white waxed paper in which they were wrapped.

"Doesn't your ex-husband send you any money?"

"He sends child support for Jeremy," she said in an even tone.

"Nothing for you?"

"I didn't want anything. I've got my sandwich money, a full scholarship to finish my last year at Manitou and some savings my grandmother left me. When I graduate in June, I'll get a counseling job with the local mental health center. Jeremy and I will do all right."

Tim had to admire her spunk. He'd heard her setting out on

her route every morning when it was cold and dark, before the sun had inched up from the horizon.

"Jeremy goes with you when you run your route?"

"Sure. I warm up the camper before I take him outside, and he rides along in his car seat. If he gets cranky, I give him a bottle of juice or milk."

"Speaking of milk, I wonder if you might have some around. My refrigerator isn't working properly, and my milk's gone sour. I need milk for my cornflakes."

"I always have milk. Help yourself. There are cornflakes in the cabinet."

Mindful now of Cricket's precarious financial position, Tim said, "I'll go up and get my own cornflakes. I've poured them in the bowl already."

When he returned with his bowl of cereal, Cricket was taking the milk container from the refrigerator.

"I'll pay the milk back as soon as I get some more," he assured her as he poured it over his cereal.

"Oh, there's no need—" she began.

"No, I want to," he said sternly.

"Well, if your refrigerator isn't working, you can keep your milk in mine. Or any other perishables you might want to keep here until you get your refrigerator fixed."

"I might have to do that," he agreed.

Cricket was gazing out the kitchen window, an expression of perplexity on her face. "Here comes Trudy, looking as though she's on an important mission," she said. "I wonder what she wants. She's usually at work by this time."

Trudy, wrapped up in a long, fringed wool shawl, was plodding across the winter-brown grass.

"Why didn't she just phone? It's cold out there."

"Trudy doesn't like to phone. She lives so close that she likes to run over when she has something to say." Then, to her dismay, Cricket thought of what Trudy might want. "Oh, she probably wants me to meet her new friend, Walt," she groaned.

"I take it that you'd rather not. Well, sit down. I'll be your excuse—tell her anything you want."

Cricket sat. She poured herself a glass of milk. "Trudy wants me to come over and have coffee with them," she said with great certainty.

"You're already having coffee. Or milk, anyhow. With me."

By this time, Trudy was knocking on the door. Cricket called, "Come in!"

Trudy greeted the sight of Cricket and Tim sitting together while Tim shoveled cornflakes into his mouth with a surprised, "Oh! I didn't know you were busy."

"Tim's just eating," said Cricket, hopping up. Tim was amused. He might have known that Cricket wouldn't stay in one place for long. "Can I get you a cup of coffee or something?" she asked Trudy.

"Well, no, I'm sorry to interrupt," said Trudy. "I was going to ask you to come over to my place for a while, Cricket. I wanted you to meet Walt. I've taken the day off, Mary Sue is filling in for me at the shop, and Walt and I are going away for the weekend, so he won't be here later. But if you're busy..."

Tim sensed Cricket's reluctance to lie to her friend, and he decided in that split second to speak up. "We just sat down," he offered brightly. "Cricket's been telling me about some of the recreational advantages of living in Manitou."

"Oh," Trudy said. "In that case I'll run along back home." With a puzzled but meaningful look at Cricket, Trudy rewrapped herself in the big shawl and took off at a run across the backyard.

"Quick," Tim said conspiratorially. "Tell me a few things to do in Manitou so I won't be a liar."

"You can go to the movies. There's a movie theater in the Ojibwa Mall. And the college has lots of things to do. Like the Manuel Susurro concert."

"I can't tell you how much better I feel now that you've made an honest man out of me. By the way, who is this Walt that Trudy wants you to meet?"

Cricket shrugged. "He's a friend of her brother's. They're both assistant professors at the University of Wisconsin at La Crosse. Talbot brought Walt to spend semester break with Trudy so that Walt could check out employment opportunities at Manitou College. Trudy has become very fond of Walt. And now they're going away together for the weekend." The idea of what Trudy was getting herself into—again—made Cricket's stomach queasy.

"It doesn't sound as though you approve."

"Oh, Tim, I feel so guilty for not wanting to meet him. But Trudy falls in love so easily. And always with the wrong person."

"Who are you to judge?" Tim asked.

"I don't judge, Tim. But when romance after romance ends in disaster, and always because Trudy used poor judgment in the first place, it's easy to come to the conclusion that she's choosing men who aren't any good for her."

"Maybe they choose her."

"I've seen Trudy pursue a guy even though it's perfectly clear to everyone else who knows them that he's a scoundrel who will end up breaking her heart."

"Do you talk to her about this?"

"Trudy carries on endless postmortems after each and every man has gone his merry way, leaving her to nurse a torn ego and a bruised heart. I always agree with her belated assessment of the guy's character, if that's what you mean. I try not to say I told you so, but it's getting harder all the time."

"Don't any of your psychology courses teach you what to do for someone like Trudy?"

"Yes, but it's not that easy when it's a good friend." Cricket sighed.

"What do you suppose Trudy thinks of you this morning, Cricket? Her stumbling on the two of us having breakfast together must have given her all sorts of ideas."

Cricket stared at him in dawning understanding. "Oh, Trudy knows that I wouldn't have...that I don't..."

"That you don't *what*, Cricket?" Tim said, suddenly still.

"Trudy's been trying to get me to date for months. She knows I haven't." For the first time, Cricket realized that Tim's T-shirt bore the slogan, Lefties Make Better Lovers. He held his spoon in his left hand. Cricket covered her consternation by sweeping a surprised Jeremy out of his playpen and hurrying into his room with him.

Tim followed slowly, carrying the bowl containing the last of his cornflakes.

"You don't date anyone?" he said. "Really?"

"Really," said Cricket, giving her full concentration to unsnapping Jeremy's playsuit.

"What a shame," he said.

When Cricket didn't reply, Tim said casually, "My cornflakes are soggy. Mind if I put them down for Mungo?"

"He'd love it," Cricket said, and was relieved when Tim took his disturbing presence back to the kitchen and set his bowl down on the floor for the cat.

He was back again in a few minutes.

"Our date for tonight is still on, isn't it?" he asked her. Her back was toward him, and he wished he could see the expression on her face.

"I—I'm not sure if the sitter can come," she hedged.

"Oh, I've been meaning to mention that Haggerty's grand-daughter, the oldest one, told me the other day that she's looking for baby-sitting jobs. She's a sweet girl, and she baby-sits a lot with her younger sister who is just about Jeremy's size. So if your regular sitter can't come, just holler. I'm sure that Kimberly would be delighted."

"Okay," Cricket said in a very small voice. He was only trying to be helpful, she knew, but he had taken away her only excuse to back out of having dinner with him. In spite of looking forward to it, in spite of the free meal, she wasn't sure that she really wanted to go anymore. For some reason, she now felt very self-conscious and shy.

Tim retreated, smiling to himself. He hadn't been much interested in women or anything remotely resembling a relationship with one since he'd left Curtisville. He didn't know why not. Women today were so accessible, as interchangeable as tires on a car. There was always one *there* for his comfort and convenience. At least that's the way it had always seemed to him.

He hadn't bought an automobile tire in a long time, and he hadn't had a woman in almost as long. Finally, far removed from the depressing problems at home, he was feeling the faint stirrings of something that he identified as desire, and this pleased him. He'd been beginning to think that he wasn't normal.

It was odd that Cricket, tiny and freckle faced and always running in several directions at once, should be the one to spark his interest. He usually liked voluptuous blondes like Amethyst, the woman he'd met in Florida the night before his accident. Cricket was just the opposite, but she was warm and vibrant and cheerful. Also, she was so oriented toward her goals. As a person without any goals of his own, Tim couldn't help but wonder what made Cricket the way she was. He wanted to get to know her better. To find out what made her tick.

What could be more natural than for the two of them to get

together? Cricket was available and he was here, and he liked her and he thought she liked him. That was pretty simple, pretty basic. Nothing complicated or complex. Which was fine with him. For now, Tim Vogel intended to enjoy it. And her.

Chapter Four

That afternoon Tim pulled into the drab airport parking lot beside the trailer where Haggerty kept his office. Sure enough, Haggerty's pickup truck was there. That meant Caesar Augustus Haggerty had to be around somewhere.

"Tim," rasped the unmistakable voice, and Tim wheeled to see Haggerty puffing up behind him.

Haggerty, as everyone, even his wife, Gracie, called him, was a sturdy triangle of a man who, due to years of smoking, was afflicted with emphysema. He didn't fly anymore; he couldn't. His addiction to tobacco had left him medically unfit. He ran the aerial applicating business almost completely by telephone out of his trailer at the airport, delegating the actual flying to "gypsies" with aerial applicators' licenses. Last summer Tim had been one of them.

"Come on over to the trailer," Haggerty wheezed. "I'll make out your paycheck."

"Some job you've got, Haggerty," Tim said as they walked past the hangar where Haggerty kept his planes and the chemicals he used in his work. "It's the only job I can think of where you can work hard five months out of the year and lounge around the rest of the time." Tim liked to josh with Haggerty, and the older man seemed to enjoy it.

"In my younger days, before Gracie and I got married, I took other flying jobs during the winter months. Went to Florida to spray crops like you did. Did some charter piloting for big-time farmers who were in a hurry to get across the state."

"Like I say, it's not a bad way to make a living. I'm champing at the bit to get up in the air again, you know," Tim said.

"How're you feeling, Tim?" Haggerty swung the door to the trailer open and waited for Tim to go inside.

"My ribs are a little sore. I don't dare sneeze because it makes me feel like I'm ripping apart. Other than that, I'm on the mend." He sat down, facing Haggerty across a big metal desk.

"Good. What happened down there in Florida, anyway?"

"The plane stalled in the turn. My fault." Tim's gaze darkened. He didn't like thinking about it.

Haggerty seemed to understand. "I've had a few narrow escapes myself, son. It happens to all of us now and then. Whatever you did wrong that day, just don't do it again."

"Don't worry, I won't," Tim assured him.

"Tim, on Monday I'll be in late. I want you to try to collect the money these guys owe me." He pushed a list across the desk, along with a key to the trailer. "And, since you don't mind bookkeeping, you can write out the checks for the bills I need to pay. I'll sign them when I come in Monday afternoon."

"Okay. Anything else?"

"You can answer the phone in the unlikely event that it rings. That's about it."

"Sounds good to me. Thanks, Haggerty. I appreciate the job."

"You're helping us both out," Haggerty said. "One other thing. Keep up the good work. I've got other things in mind for you, Tim." His look was kindly.

Tim was surprised. "Like what?" he asked.

"Oh, tell you later," Haggerty said mysteriously, and with a cackle of laughter, he pulled out his checkbook and wrote Tim's paycheck for the past week.

"So you're taking that little O'Malley girl out tonight, are you?" said Haggerty as he jabbed the cap onto his pen.

"I'm taking Cricket Erling to dinner," Tim said in puzzlement.

"O'Malley, Erling, same thing. Cricket O'Malley married Hugh Erling, and I'm not surprised it didn't last. She never should've married him in the first place."

"How did you know I'm taking Cricket out?"

"My granddaughter. You called her about baby-sitting."

"So I did," Tim said with a grin. "Cricket's regular sitter couldn't make it."

Haggerty favored him with a shrewd once-over as he handed Tim his paycheck. "Don't go making that little girl's life any harder than it's already been," he warned.

"Would I do that?" said Tim, snapping the check from Haggerty's fingers and digging into the pocket of his jeans for his wallet.

Haggerty reached out and, in a flash, lifted the check out of Tim's fingers. He held it just out of Tim's reach.

"You look like the original heartbreak kid," Haggerty said gruffly. He glowered at Tim. "Like I said, don't go breaking Cricket's heart. If you do, I'll break your—well, let's just say that what happened to you in that plane crash would be mild compared to what I could do to you."

Tim had never seen Haggerty so serious. He was taken aback.

"Haggerty," he began uneasily.

"I mean it, Tim."

"I have no intention of doing anything to hurt Cricket Erling," Tim said with dignity. "What do you think I am, anyway?"

"Just another crop-dusting gypsy," growled Haggerty, handing Tim his paycheck.

"Yeah, but I'm nice," Tim said as he pocketed his wallet. "Even your dog likes me."

"My dog, my grandchildren and my wife all tell me you're a great guy. 'When is Tim coming over for dinner?' my grandson wants to know. When *are* you, anyway?"

"Whenever I'm invited."

"You're invited next week. I'll have my wife call you."

"She can call me in care of Cricket. I don't have a phone yet."

"Fine," Haggerty said, stifling a cough.

"When are you going to do something about that cough?" asked Tim with concern.

"Soon, if everything goes well," Haggerty said. He opened his desk drawer and popped a menthol cough drop in his mouth. "Want one?" he offered.

Tim shook his head. "No, thanks," he said. He started out the door, and a wintry wind almost wrenched it from his hands.

"Remember what I said about Cricket," Haggerty called as the door slammed.

When Tim got home, there was no sign of Cricket. The big house seemed empty without her. Tim went upstairs, showered and shaved, and wondered what to wear. He finally decided on one of his newer pairs of blue jeans and a plaid lumberjack shirt. He hummed as he pulled on his socks. Downstairs, the kitchen door slammed as Cricket came in.

The house was built so that Tim could hear many of the words that were spoken downstairs. He'd become accustomed to listening to Cricket croon to Jeremy as the baby fell asleep, to Jeremy's wails and cooing and crying. He smiled now, listening to Cricket in the kitchen as she fed Jeremy his supper. Soon she took Jeremy into her room while she dressed. He heard the knock of the plumbing as Cricket took a quick shower, and he listened to Jeremy crooning to himself in his playpen.

"What'll I wear, Jeremy, hmm?" Cricket said. Her bedroom was directly beneath Tim's. He heard her so plainly that he almost started to answer her, but then he lay back on the bed and thumbed through a new copy of *Flying* magazine. He and Cricket weren't supposed to leave for the restaurant for another half an hour, and he found himself glancing impatiently at his watch every few minutes.

"I shouldn't have washed my hair," Cricket said, either to herself or to the baby. "It's going to mean it takes longer for me to get ready." And then, "Oh, there's a run in my panty hose. Hope I have another pair." And, "Which cologne, Jeremy? Does Tim like Chloé or Anaïs Anaïs better?"

Tim almost said, "Chloé," and then he laughed. Listening to Cricket run on and on in her clear, high voice, he almost felt as if he were in the room with her. He wished he *was* in the room with her, watching her pull on her panty hose, her fingers unfurling them all the way up her smooth legs. He'd like to watch her lean over to dry her hair with the blow dryer, her body graceful and supple, her arms moving rhythmically as she wielded both hairbrush and dryer. Her hair would gleam, burnished as bright as new copper by the bedroom lights. When she straightened, ready to slip into the dress she planned to wear—he had no idea why he thought it was a dress. He simply knew, that's all—her eyes would shimmer like a sunlit sea in summer.

He stood up abruptly and walked to the window. His imagination was running away from him. He had no business thinking of Cricket Erling in such intimate terms.

"Tim?"

Her voice at the bottom of the stairs startled him out of his reverie. He hurried to the door and opened it. Cricket stood in the foyer holding a suited and capped Jeremy in her arms.

"Tim, I'm running a little late. I'm going to go pick up the baby-sitter now, and we'll be back in ten minutes or so." She looked tinier from this angle. Maybe it was because the baby was so bundled up, making him look rounder and fatter. Cricket hadn't put her coat on yet, and yes, she was wearing a dress. A royal-blue one. Her hair was a shiny aureole around her face.

Suddenly Tim realized that Cricket was going to have to take Jeremy out in the cold.

"I'll go get Kimberly," he said. "I wish I'd thought of it earlier. I guess I thought baby-sitters materialize out of nowhere when you need them."

"There's no need," Cricket began, but stopped talking when Tim shrugged into his coat and ran downstairs.

"You stay here," he said. "I'll be back with Kimberly in a jiffy." He tweaked the openmouthed Jeremy's nose and went out the door.

"Thanks," Cricket called lamely as he started up his car at the curb. It was a nice thing for him to do. He wouldn't have had to do it.

He smiled at her as he drove away.

While Tim was gone, Cricket divested Jeremy of his snowsuit and cap and settled him in his musical swing. She had just wound it up when the door opened, admitting Tim and the baby-sitter, Kimberly Haggerty.

Cricket knew Kim and liked her. To the accompaniment of the tinny "Rock-a-Bye Baby" lullaby played by Jeremy's musical swing, she quickly outlined Jeremy's evening routine and showed the sitter where to find Jeremy's clean diapers. Kimberly sat down and started to amuse the baby while Cricket hurried to the closet. Tim helped her on with her coat.

"Bye," said Kimberly as they walked out the door, and then Cricket was walking down the outside walk toward Tim's car.

I haven't even had time to think about what to say to him, thought Cricket as Tim opened the car door for her. While he walked around to his side of the car, she almost panicked. What if she couldn't think of anything to talk about except Jeremy's teething problems or her college classes? She didn't consider herself particularly well-rounded these days.

"So we're off to the—what is the name of that restaurant where we're going?" he asked when they were riding down the street. He glanced at her sideways, noting how pale she looked, how unlike herself. He wasn't used to seeing her without the baby in her arms. It seemed strange to see her sitting still.

"It's Nickelodeon's," Cricket said, licking her lips. Then she wished she hadn't. In this kind of weather, they'd only get chapped. Nervously she pulled a Chapstick out of her purse and spread some on her lips. Tim braked the car to a stop at a stoplight, and his eyes lingered a bit too long on her mouth. Cricket dropped the Chapstick into her purse and snapped it shut. The noise it made sounded as loud as a trapdoor clanging shut.

The restaurant was crowded when they got there. A younger crowd dominated. It was the weekly happy hour, and there weren't any tables available.

"I should have called for reservations," Tim said.

"They don't take reservations," Cricket replied.

"It'll be about forty minutes before we have an available table," the hostess informed them.

"Put our name on the waiting list," Tim directed her, and then he and Cricket walked out into the shopping mall.

"Is there anything you need to buy while we're here?" Cricket asked nervously.

"I need shaving cream," Tim said.

"There's a drugstore to the left," Cricket said, leading the way.

She had unbuttoned her coat, and it swung loosely from her shoulders. He got a glimpse of royal-blue wool. Her silk scarf parted to reveal the swelling of her breast against the jersey. He pulled his eyes away.

"Here it is," said Cricket.

She walked ahead of him, and he caught a whiff of her cologne. It was Chloé, his favorite. He smiled, and she saw the smile as she glanced over her shoulder when she went through the drugstore turnstile. "What kind should I get?" he asked her as they surveyed the array of aerosol shaving creams on the drugstore shelf.

"I don't know," Cricket said, looking uncomfortable, and Tim wished he hadn't asked the question. It was only his way of trying to put her at ease, but it hadn't worked. He picked up a can of lemon-lime shaving cream.

"This will do," he said.

Out in the mall they stopped before a display of furniture in a furniture store window.

"That's the kind of couch I'm going to buy when I get new furniture," she said. The couch was upholstered in white leather, a sectional with a recliner at one end. One of the sections made into a bed.

"White leather doesn't seem too practical if you have a baby," Tim said doubtfully.

Cricket's face fell. "I'd better readjust my home-furnishing ideas, I guess. I still don't think in terms of having a baby. After over eight months of motherhood, you'd think I would, wouldn't you?" She smiled as if to make fun of herself.

"Kids are permanent," Tim said.

Cricket laughed. "Yes, indeed. Jeremy has certainly changed my life. I never thought I'd be a single mother. I wouldn't have dreamed that I'd *like* being a single mother." She turned away from the window and walked on.

"Obviously you do like it," Tim said. He couldn't imagine being a parent. Before he'd held Jeremy, he hadn't ever held a baby before, at least not that he could remember. He'd never even held his nieces and nephews.

"It's different from the way I'd imagined parenthood. I always thought that I'd have someone to share the parenting with," Cricket said thoughtfully. "I became pregnant when my husband and I were attempting a reconciliation. The reconciliation didn't take, but the pregnancy did. I knew at that point that it would be hard to raise a child on my own, but I've never regretted the decision to have the baby. Never." Cricket's voice was soft, but determined.

"You must have been in school when you found out you were going to have a baby," Tim said.

"I was. When I found out I was expecting, I had to decide whether or not to drop out of school. Now I'm five months away from getting my degree, so I'm glad I didn't quit."

They stopped for a few minutes to watch a performance of the high school chorus on a dais in the middle of the mall. The choir sang several songs, and Cricket, leaning on the railing separating the spectators from the performing area, watched avidly, her lips parted, her eyes shining.

"Anyway," Cricket said, strolling on after the choir finished their fifteen-minute performance, "when I became responsible for another human being, it became even more important to finish work on my degree so that I could get a better paying job than the restaurant-hostess job I had while Hugh and I were married. So I suppose I could say that having Jeremy gave me the impetus I needed to finish school."

They had made a full circle of the mall and found themselves in front of Nickelodeon's again. Inside, after they had been seated at their waiting table, Tim leaned toward her.

"Well, Cricket Erling, that's an inspiring story you've just told me. I wondered what gave you all your get-up-and-go. Now I know. I wish I had the same kind of commitment toward a goal. Do you have any advice for me?"

Cricket grinned at him impishly over the top of her menu. "You could have a baby," she suggested.

Tim laughed. "Unfortunately, that's not a physical possibility. You've got to do better than that."

The waiter arrived to take their order, and their conversation drifted naturally to other things. Nickelodeon's was a place catering to the local young set, and peals of laughter could be heard from the people sitting around the bar. An electric train chugged around the inside of the bar, and music played over loudspeakers. Every time the bartender was given a tip, he rang a ship's bell.

The drinks were strong, the food was good, the atmosphere was congenial, and soon they were laughing together as though they were old friends. Several people stopped by to say hello to Cricket, looking surprised to see her there. When she introduced Tim, they looked even more surprised.

"Have you seen Trudy?" asked a girl who stopped by their table.

"No, Mary Sue. I think she's out of town for the weekend."

"Oh," Mary Sue said with a knowing look, before wandering away.

"How is the romance with Walt going?" Tim asked.

"The same as all the rest of Trudy's romances. Blissfully, at least for the time being."

"You sound as though you don't have much hope."

"Walt hasn't left his girlfriend, Rona, yet. He has to sneak away from her to see Trudy. I wish that Trudy would see through him, and soon."

"Why don't you talk to Trudy?"

"She'd only get annoyed with me, and she's going to need me."

"Why?"

"To comfort her once they break up," Cricket said.

"Good grief," Tim muttered.

"Well, it's true. I don't have to fib to you like I do to Trudy." Her eyes were clear and trusting, and he smiled back.

"That's right. And there's another thing I want you to tell me. What's the best dessert they serve here?"

She grinned at him. "The mud pie. It's fabulous."

"Will you have a piece?"

"I couldn't eat a whole one," she said.

"Share?"

"Well—"

Tim beckoned to the waiter. "We'll have one piece of your fabulous mud pie. And two plates."

Tim split the piece of pie right down the middle with a table knife. "You choose which piece you want," he said, pushing it toward Cricket.

"I don't care," she said.

"The one who cuts it always lets the other one choose. It's the rule."

He looked so serious that Cricket almost laughed. "Whose rule?" she wanted to know.

"Sarah's rule."

"Who's Sarah?" Cricket asked as she slid the piece that looked slightly smaller onto her plate.

"My friend back in Curtisville. She used to be my baby-sitter when I was a kid."

"She's that much older than you?"

"Yeah. She's like a sister to me, Sarah is." His face clouded momentarily. He hadn't been in touch with Sarah since he left Curtisville in the middle of one hot August night.

"You don't have any sisters, do you, Tim?" Cricket asked.

"No. Just two brothers, Leonard and Bernie. I had an older

sister, but that's another story." Tim paused. He wanted to change the subject. "How about you, Cricket? Any brothers or sisters?"

She shook her head. "I'm an only child, and I was raised by my grandmother. That's why I never heard of the rule you just made up."

"I didn't make it up!"

She smiled. A piece of shaved chocolate stuck to her upper lip, and her small pink tongue licked at it so that it disappeared. "Just testing you," she admitted. "Still, it's things like that that make me want to have a brother or sister for Jeremy."

"Don't you have your hands full enough as it is?" Tim polished off the last of his pie and stared at her.

"Yes, at least for now. But later—well, a child should have brothers and sisters. That's what I've come to believe from my study of psychology. The trouble is, experience tells me it's not such a good idea to have a baby if you don't have a husband." Her smile was plucky, but Tim sensed an underlying sadness.

After Cricket and Tim left the restaurant, they walked reluctantly to Tim's car. Their breath trailed behind them in white vapor trails. "Like jet planes," Cricket said playfully, spreading her arms like wings.

"Like steam locomotives," said Tim, chugging around her in a circle so that she laughed. He unlocked the car, and Cricket slid inside. She reached over and unlocked the door on his side.

"I'm not ready to go home yet," Tim said. "Is there anyplace we can go? Maybe for dancing? A drink?"

"I have to run my sandwich route in the morning," said Cricket. She couldn't believe, given her earlier worry about spending the evening with Tim, about finding things they could talk about, that the evening had gone so smoothly.

Tim slid the key into the ignition and started the car. It began to snow, and snowflakes sifted past the windshield.

The car warmed up slowly, and Cricket started to pull her gloves from her purse. Tim, however, reached over and covered her cold hands with his warm ones.

"I've had such a nice time," he said, and his earnestness made her heart flip over.

"I have, too," she said, her voice just above a whisper.

"I mean, nicer than nice. Wonderful."

Cricket swallowed. "Me, too," she said.

His eyes were dark and expressive. She could have drowned in their depths.

But then the moment was over. Tim shifted the car into reverse and backed out of the parking space. They exchanged small talk on the way back to the house, and as they drew up to the curb, Tim offered to take the sitter home for her.

"Oh, no," Cricket objected. "It's my job to do that."

"Remember what you said about thinking that you'd have someone to help you with the parenting when you eventually had a child? I'm not exactly offering to be a parent, but I don't mind taking Kimberly home. Honestly."

Shaking her head in amused acceptance, Cricket gave in. When Tim came back, the aroma of perking coffee filled the house.

"I thought this would warm you when you came in from the cold," Cricket said as she met him at the door and handed him a full cup of coffee.

"Why—"

"I'll hang your coat up in the closet," she said, taking it from him and brushing off the snowflakes.

"Is Jeremy asleep?" he asked as he followed her into her living room.

"Yes, Jeremy's a sound sleeper, thank goodness." Cricket settled herself on the couch, and he sat down next to her. She slipped off her shoes and folded her stocking feet under her full skirt.

They talked about her college courses, and he told her about flying, and he mentioned his years in the air force, and she described growing up in Manitou. When they thought to look at the clock, it was almost midnight.

Tim was embarrassed. "I didn't mean to stay so late," he said. "I know you have your route to run in the morning. I mean, that's why we didn't go anywhere else after the restaurant." He stood and walked to the stairway to his apartment.

Cricket followed him, and her smile was gentle. "I don't mind," she said. "I've had such a good time, Tim. I know I told you that before, but—well, I did."

He wanted to kiss her. She looked so pretty, standing there in her royal-blue dress and her stocking feet, waiting for him to climb the stairs to his room. He wanted to kiss her, but he couldn't bring himself to do it. A kiss would put their relationship on a different plane altogether. He wasn't ready to change the status quo.

"Good night, Cricket," he said.

"Good night, Tim."

The last glimpse he had of Cricket was of her standing at the bottom of the stairs, her small figure outlined by the light in the living room behind her and her hand stifling a yawn.

Hours later, a plaintive meow at the door of his apartment woke Tim. Immediately he thought of Cricket. He was afraid that the cat's meowing might wake her. Tim stumbled from his bed, opened the door, and Mungo scooted inside, disappearing into the dark void of his apartment.

"Hey," Tim said feebly, but the cat didn't reappear. Tim closed the door and felt his way through the blackness to the bedroom. He heard the cat purring before he ran into the dresser and stubbed his toe.

"Ow," Tim said halfheartedly, thinking that his "ow" sounded a lot like the cat's meow. Mungo must have thought so, too, because he stopped purring momentarily, then resumed. It was then that Tim realized that the cat occupied his bed.

"Move over," Tim grumbled, and Mungo complied, although grudgingly.

Tim yawned and curled himself around Mungo's comforting warm body, and before he knew it, he was sound asleep. The big cat slept beside Tim all night on Cricket's blue plaid sheets, his tail curled over his nose. Tim didn't awaken until both he and Mungo heard the cranky start-up of Cricket's camper just before dawn.

At that point, Tim jolted wide awake. He pulled on his bathrobe and hurried downstairs, thinking that he could offer to take care of Jeremy for Cricket while she ran her route. It was the least he could do after keeping Cricket up so late the night before.

He was too late. The camper lurched into the street just as Tim reached the door. It disappeared into the misty morning, its tail-lights glowing eerily through the camper's exhaust.

The ever-present Mungo twined around his ankles, and Tim automatically reached for the Cat Chow in Cricket's kitchen cabinet. He poured some into Mungo's dish.

"I guess I could have coffee ready for her when she gets

back,'' Tim said to the cat as though it was a person, and he plugged in the coffeepot before he went back upstairs to dress and shave.

Chapter Five

During the following week, Tim established a routine. In the morning he'd wake up at the first sound of Cricket and Jeremy's moving around downstairs just before dawn. He'd lie in his bed, watching the cold gray fingers of light creep through the interlaced bare branches of the tree outside his second-floor window.

He'd listen to Cricket's solicitous murmuring as she busied herself feeding Jeremy and to her shushing of her infant son when she thought he was too loud and might awaken Tim. And he'd wish with all his heart that he was downstairs with them, part of their warm circle.

Later, after the sound of Cricket's camper had faded down the street, Tim would slide out of bed, pad downstairs in the comfortable slipper socks his mother had knit him, and plug in Cricket's coffeepot. Then he'd feed Mungo and return to his apartment to shower and shave, after which he'd descend the stairs again, reach outside into the cold to pick up the paper from the front porch, and sit in Cricket's kitchen to read it.

Cricket apparently didn't mind his intrusion. His tiny refrigerator remained out of order, and he kept his meager food supply in hers. Cricket always seemed glad to see him when she came in from running her route, her cheeks red as apples from the cold.

She'd set Jeremy down on the rug in the living room and lean against the kitchen counter while she kept an eye on her small son as he bulldozed around the room on hands and knees. She'd drink a cup of coffee, and sometimes she'd eat a bowl of cornflakes if there was enough time. She and Tim would chat companionably before she rushed off to class and he hurried out to the airport.

"Why don't you eat breakfast? You should," said Tim one day.

"No time," Cricket said with a shrug, before slinging Jeremy in his blue baby carrier across her chest and hefting her book bag in one hand. With a cheerful wave, she disappeared out the back door, heading for the college.

"If I had breakfast ready for you when you came home in the morning before class, would you eat it?" Tim asked the next day.

"If I had time," she said.

"I was thinking that I'd like to eat more than cereal on these cold mornings, but my kitchen is too small and cramped for cooking. If I could cook down here, I'd make enough eggs or whatever for both of us."

"You're welcome to do that if you like," was all Cricket said before she left.

The next day, Tim bought a dozen eggs and a pound of bacon and left them in Cricket's refrigerator. When he came in late that night after knocking around a few of Manitou's bars and lounges, Cricket was studying at the kitchen table. She was barely visible from the foyer, and at the sound of the front door latch, she looked up from her book.

"How do you want your eggs in the morning?" Tim called to her.

"You mean you bought those eggs for me?"

"For both of us. Jeremy, too. Does he eat eggs?"

Cricket stood up. She looked tired. "You don't have to fix breakfast for me, Tim."

"We discussed it. I thought you said you'd eat it if I fixed it. And if you had time."

"I didn't really expect you to do it."

"Well, I am," he assured her.

"All right then. How about sunny-side up?"

"Sunny-side up it is," he said. He hesitated. He didn't want to go upstairs to his lonely apartment.

"Have you made your sandwiches yet?" he asked helpfully.

"Yes, they're ready to go."

"Oh," he said, still hesitating. Maybe she'd invite him into the kitchen for a cup of coffee. But she sat down on the kitchen chair and bent her head over her book. Tim climbed the stairs slowly, half hoping that she'd call him back. She didn't. He heard her running the faucets in her bathroom about an hour later. He heard the toilet flush, and then it was quiet downstairs.

Tim glanced at his clock. It was almost midnight. That was a late bedtime for someone who had to be up at the crack of dawn every morning.

The next day, a Saturday, Tim got up while Cricket was running her route and cooked bacon and eggs. How many eggs could Cricket eat, he wondered. He finally decided on two for her and three for him. He whistled cheerfully until he saw Trudy slipping through the hedge behind the house. It was early for Trudy to be out and about on a weekend.

He opened the door before she arrived.

"Why, Tim," Trudy said. "Is Cricket—um, around?"

"She's running her sandwich route," Tim said.

"I see," said Trudy, looking at the eggs Tim had just cracked into the frying pan. They were beginning to sizzle and curl around the edges. Tim turned the heat down.

"When will she be back?" Trudy asked.

"Any minute. She's going to eat these eggs."

"Oh. Well, tell her I stopped over. I'm going to go to work in a few minutes, and I want to leave the key to my house here. She can give it to Walt when he comes." Trudy plunked her house key down on the counter.

"I'll tell her," said Tim. "Do you have time to stay for breakfast?"

"I've eaten," Trudy said. "Anyway, I've got to open up my shop. Tell Cricket to call me sometime. Or to come over."

"Sure thing," Tim said.

"Well, goodbye, Tim."

"Bye, Trudy," Tim replied. He waved the spatula at her in farewell. Clearly Trudy wondered what his role was in this household.

"Chief cook and bottle washer," Tim told Mungo, who sat underneath the high chair waiting for scraps of food. The idea of becoming the self-appointed chief cook and bottle washer in this house wasn't a bad one. It felt good to have a defined role in life after all his drifting.

At that moment Cricket's camper rolled into the driveway, and she jumped out. She unfastened Jeremy from his car seat and hurried toward the house.

"Mmm," she said appreciatively as she pushed the door open. "It smells good in here. So homey." She closed the door behind her, tugged Jeremy's hood off with her teeth and sat him on the edge of the kitchen counter while she pulled his arms and legs out of his snowsuit.

"Breakfast is served, *madame*," Tim said with a grand flourish as he set their plates of eggs and bacon on the table. The toast popped up in the toaster, and he proceeded to butter it.

"Jeremy ate before we left," she told him.

"Maybe he'd like some toast," Tim suggested.

Cricket fastened Jeremy in his high chair.

"Would you like toast, Jeremy?" she asked.

Jeremy said something that sounded like "Babababaha," which Tim took to mean yes, and so he dropped another piece of bread in the toaster.

"Sit down, Cricket," he said.

"I was getting the jelly," she said.

"Sit down and eat. I'll get whatever we need," Tim told her.

Cricket sat and dug into her eggs. "They're perfect," she said. "Just the way I like them."

Tim was glad to see that Cricket enjoyed her breakfast. He sat down across the table from her and picked up his fork. Jeremy clamped his gums down on the toast and gnawed on it, seemingly content.

"I'll fix breakfast every morning," Tim said. "That is, if you don't mind me in your kitchen."

"Of course I don't. I don't want you to go to the trouble of cooking on my account, though. I've been getting along without breakfast for ages with no ill effects. Anyway, sometimes I won't have time to eat in the morning. I have to get to my first class on time."

"And what's your first class?"

"Psychological measurement. It emphasizes psychometric theory, concepts of correlational analysis, norms, reliability, validity and item analysis. We're working on statistical analysis right now."

"You're really into this psychology stuff, aren't you?" he said in admiration.

"It's interesting," Cricket said. She spread her toast liberally with jelly.

"And Jeremy goes along with you to class?"

Cricket's mouth was full, but she said "Mm-hmm." She swallowed. "He's getting to be a bit of a problem. He used to sit in his infant seat and either doze or watch whatever was going on in class, but now he's at the point where he wants to crawl around on the floor. I can't let him do that, so sometimes I'm at my wit's end to entertain him and take notes at the same time."

"I guess your professors must get annoyed if he's disruptive," Tim said.

"Oh, Jeremy has hardly ever interrupted class. Once when he was tiny he spit up all over my sweater and I had to leave the classroom, and once he cried during a test, but other than that he's been perfectly wonderful until now. Haven't you, Jeremy?" She turned bright eyes upon her son.

"Babababababa," said Jeremy, uttering what appeared to be his all-purpose word for everything. Tim had to admit to himself that the kid was kind of cute.

"By the way, Tim, I got you a ticket to the Manuel Susurro concert. It's Tuesday night." She reached for her coat hanging on the back of her chair and dug in the pocket. She pulled the ticket out and handed it to Tim.

"Wonderful," he said with satisfaction. "You'll go with me, won't you?"

"I hadn't planned—" Cricket began with some dismay.

"Oh, but I wouldn't go without you. I don't like to go to concerts alone."

"I'm not sure my regular baby-sitter can make it. Renee's a part-time college student and might want to go to the concert herself."

"I can call Kimberly again if you'd like." His eyes pierced through her. They were electric blue and brilliant.

"I'll check with Renee," said Cricket, trying not to stammer.

"Will you? I really want you to go with me, Cricket."

Cricket stood up and took her plate to the sink, where she washed off the egg yolk.

"Tim, I—I don't know how to tell you this," she said, turning toward him abruptly.

"You don't know how to tell me that the last time you went

to see a guy play the guitar, his teeth fell out, rolled across the stage and fell into your lap,'' said Tim.

She stared. ''Oh, you're joking,'' she said in relief when she realized that his expression was mischievous.

''Of course I'm joking. But I feel an excuse coming on. What is it?''

''I just—I just,'' she said, and then she threw her hands up in the air. ''It's hard to have a serious conversation with you when you're looking at me like that.''

''Like what?''

''Like Mungo when he's playing with a mouse. By the way, I think we've got mice in this house. I've heard them running around inside the walls and ceiling.''

''Why doesn't Mungo catch them?''

''So far they haven't come out where he can get them.'' The mice were like her—afraid of getting caught.

''I'll buy a couple of mousetraps. Why do you avoid talking about going to the concert with me? Don't you want to go?''

''It's not that I don't *want* to go,'' she said slowly.

''Good. Then we can leave home around seven-thirty so we'll get good seats.'' He stood up, walked over to the sink and rinsed his plate off, too. Under his front-zipping sweatshirt, she saw that he again wore the T-shirt that said Lefties Make Better Lovers.

''I had mice in this house once before,'' Cricket said, determined to start over. ''I put poison out and they disappeared.'' She saw the pulse beating in the vein in Tim's neck. She smelled the lemon-lime of his shaving cream. She swallowed and took a step backward.

''Somehow,'' Tim said carefully, taking one step forward so that they remained the same distance apart as they were before, ''I get the idea that I make you uncomfortable, even though we had such a good time together when we went out. I'd certainly like to know why that happens.''

''It just happens,'' said Cricket. Her voice squeaked, betraying her nervousness.

Tim didn't seem to notice. ''I'd hate to think that it happens because you don't like me,'' he said.

''It isn't that,'' Cricket said quickly.

''What is it, then?'' he said. His voice issued from low in his throat. She sensed something very virile and masculine about him, a quality of Tim's that she had ignored for too long.

"I'll be honest," she said, surprising him with her decision to be candid. "You're a man. I'm a woman. I haven't been seeing anyone since Hugh and I split for good. I'm very self-conscious around you. I almost don't know how to act around a man. Is that good enough for you?" She held her chin up in a kind of proud defiance.

This time Tim stepped backward. He lifted his hand and rubbed the back of his neck, looking ruefully down at the floor.

"Well, yeah, I guess that is good enough," he said in a tone of surprise. He looked her in the eye. "So what do I do about it? I enjoy your company, not only because you're an attractive woman but because you're fun to be with. Am I supposed to back off just because I make you uneasy?"

"Sometimes I need space," Cricket said in a low tone.

"I see," Tim said. There was a silence. "Is today one of the days I should back off? And how will I know when I should back off and when I should charge full speed ahead?"

Cricket amazed herself by feeling a tickle of amusement. "I wonder what you mean by full speed ahead."

"Asking you to go to the concert with me is full speed ahead," said Tim. "If I go back to my room now, that would be backing off." He ventured a smile.

The edges of Cricket's mouth twitched. "Maybe you could go full speed ahead before you back off. This morning, anyway."

He blinked at her. "Does that mean you'll go to the concert with me?"

"Yes, Tim." Her smile exploded all over her face, and she pushed him out of the kitchen. "It also means I want you to back off while I clean up after breakfast."

He let her nudge him into her living room, then turned to watch her run water in the sink.

"In case you didn't know," she called over her shoulder as the water ran, "that's another rule. The one who cooks doesn't have to clean up."

"What rule is that?" he asked, puzzled.

"Mine. I just made it up." She turned long enough to wrinkle the freckles on her nose at him and then began to suds the dirty dishes.

Tim laughed. Everything was all right between them, then. He turned to go upstairs, then remembered something.

"By the way, Trudy stopped by this morning. She left her house key on the counter. She said to give it to Walt when he arrives in town so he can get into her house. So I guess you're finally going to meet Mr. Wonderful," Tim said.

"Great," he thought he heard her mutter as he rounded the balustrade. "Just great."

And from his high chair, Jeremy said, "Babababababa."

LATE THAT NIGHT Cricket was balancing a full glass of milk and a brownie on a plate as she maneuvered through a veritable mine field of Fisher-Price toy people on the living room floor. She held up the hem of her long chenille bathrobe with her free hand and winced as she stepped on her third Fisher-Price person. She kicked it the way of Mungo, who batted it under the couch before threatening to make Cricket lose her balance by throwing himself against her ankles.

"Mungo!" she exclaimed as the front door swung open.

Tim closed the door behind him and looked at the condition of the living room. "What happened, Cricket?" he said. "It looks like Jeremy had a free-for-all."

"You should have seen him with two little wooden people sticking out of his mouth," said Cricket. "He looked like a cannibal chipmunk."

"Those cannibal chipmunks are the worst kind," Tim said. Cricket stood in front of him in the foyer now, and as always, he was surprised at how small she was.

From somewhere he heard the blare of the familiar words, "Live from New York, it's Saturday night!"

"Say, isn't that *Saturday Night Live* on TV?" he said.

Cricket, still carrying her brownie and her milk, nodded. "I'm going to watch it," she said hesitantly, and then because he looked so envious and because she knew that he didn't own a TV, she said, "Would you like to watch it with me?"

"Why, yes," he said in surprise after a slight hesitation.

"This way," she said, going into her bedroom. Her chenille robe flapped around her ankles, revealing her bare feet, their heels as smooth and round as a baby's.

Amazed that she would invite him into her inner sanctum without so much as a bat of an eyelash, Tim followed.

Cricket was unprepared for how awkward she would feel to see Tim Vogel standing in the middle of her bedroom. Her eyes met his, and their gaze remained locked for a few seconds too long. He finally pulled his eyes away and rested their gaze on the one straight-backed chair in her room with an expression of resignation.

Cricket wished she had thought this through before she'd so casually issued an invitation. In her bedroom there were only two places from which one could watch her television set—the chair and her double bed. She automatically excluded the floor. It was too cold and drafty at this time of year.

He saw the look on her face and said, "Hey, if it's going to make you feel uncomfortable—"

"Nonsense," she said, adopting a brisk tone. She set her brownie and milk on the nightstand with a clatter.

"It's just that I didn't realize," he began.

Cricket rested her hands on her hips. "We're two adults," she said rapidly. "I mean, I don't see why the two of us can't sit on my bed together. It's not as though I'm wearing a sheer negligee and am trying to lure you in here, is it? And you're not lunging after me, are you? Let's act like two mature grown-ups and sit on the bed to watch this show, which happens to be one of my favorites."

It was a long speech for Cricket, and Tim was glad that she could be so pragmatic about the situation. Clearly she hadn't given this idea much thought before she'd invited him, but at least she was living up to her invitation, for which he was thankful. He was at loose ends tonight, feeling out of place in the Manitou bar scene and having nowhere else to go.

He sat on the bed.

"I'll get some pillows," Cricket said, turning away to hide her confusion. She tossed a few fluffy pillows down from the closet shelf, and when she turned around, Tim had propped himself up against one side of her headboard. On the television screen somebody was taking a pratfall. Gingerly Cricket sat down beside Tim, and after a moment, she swung her legs up on the bed, making sure that her robe didn't gap.

It seemed odd for Tim to be on the other side of her double

bed. His arms were crossed over his chest, and his biceps bulged. She had to lean toward the edge of the bed to keep from rolling toward the depression his body made in the mattress. She kept fidgeting with the front of her robe, making sure that it didn't flap open. That was silly, because if it did, all Tim would see were her red-and-white striped flannel pajamas.

On-screen, one of the *Saturday Night Live* regulars was suing Mephistopheles in *People's Court*. Tim started to laugh. It was a mere chuckle at first, broadening to a deep belly laugh after a few seconds. Cricket laughed, too, whether in response to Tim's infectious laughter or to the funny skit, she didn't know. After that skit, which ended in an award for the plaintiff, a visiting comedian started a monologue. Tim began to chuckle again, and so did she.

After their laughter leveled off, Cricket was amazed to look down and see that Tim was holding her hand. How could he have taken her hand without her knowing it? It must have happened while they were absorbed in the television program. All of a sudden her hand felt too warm, and her fingers jerked reflexively within his grip. He squeezed back, and she realized that he must have thought she was squeezing his hand. She was too embarrassed to pull her hand away.

When the commercial break came on, Tim released her hand and said, "I'm going to get a glass of milk. Do you want a refill?"

"Please," she said, handing him her glass. "Bring the pan of brownies in here, too," she called after him, acting for all the world like a wife instructing her husband. Did Tim make that connection? Maybe not. He'd never been married. Maybe he didn't know what marriage was like. In its better days, her marriage had been a lot like this. She and Hugh used to stay up to watch *Saturday Night Live* every weekend.

She watched the commercial through a haze. Why had she invited Tim into her bedroom to watch television, anyway? What was her unconscious motive? Why had she fallen into a pattern that reminded her of being married? She was asking for trouble. There were inherent dangers in this situation, and Cricket was belatedly beginning to realize what they were.

I'll get Mungo in here, she thought in desperation. Mungo would seem like a third person. That would make this cozy little scene a lot less intimate.

When Tim returned to the bedroom, he found Cricket sitting

cross-legged on the bed, stroking Mungo's thick coat. He found nothing amiss in this, except that Cricket seemed to be repositioning Mungo so that the cat would be between them.

"Let's see if Mungo likes brownies," he said, holding a large crumb toward the cat, who sniffed it and gobbled it down.

"I never knew he'd eat sweets," Cricket said. She gave Mungo part of her brownie, too.

They settled back amid the pillows to watch the rest of the program. They laughed at all the same things. Cricket felt a stab of sadness because she so seldom had another adult with whom to share the things she found funny. She'd never realized before just how much she missed that intimacy in her life.

When the program was over, Tim said, "The brownies were delicious. And I enjoyed this. I'd better get serious about buying myself a television set."

"You can always watch mine," Cricket pointed out. "I don't mind."

"I don't want to intrude on your life in any way," he said earnestly. "I mean, it occurred to me when I was in the kitchen getting my milk out of your refrigerator that I'm acting like a roommate. You'd better let me know if I overstep my bounds."

"I—I like having you here," Cricket said truthfully.

Tim sat up. "Well, thanks," he said. His awkwardness made him seem even more appealing. Cricket used the remote control to turn off the television set. The silence crowded in on them. Cricket wanted to turn the TV set on again, but her fingers seemed frozen around the remote control unit and would not push the button when her brain gave the command.

"Cricket," Tim said softly, bending toward her as though she were an irresistible force. His eyes mesmerized her with their magic, and the soles of her feet began to tingle before his lips met hers.

Her eyes stayed open in surprise. He closed his eyes, pressing his mouth to hers gently, softly and in an undemanding way. He kissed her lips no more passionately than one would kiss a child on the cheek.

He straightened, looking down at her as though from a new perspective.

"Like I said, Cricket, let me know if I overstep my bounds," he said, and then he walked softly from her room.

Mungo stood up, stretched and followed him up the stairs.

And then Cricket did turn on the television set again, watching a mindless movie on the *Saturday Night Creature Feature* rather than lie alone in the dark and admit to herself that she was falling in love.

Chapter Six

The next morning Tim wore a T-shirt that said: Curtisville, Kansas, Isn't the End of the World, but You Can See It from There. Tim's T-shirts always piqued Cricket's sense of humor. This time Tim noticed her smile when she came in the back door, although he didn't suspect that the slogan on his shirt was the cause of it. Cricket's smile could dispel the gloom of a Wisconsin winter morning, and he found it impossible not to return it.

"I guess you got to meet Trudy's Walt yesterday," Tim said when they were sitting at the table eating their eggs.

Cricket made a face. "I certainly did," she said.

"I take it that you weren't impressed with Mr. Wonderful."

"He had sad eyes," said Cricket.

"Is that a plus or a minus?"

Cricket cut a sausage link into three pieces. "In Trudy's opinion, it's a plus."

"Are he and Trudy spending this weekend at her place? Or have they gone out of town?"

Cricket glanced out the window toward Trudy's hedge. She saw a light on in the kitchen. "I think they're at Trudy's. She's been seeing him for the past couple of weekends. I can't imagine what Walt tells his live-in girlfriend about his travels."

"He tells her that he's still checking out Manitou College for a job," Tim said with certainty.

"How do you know?" Cricket asked.

"That's what I would do if I were in Walt's position," Tim said with a shrug.

"And have you ever been in a similar circumstance?" Cricket

asked. She was curious to know more about Tim, and he'd been very quiet about his background.

Tim shook his head. "No, I'm not like Walt," he said.

"I'm sorry," Cricket said hastily. "I shouldn't have asked."

"Why not? I don't mind."

She toyed with a crust from her toast. "I was prying," she said.

"You want to know more about me," he said softly. "That's only natural."

Natural in what circumstances? Cricket thought. "We're housemates, not—" she said.

"Not what?" Tim said.

She stood up and dumped her half-eaten breakfast in the garbage.

"Not anything else," she said.

There was a pause lasting several beats while they each charted the direction in which their conversation was heading. It was clear to them that they both knew what they were talking about. Neither of them said anything until Tim arose from the table.

"I guess I'll go out to the airport," Tim said abruptly, and then he was gone.

Cricket spent the afternoon studying, but she was easily distracted. She had learned to recognize the sound of Tim's car as it rounded the corner, and she knew the ring of his heels on the front porch. This afternoon she heard neither, and she wondered what Tim Vogel found to do on Sunday afternoons in a strange town.

It was after dark when Trudy dropped by. Cricket had put Jeremy to bed and was trying to decide whether to wash her sweaters or go to bed with a good book. She had made up her mind in favor of the book when Trudy knocked on the back door.

Trudy, heavily bundled in a down jacket, blew in on a snow flurry, and she rubbed her cold cheeks to warm them as Cricket hung her coat in the closet.

Trudy seemed tightly strung tonight, her eyes bright and her smile a bit too brittle. She balanced on the edge of one of the kitchen chairs while Cricket filled the teakettle.

"He's going to tell her this week," Trudy said without preliminaries.

Cricket set the teakettle on the stove burner.

"Who is going to tell whom? And what is he going to tell her?"

"Walt is going to tell Rona he's leaving her," Trudy said.

"Good," said Cricket. "Did the job at Manitou College pan out for him?"

"Not yet. He's still working on it." Trudy crossed her legs and began to jiggle her foot.

Cricket wished that Trudy would relax. She pushed a box of cookies across the table to Trudy, but her friend impatiently waved it away.

"Anyway," Trudy went on, "Walt's going to rent a room in a student boardinghouse for the rest of the semester. It'll be cheap, and—"

"Wait a minute, Trudy," Cricket said, shaking her head as if to clear it. "Does Walt have money problems?"

"Well, doesn't everyone?" Trudy asked sharply.

"You know what I mean," Cricket said.

Trudy sighed. "Walt supports his mother, who is very old and sick."

"I see," Cricket said.

"If it weren't for me, Walt says, there wouldn't be a bright spot in his whole life. Oh, Cricket, I sobbed when he told me about his ex-wife. You wouldn't believe what that woman has done to him." Tears shone in Trudy's blue eyes.

"Tell me anyway," Cricket said.

Trudy blinked her tears away. "The story is too long to go into right now, but believe me, I don't see how she could have treated him the way she did. That's why he got so deeply involved with Rona. He was lonely after his divorce, and Rona happened to be there, and before he knew it, he was living with her, and her children had come to depend on him. Walt's so kindhearted that people take advantage of him."

"I met Walt yesterday when he came to get the key to your house," Cricket said.

"What did you think of him?" Trudy beamed.

Cricket strived for a neutral tone. "He was very polite," she said.

"Oh, he *is*. And thoughtful. He brought me a huge bouquet of roses, can you imagine? And as a lover—well, all I can say is, his eyes are *not* his *best* feature."

"Trudy!"

"I absolutely adore him, Cricket."

"I'm glad," Cricket said weakly. The things that were obvious to her were certainly not clear to Trudy, who seemed blind to everything except Walt's best features.

To escape Trudy's rapt expression, Cricket got up to pour the tea, and Trudy mercifully dropped the subject of Walt.

"By the way, you're certainly getting chummy with Tim," Trudy remarked when Cricket sat down again.

Cricket, who was stirring her tea, raised her eyes to Trudy's. Trudy was eyeing her coyly and curiously, waiting for Cricket to explain.

"Chummy? I don't know about that," Cricket hedged. She lifted her cup to her lips, but the tea was too hot to drink.

"You're eating breakfast together every morning. It's almost as though he's moved into your part of the house."

"Tim's refrigerator is broken. I let him use mine," Cricket said. She resented having to define her living arrangements for anyone else, even her closest friend.

"I heard he's a barfly. He makes the rounds of the Manitou watering holes almost every night."

"Last night he was right here," Cricket said before she thought. Then, thinking of the chaste kiss they had shared, she blushed.

"Why, Cricket, I do believe there's something between you and Tim Vogel," Trudy said with obvious delight.

"Trudy," Cricket warned.

"If there is, it's fine with me," Trudy said quickly. "I've always thought you needed someone."

"Tim and I happen to live in the same house," Cricket said. She suddenly felt exhausted, as though she couldn't go on with this conversation.

"And he cooks breakfast for you," Trudy added.

"Yes. And that's all," Cricket replied as firmly as she could.

But secretly she wondered if that was really all or if, given the opportunities they had, there would soon be more.

On Tuesday night, Tim and Cricket attended the Manuel Susurro concert as planned. The concert was packed, and the guitarist was in top form. The music was more sensuous than either of them had expected. The program consisted of many soulful Spanish pieces.

Cricket was borne away on the lush strains of the melodies. The guitarist was short and swarthy, but something about the line of his lower lip reminded her of Tim. She sneaked a look at Tim, only to find that he was staring down at her. She shifted away from him, in her seat, suddenly self-conscious.

When the music was over, it was hard to break its spell. Cricket preceded Tim up the aisle, overly aware of his presence behind her.

"We could go to the Rathskeller," Tim suggested as they pushed their way through the crowded lobby of the concert hall. Many of their fellow concertgoers were walking in the direction of this popular off-campus hangout.

"Okay," Cricket said, wrapping her scarf more tightly around her neck.

The air outside was bitterly cold, and snow from the latest snowstorm was heaped at the curbs. In the glow from converted gaslights, snow sparkled on the tree limbs and looked like sugar frosting. Tim took Cricket's arm in case she stumbled on the sand-strewn sidewalk. Her warmth emanated through the sleeve of her coat.

"So what did you think of the concert?" he asked.

"Manuel Susurro is a very good musician. I don't know why his music left me feeling so unsettled."

He regarded her with mild surprise. The voluptuous music had had that effect on him, too. He had expected Cricket merely to say that she enjoyed the concert. That was what most women would have done.

"I think it was the way the man played the guitar," he offered.

Cricket recalled how Susurro had cradled the guitar in his arms, almost the way he might have held a woman. He played it the way he might make love to one. Cricket shivered, but not from the cold.

The Rathskeller was smoky and crowded, but its stuffy warmth was welcome after the glacial outside temperature. Cricket and Tim found a tiny table littered with other people's empty glasses, and Tim shouldered up to the bar to get their drinks.

She felt uncomfortable and out of place while she waited for him to return. She hadn't visited the Rathskeller in so long that she had forgotten how noisy it could be. Someone punched a selection on the jukebox, and the music was so loud that the table vibrated with every beat. Cricket was still swaying inside to the rhythm of a Spanish guitar. The jukebox music made her feel out of sync.

A couple of friends from school pushed past her table and said hello. They looked carefree and had a certain devil-may-care air about them. They seemed to be everything she was not. The difference depressed her. By the time Tim came back with their drinks, a seltzer with lime for Cricket, a beer for himself, Cricket knew she was out of her element.

Tim said something, but Cricket couldn't hear him. She asked him to repeat it.

"I said, I've never seen it this crowded in here before," he shouted.

"Do you come here often?"

"I've been here a few times," Tim said.

"Does Curtisville have any places like this?" she asked. She had to scream in order to be heard.

"Curtisville? Are you kidding? There isn't even a place where you can buy a drink in Curtisville," he said.

"What is Curtisville like?" Cricket asked. The song on the jukebox was taking a long time to rise to a loud and crashing conclusion.

"What?"

"I said, what's it like?" she yelled back. Her throat felt scratchy from inhaling other people's cigarette smoke and from shouting.

Tim shook his head and placed his lips close to her ear. "I give up. Would you mind if we go? I can't stand it in here."

Cricket had been thinking the same thing, but she'd been reluctant to suggest leaving. Now she smiled in instant relief. "That sounds good to me," she said.

They abandoned their drinks, which they had barely touched, and pushed through the crowd to the door. Outside, they headed into the teeth of an icy wind. They had walked to the concert, for the house was only a few blocks away.

"Anyway," Tim said, keeping his eyes to the front, "you asked about Curtisville. It's not as big as Manitou." The breath burst from his mouth in frosty balloons, like in a comic strip.

There was nothing either amused or amusing in his expression, however. If anything, he looked distressed, and Cricket couldn't figure out why.

"And your family still lives there?"

Cricket thought she detected a slight hesitation, but Tim said, "Yes, more or less."

She wondered what that meant, and she waited for him to elaborate. He didn't.

"I've wondered how you ended up here in Manitou in the dead of winter," she said.

"It's a long story. You wouldn't be interested," he said gruffly.

"Try me," she said.

He looked down at her, plodding along so determinedly beside him. He longed to tell her all of it. He didn't know how he knew that Cricket Erling wouldn't think less of him for what he had done; he just knew. He cleared his throat, and she slid an inquiring look up at him.

"I—" he began, but he found that the words wouldn't shape themselves.

"Yes?" she said.

"I don't want to talk about it," he said.

Cricket's mouth formed a silent O.

"I miss my family," he said in a cracked voice. "I've never said that out loud before."

"It's okay," she said.

They turned up the walkway in front of the house. Cricket paused at the steps and sighed a plume of vapor into the air. It froze on her eyelashes.

She turned and looked up at him, surprised at the anxiety on his face. She was raising her hand to brush his cheek in a gesture of silent comfort for his anguish, whatever it was, when the babysitter opened the front door. Turning away from Tim, Cricket found that it was hard to walk inside and pay the sitter. The past few minutes had drawn a net of intimacy around the two of them.

Renee, the baby-sitter, lived within walking distance. She left, and Cricket and Tim faced each other in the foyer.

"Thank you for going to the concert with me," Tim said.

Cricket wondered what was running through Tim's mind now, and she expected him to kiss her. She kept her eyes fixed on his face.

"The concert," he began uncertainly, not knowing what he wanted to say about it. He was only now beginning to realize, as he gazed at Cricket's parted lips, how erotically it had affected him.

"It was—different," she agreed. She didn't move from where she stood in the doorway between foyer and living room.

He wondered if she felt what he felt as a result of watching and listening to the guitarist. He thought about the way Susurro's hands had moved so intimately over the guitar, plucking and stroking—

Cricket moved toward him, and he opened his arms. There was a light in the living room, but not in the foyer. Backlighted, Cricket seemed wraithlike and delicate, her features exquisitely wrought. She positioned herself within the circle of his arms, and she lifted her head.

He kissed her as though it was what he had planned to do all along, and indeed perhaps he had. He was conscious of her body pressed against his. Her breasts felt bigger than they looked. Her bones felt fragile, birdlike.

Cricket let herself relax, put in mind of flowing strains of guitar music and her own melting response to it. Tim's mouth against hers fit perfectly, and it was an extremely satisfying kiss, expressive in the extreme.

He let her go, and despite the surprising level of her arousal after only one kiss, Cricket saw that he was just Tim again, familiar Tim with his blond hair and lopsided smile, a Tim who was staring down at her tenderly and as though she had just said something he didn't understand.

"I was thinking of making an omelet in the morning," he said.

"There's cheese in the utility compartment of the refrigerator," she said.

This mundane exchange put a damper on all imagined future proceedings and made it clear that nothing else was going to happen. Jolted back to reality, Tim stammered his good-night and retreated slowly upstairs.

Cricket fled from the foyer under the pretext of checking on Jeremy, and in her nervousness she caught a glimpse of her face in the mirror on the back of Jeremy's door. She looked the same except that her lipstick was slightly smeared. She wiped it with her little finger, wondering why she bothered, and then she realized that she was hoping that Tim might come downstairs again.

He didn't. After a long, hard look at the closed door at the top of the stairs, she went to bed, leaving her bedroom door open as usual and wondering if that was a wise thing to do. Maybe it wasn't, but it was her custom and the only way she could hear Jeremy if he cried during the night.

Upstairs, Tim threw himself across his bed and pondered the interesting question of what he would have done if Cricket had invited him into her bedroom tonight.

He decided that he would have gone, but afterward he wouldn't have felt good about it.

In the end, he was glad she hadn't asked him. He was suddenly afraid that he might hurt her, and he had promised Haggerty that he would not.

The only way that he could keep from hurting her, he was certain, was to lessen his involvement with her. He should never have revealed so much of himself to her tonight. Anybody could see that she was half in love with him already.

Or was it only that he was an antidote to her loneliness? And that she was the antidote to his?

Either way, he'd better play it cool.

TIM SLEPT RESTLESSLY that night, and when he finally woke up the next morning, he didn't hear Cricket moving around below as usual. He jumped from bed, thinking that she had overslept. Today was Monday, and he knew it was important to her to run her route so that she could get to her first class on time.

He rushed barefoot down the stairs, peering around the edge of Cricket's open bedroom door. She wasn't in bed, and with the shades pulled down, the house was silent and gloomy. Fear clenched his stomach. What if something had happened to her?

He hurried through the living room and swung open the door to the sun room that served as a nursery. And Cricket was there, sitting in the old rocker beside Jeremy's bed, nursing her child.

She had fallen asleep. Tim wasn't prepared for the supremely emotional response he felt at seeing Cricket, her breast bared, as she suckled her baby. He was frozen on the spot, unable to move.

A ray of winter light slanted through the window to halo her bright hair, and her skin glowed with health and radiance. Her arms held her child loosely, and her head was bent forward and slightly to the side, resting against the back of the chair. Her face in repose was gentle and Madonna-like. She wore her same old blue chenille bathrobe. Her breast was round and full, with Jeremy's small hand resting against the bottom curve. Her nipple was in Jeremy's mouth, and he sucked on it, making little contented swallowing noises deep in his throat.

Tim didn't want Cricket to wake up and find him there. He didn't want the scene spoiled by the startled expression that he knew would leap into her eyes at the sight of him.

He backed slowly out of the room and silently closed the door. He stood there for a moment, undecided and, for some reason, numb. And then, more quietly than he came, he retreated to his room, where he sat on the edge of his bed and discovered that he was trembling.

He hadn't realized that Cricket still nursed Jeremy. She'd never given him any idea.

Tim had grown up on a farm, and animals giving birth and suckling their young were nothing new to him. Why, then, had the sight of Cricket and Jeremy, mother and son, in such an intimate relationship almost unhinged him?

Finally he heard Cricket talking to Jeremy downstairs, opening and closing the refrigerator door, running water in the sink. When she left, Tim got up and dressed, moving like an automaton. He vaguely recalled that he had planned to cook an omelet this morning.

He made the omelet before Cricket came home from running her route, and he served her wordlessly, which was unusual for him.

The T-shirt he wore this morning was yellow and said: Gee, Toto, I Don't Think We're in Kansas Anymore. Cricket smiled and said, "I saw graffiti on a wall at the college. It said, 'Aunt Em—hate you, hate Kansas. Taking the dog. Dorothy.'"

She thought this would amuse him, but he only replied with a grunt.

By the time Cricket and Jeremy left for class, Tim was still acting gruff and moody. He saw her shoot one last perplexed look at him over her shoulder as he stood at the kitchen door, watching her go.

Tim didn't come home until late that night, and he made sure that it was after Cricket was asleep. He paused in the hall, peering toward the dark and open doorway of her bedroom. He wondered if she was awake.

On his way up the stairs, he stumbled twice. He had managed to get himself very drunk.

CRICKET WALKED OVER to Main Street later that week one day during her lunch period. She had to buy poison to put out for the mice. The traps Tim had set for them had produced no results. She also wanted to look in on Trudy. She felt guilty about not being more supportive of her friend in her new romance.

"Cricket! And Jeremy!" Trudy darted out from behind the cash register in her shop and hugged both of them.

"It's time for lunch," Trudy said. "Why don't we get some sandwiches from the Lunch Box Café across the street?"

"Sandwiches are my stock in trade," Cricket said, holding out a brown bag. "I brought ham and cheese for you and tuna fish for me."

"My favorite!" said Trudy, appropriating the bag. "We're going to eat lunch in the back," she called to her assistant, Mary Sue.

Trudy's small desk in her office behind the store was pressed into service as a lunch counter. Trudy insisted on holding Jeremy on her lap while she ate. "He's getting so big," she marveled, cuddling Jeremy close with one arm.

Cricket produced a bottle of juice for Jeremy. "I know. He's outgrowing his clothes so fast he hardly has anything to wear anymore. I'm weaning him, you know. He eats more solid food now."

Trudy kissed the top of Jeremy's head. "I've been thinking that maybe it's not too late for me to have a baby after all, Cricket," she confided between bites of her sandwich. "If things work out between Walt and me, who knows? Maybe I'll be wearing maternity clothes by this time next year."

"Why, Trudy! Do you think marriage is a possibility with Walt?"

"Definitely. He hasn't actually said it, but we know how we feel about each other. By the way, we're going to Wintermont to ski this weekend."

"Wintermont! How nice," exclaimed Cricket. She had made

up her mind to be as enthusiastic as possible about Walt today, and besides, Wintermont was the best ski resort in the northern part of the state.

"Yes, and it was Walt's idea. I can hardly wait. All that skiing, and après-skiing, and after the après-skiing..." Trudy's face glowed.

"While you're anticipating your weekend, I'd better get back to the campus," Cricket sighed. She stood up, brushed the crumbs off her lap and held out her arms for Jeremy. He laughed and kicked his feet so hard that she could hardly get him back in his baby sling.

"It was a nice visit," Trudy said. "Let's do it more often. By the way, what are your plans for the weekend?"

Cricket tucked Jeremy's juice bottle in her purse. "I have to finish a term paper, put out some d-CON before the mice take over the house, and run my sandwich routes," she said. Trudy made a face. "What about Tim?"

"What about him?" Cricket managed to keep her expression blank.

"Oh, you know. I thought that you and Tim were an item. Since he's been living in the same house, you seem more *normal*."

"Normal? You mean I've seemed *abnormal* before?"

"Not abnormal, but certainly you've been intensely involved in motherhood and in getting your degree to the exclusion of other pleasures. I thought you might be opening yourself up to dating again after you started to go out with Tim."

"Trudy, dear, you're my closest friend. You tend to overestimate my attractions, though, don't you think? Even you must realize that not many college men are interested in a woman who appears to have a baby growing from her hip."

"But Tim—"

"Tim and I are only friends," said Cricket.

"If only you'd try," said Trudy.

"Try?"

"You know, try to impress him with your feminine charms."

Cricket laughed. "You're a dreamer, Trudy. I hope you and Walt have a terrific time at Wintermont."

Trudy beamed. "We will, you can count on it." She waved at

them through the window as Cricket began her hike up Main Street.

Impress him with my feminine charms, Cricket said to herself as she hurried toward the campus. Trudy certainly lived in a dream world.

Cricket had stopped to wait for a light to turn green when her eyes fell on a blouse in a store window. She sauntered over and gazed through the plate glass, holding Jeremy's hands so that he wouldn't leave his fingerprints all over the window.

It was such a lovely blouse. Cricket was sure that she'd never owned one nearly as pretty. It was a pale eggshell-beige silk in a shimmering jacquard pattern, and it had an intricately embroidered lace collar. It was long sleeved, with a fitted bodice and padded shoulders. She was sure it would cost entirely too much money.

With her pale red hair, the color would be perfect. She lingered until the light had changed again, and then she thought she might as well go inside and inquire how much the blouse cost. The salesclerk on duty, who knew Cricket slightly, quoted her a price that made Cricket bite her lip in disappointment. The blouse was far beyond the amount of money Cricket had to spend.

"It's going to be on sale tomorrow," the clerk said as Cricket turned to leave.

Cricket paused to look at the blouse again. It was such a neutral shade that it would go with almost every suit, skirt and pair of pants she owned. It would be a wonderful wardrobe expander.

"I could ask my boss if he'd let you have it at the sale price," the clerk suggested.

When she had gone to ask, Cricket fingered the silk fabric. It felt so fine and luxurious. She would love to own it.

"Good news—my boss will mark the blouse down for you right now," the salesclerk reported.

With the money she had collected from her sandwich customers that morning, Cricket could just swing the purchase.

"I'll take it," Cricket said in a rush, and before she knew it, she was walking out of the shop carrying a bag containing the prettiest blouse she'd ever owned.

"That was probably a dumb thing to do," she told Jeremy. Not only had she bought the blouse, but she was late for class. Jeremy laughed and clutched at the bag.

"I don't know what possessed me to buy it," Cricket said a few moments later. Jeremy chortled. He was in fine fettle today.

And then Cricket recalled what Trudy had said about impressing men with her feminine charms. She had to admit that if she couldn't impress someone with her feminine charms while wearing a blouse such as this, then most probably she didn't have any.

"Feminine charms," muttered Cricket as she slid into her seat in the back of the big teaching auditorium where her class was held.

"Babababababa," Jeremy said loudly, causing the professor to stop in mid-sentence, take a deep breath and pierce Cricket with a glare of pure annoyance.

Chapter Seven

The next day was Friday, and Cricket felt a new sense of freedom when she left her last class. She wasn't sure why. Maybe it had something to do with buying an expensive blouse on the spur of the moment. She hadn't done anything that reckless in ages.

When she got home, she put Jeremy in his crib for his nap. As she was leaving the room, she heard the scratch of tiny feet above the ceiling.

"It's those mice again," she told Jeremy, who was already half-asleep.

She closed the door to Jeremy's room and went to get the poison she'd bought.

"Where should I put it?" she said to herself. She glanced out the window, and saw Tim's car parked at the curb. That meant that Tim must be upstairs. She wanted his advice. After all, the mice in this house had to be regarded as his mice as well as hers.

"Tim?" she called in the direction of his door. She didn't call too loudly in case he was taking a nap.

She heard the footsteps overhead, but they were human footsteps this time. Tim opened the door and stood smiling down at her. Briefly she wondered if she'd made a mistake to consult him.

"Tim, I bought some poison for the mice, but I'm not sure where to put it."

Tim considered this. "There's an attic space under the eaves. I can get to it through a small door in the wall in my kitchen. We could put the poison in there. That seems like a good place, since I'm pretty sure they'd have access to the space between the walls from the attic. We should put some poison in the storage area under the stairs, too.''

"Okay," she said. "Here's the d-CON."

"Bring it upstairs, and we'll put it in the attic," he said.

The poison came in little trays, the top of which was peeled back to expose baited grain. Tim crawled into the space under the eaves with two of the trays while Cricket held a flashlight so that he could see.

"There," said Tim, backing out of the space after positioning the bait trays. He stood and washed his hands at the small sink.

"Thanks, Tim," Cricket said.

"You're not leaving, are you? I was going to ask you to stay."

"Well, I—"

"Where's Jeremy? Taking his nap?"

Cricket nodded.

"I've never shown you how I've fixed this place up," he said. They were still standing in his kitchen that had once been a closet and where there was hardly room to turn around. Cricket resorted to backing out, and Tim followed.

"I bought some curtains for the lower half of the dining room windows," he said. He had mounted café rods and put up red-and-blue café curtains in a snappy print. They livened up the room considerably.

"I bought this rug at a garage sale," he said, pointing to the small oriental on which they were standing.

"It's pretty," she said. "I didn't know anyone had garage sales at this time of year."

"These people were settling the estate of their parents. Haggerty knew them, and when I told him I needed a few things for the apartment, he sent me over there. I bought this good reading lamp, too," he said, leading the way into the living room.

"This is nice," Cricket said as she admired a large globe with black oceans and multicolored continents. She pulled a chain, and the world lit up.

"I couldn't pass that up," Tim said sheepishly. "It's fun to look at whenever I get an attack of wanderlust. I can stare at Africa or Australia and almost imagine that I'm there."

"Do you have such attacks often?" Cricket asked. She sauntered around the living room, looking at the homey touches Tim had added. There was a silk flower arrangement, second hand, but only slightly faded. He'd spread the afghan out over the back of the couch so that its intricate design showed.

"I'm afraid I do think about traveling a lot," he admitted. "Won't you sit down? You can be the first guest I've had since I bought these new—or rather old—things." He turned on his most charming smile.

Cricket perched on the couch, and Tim went to get them a cup of tea. He seemed almost pathetically eager for her company, which was a direct contrast to the way he'd been acting most of the week.

He sat down beside her on the couch. His hair was brushed back from his forehead, and he wore a T-shirt with the slogan, Being Sexy Is a Tough Job, but Somebody's Got to Do It. Cricket wanted to laugh out loud, but she took a sip of her tea instead.

Noticing her strained expression, Tim asked, "What's wrong?"

She decided to tell him. "It's your T-shirt. I never know what your chest is going to say next."

Tim laughed and looked down. "I've collected these shirts from all over. Every town seems to have a shirt shop, and I like to buy one everywhere I go. That way I can remember the town after I've left."

"Where did you find that one?"

"In Andalusia, Alabama," he said.

"What were you doing there?" she asked.

"Flying."

"And then you went south to Florida?"

"Yeah, and that's where I crashed into a field. You should see the shirt somebody brought me in the hospital. It says It's Not the Crash That Kills You, It's the Sudden Stop."

"Have you flown since that crash?"

Tim shook his head. "I'll have to pass the medical exam first. Then I'll be flying charter flights for Haggerty," he said.

"I thought you were a crop duster," she said.

"I can fly charters, too. Anyway, crop dusters are called aerial applicators these days," Tim said.

"Aerial applicators," repeated Cricket. "That's going to take a while to catch on. It doesn't have quite the ring to it that crop duster has."

"Nobody dusts crops anymore. We spray them. Anyway, we have to have a complete knowledge of the crops and the pests we're trying to eradicate. Not only that, we have to know what chemicals to use and how to apply them safely. Aerial applicator may not be as easy to say as crop duster, but it's a lot more descriptive.''

''Where'd you learn all the things you needed to know in order to applicate aerially?''

He liked the way she teased him with a straight face. ''I learned to fly in the air force, I learned about crops at home on the farm, and I went to school to learn about controlling greenbugs, wheat rust and smut, and a host of other problems.''

''So you lived on a farm,'' said Cricket, pleased that she was finally finding out something about Tim's background.

''Yes,'' he said shortly, and she realized immediately that she'd somehow blundered.

Her gaze dropped. She was wearing a Fair Isle sweater in a becoming shade of green and a pair of black corduroys. She picked at a piece of lint on the corduroy, wondering how to save the conversation.

''I was thinking,'' she said slowly, ''that maybe you'd like to eat dinner downstairs with me tonight.'' She had been thinking nothing of the sort. It had popped into her head that very instant.

Then she realized that he might have other plans. He might have a date.

''I mean,'' she amended, ''if you have nothing better to do.''

He cocked his head at her. ''I don't get it,'' he said.

''Get what?'' she replied, lifting her head and wishing she didn't feel so shy all of a sudden.

''I don't understand why you would offer an invitation and then act as though it's second-rate.''

''I, um,'' she said.

''Well?''

''I thought you probably had something else planned,'' she said in a near-whisper.

''Why?''

''Trudy says,'' and she stopped.

''Trudy says what?''

''That—that you like to go out,'' she said. She could never tell him what Trudy had really said.

''I've only seen Trudy once at night, and that was at the Rathskeller where I had gone to play a quick game of pool.''

"Oh."

"And for your information, I would be delighted to join you for dinner. What can I bring?"

"Nothing," she said, getting up.

"What time shall I arrive?"

"I don't know." This conversation was making her miserable. She felt as though Tim was making fun of her in some way known only to himself.

"How about if you knock three times on the ceiling when you want me?"

"Or twice on the pipe?" she said, grinning in spite of herself.

"You've got it," he said.

She gave up. She couldn't help but respond to his outgoing personality, which was a welcome change after a moodiness that had lasted most of the week. "Could you come around seven-thirty? Is that okay?"

"Seven-thirty is fine."

"I made a pot of chili today," she said in unnecessary explanation.

"I like chili." He looked pleased.

Cricket stood at the door, wishing for some magical incantation that would enable her to get through it without making a fool of herself. Finally she resorted to, "I'll see you later," and fled down the stairs into her own territory, where she felt infinitely more comfortable.

She went into the kitchen and began to assemble a salad. It was early yet, but once Jeremy woke up, she wouldn't have time.

She still didn't know what had possessed her to invite Tim to dinner tonight. She should have let him go ahead and do whatever he had planned. It was hard to believe that he had no plans, and it was even more difficult to believe that he was actually happy to be spending the evening with her.

She'd almost forgotten that it was a Saturday. They could watch *Saturday Night Live* together again. Cricket stood undecided, a tomato in one hand, a knife in the other. After a moment's thought, she dropped the knife into the sink and went to lug her portable television set from the bedroom to the living room.

TIM AND CRICKET STOOD in the kitchen, making sandwiches after eating chili. The sandwiches were for Cricket's customers, and

Tim had offered to help after they cleaned up the kitchen.

"You have to put a little mustard in the egg salad," said Cricket, keeping a watchful eye on Tim.

"How about dill? Do you have any?" Tim sampled the egg salad.

"Yes, but my customers are likely to complain if I deviate from the way I usually do it. One time I put green onion in the tuna salad, and a couple of people called up to tell me they liked it better the old way."

"Okay, no dill. Where's the mustard?"

"In the refrigerator. Tim, you're pretty good at this."

"Ma made sure I knew my way around a kitchen."

"You hardly ever mention your parents, Tim," she said, glancing at him to see what effect this observation had.

He flushed, but he kept on spreading egg salad. "Like I said, I haven't seen my family in a while," he said finally.

"That's too bad."

"Under the circumstances, maybe not," Tim said.

She knew by the way he said it that something had come between Tim and his parents. She'd studied family interaction in her psychology courses, and the way families functioned had always interested her. She had no family left now that her grandmother was gone.

"Hand me the mayonnaise, will you, Tim? It's on the bottom shelf of the fridge."

Tim got the mayonnaise and kneed the refrigerator door to close it. Cricket spread mayonnaise on twenty slices of bread. She worked deftly, with no wasted motion.

"It's not that we hate each other or anything," Tim blurted. He had a stark look on his face.

"What?" She focused startled eyes on him.

"My family and I. We get along all right."

"Tim," she began, wanting to tell him that he owed her no explanation.

"I have a mother, a father and two brothers. I'm the youngest. I—I let them down once, and we've been out of touch." Tim stood with his back to the counter now, leaning against it. His eyes seemed to plead with her for understanding.

"Do they know where you are?" she asked.

Tim nodded. "I left home because the bank repossessed our farm. It was traumatic for all of us, because the land had been in our family for generations. They were going to auction off everything we owned, and I couldn't stand to see that happen. So I left in the middle of the night last August, and I haven't been back since." He heaved a giant sigh, but he looked immensely relieved, as though he'd managed to get something important off his chest.

"Tim, I'm sorry about your farm." Cricket kept spreading tuna salad.

"So was I. And I'm sorry I left. Someday when our wounds have healed, I'll go back. I feel rotten about what I did. It was as though I couldn't stand to *feel* it—do you know what I mean?"

"It's hard to know exactly what another person goes through in a time of misfortune," Cricket said softly as she wrapped the final sandwich. "I understand trials and hardship, though, and I've been through situations where I thought I couldn't bear the feelings I was having any longer. As though I could bear what was actually happening, like when Hugh left me to fend for myself and my unborn child, but I couldn't handle the emotions that went with it."

"You do know what I mean," Tim said, and his eyes seemed filled with his very soul.

Cricket turned away to hide her empathy for him, wondering as she did so if it would be better to show him how she felt. Who did he have, after all, who would share his pain over losing the farm?

She stashed the sandwiches in the refrigerator, ready to deliver in the morning.

"There," she said. "That's done. Thanks, Tim. We got those sandwiches made in about half the time it usually takes me."

Tim shifted his weight uncomfortably. "Thanks for listening. I haven't talked to many people about it. Just Haggerty. And you."

She rested a hand on his arm in a gesture of spontaneous encouragement. "Don't thank me," she said. "Come into the living room and tell me more about yourself." She smiled up at him until he grinned back.

She checked to make sure that Jeremy hadn't kicked off his crib blanket as he slept, and Tim thought involuntarily of Jeremy's small hand curved around Cricket's breast. Just as quickly he canceled the thought. For some reason, that was another scene he'd like to ban from his mind, like the farm auction he'd watched on television.

Cricket returned, put on the coffeepot, and sat beside him on the couch. Tim found himself telling her about the farm and how he had grown up there thinking that one day he, too, would farm the land that his family had cultivated for generations.

"I never dreamed that our land would belong to anyone but Vogels," he said sadly.

"You're not the only ones who have lost their land," Cricket said in ready sympathy.

"I know, but each situation is unique. In our case, the loss of our land fragmented our family. My father wouldn't talk to anyone after it happened. My mother went around trying to be cheerful, which only made us all more depressed. My brothers seemed isolated from the rest of us. And I flew away on a propjet. What I did wouldn't be so bad if my older sister Norrie hadn't run away years ago."

"What happened to Norrie, Tim?"

He shook his head. "She disappeared mysteriously at the age of nineteen, and no one ever heard from her again. I never even saw her. I was born after she left home."

"Tim! Didn't your family try to find her?"

"They tried, but with no results. She left at the end of the harvest. That's when the town is filled with transient workers traveling from town to town with combine crews to harvest the wheat. Pa always thought that Norrie got a ride out of Curtisville with one of the crew members. It's a small town, and once Norrie was reported missing, if any of the townspeople had helped her leave they would have come forward. And we're sure that she didn't leave on a Greyhound bus, which is the only way out of town except for car or truck."

"That's so sad, Tim. Your family has certainly had its share of difficulty, hasn't it?"

"Yes, and I've only given them more heartache."

"Why don't you go home, Tim?"

He lifted a shoulder and let it fall. His eyes were troubled.

"I still can't face it, I guess," he said quietly.

They sat for a long time, thinking private thoughts. Then

Cricket jumped up and said, "Oh, I nearly forgot. It's time for *Saturday Night Live!*"

When she rushed to the corner of the room to turn on the TV, Tim smiled. He hadn't realized that she'd moved the television set in here. It was a needless precaution, although she didn't know that. He had made up his mind that nothing was going to happen between Cricket and him. He had promised Haggerty, and besides, he valued his friendship with her even more than he had before. He didn't want to jeopardize it by becoming Cricket's lover.

Cricket's lover. He repeated the words to himself. No, they didn't apply to him. He had known from the beginning that Cricket wasn't his type.

"Go ahead and prop your feet on the coffee table," Cricket urged.

He looked at her.

"I mean it. I'm going to," and she slipped off her shoes and rested her feet on the table in front of them. Her socks were blue and had beige-and-red paisley figures on them. Tim thought they were cute. He followed suit, thinking how much bigger his feet were than hers.

"What are you looking at?" Cricket asked as the theme music began.

"Your feet," he said.

"What about them?"

"Cute socks." He grinned at her.

"Cute socks!" she said, laughing, and she reached over to take his hand.

Tim decided that holding hands was all right. There was nothing explicitly sexual about holding someone's hand, and all he had sworn off with her was a sexual relationship. Friends held hands; kindergarten students did, too. He tried to forget about her small hand clasping his and concentrated on the show.

This program was funnier than the previous week's program, and Cricket laughed even harder than he did. It was fun laughing with her. He kept stealing glances at her, thinking how pretty she looked with her cheeks flushed, and how her eyes sparkled with glints of green in the flickering light from the TV.

Cricket had baked a lemon Bundt cake, "from a mix" she said. They each ate a slice, and then Tim ate another. By the time he had finished it, the program was over. Tim wasn't really ready to go to his apartment, but he realized that Cricket had to get up early in the morning.

"Tim?"

Cricket was staring up at him, and he realized that she must have asked him a question that she apparently expected him to answer.

"I'm sorry, I was watching the TV," he said. A used-car dealer in a shiny striped suit was thumping the fenders of various "cream puffs" in an effort to draw customers to his lot.

"I asked you if you wanted to take some of the cake upstairs," she repeated.

"Sure, that would be good," he said. He followed her to the kitchen and waited while she wrapped a wedge of cake in aluminum foil.

She handed it to him and reached to turn out the kitchen light. They were stranded in darkness, and he knew that she expected him to kiss her again. Instead he walked through the living room to their shared foyer.

It was becoming harder and harder to maintain the separation between his feelings of friendship for her and her sexual attraction to him. Well, he might as well admit it, he was attracted to her in a sexual way too, although, he hastened to remind himself, she was not his type.

They stood in the foyer now, and he felt unbelievably awkward holding the cake in his hands.

"The chili was delicious," he began in preamble.

"Thanks," she said. She was looking at him questioningly and with such vulnerability that his heart melted.

He put his free hand under her chin and tilted her face up to the light. She regarded him with frightening openness.

He reached out and set the cake between the newel post and the banister, wedging it into the angle so that it wouldn't fall. Then, very deliberately, he took her face between his hands and kissed her, powerless to do anything else. He felt a surge of emotion toward her, realized that she was holding her breath and released her lips. When she breathed, her breath tickled his cheek. Titillated, he kissed her again.

He felt her tenseness, and he knew what would dispel it. He also knew that he wouldn't do anything about it.

Did she know how transparent she was? Did she know that he could read her longing and desire as though it were written in a book? Did she know that he wanted her at this moment as much as he'd ever wanted any woman?

"Good night, Cricket. It was a lovely evening," he said, forcing himself to end it then and there.

She nodded, swallowed and backed away. By the time he had retrieved his cake from the banister, she had fled into her bedroom. She had, however, left the door open.

He lay awake for a long time that night, wondering what would be the honorable thing to do about Cricket Erling. One thing was for certain: if they kept on like this, he'd be taking a lot of cold showers.

Chapter Eight

"Move to the left," Cricket said. "A little more."

"Is this all right?" Trudy asked, her voice muffled by the running water from the faucet at the kitchen sink.

"Perfect," Cricket said. She pressed the water from Trudy's wet hair so that it ran down the drain and wrapped a towel around her friend's damp head.

"There!" she said.

"Good, now I'm totally blond again," Trudy said. She wiped the water out of her eyes and blotted at her hair with the towel.

On Saturday afternoon Cricket and Trudy were in Trudy's kitchen performing the ritual they repeated every few weeks when Trudy's dark roots needed touching up. Cricket was almost a pro at this. They'd been doing it for years, ever since Trudy had decided to be Bijou Blonde. Cricket persisted in calling Trudy a kitchen blonde, since that's where the work was done, but Trudy drew the line at that.

"This is serious business," she told Cricket. "Don't make fun of it. Being blond is going to help me find a husband. Why, I've never had so much attention from men as I've had since I became Bijou Blonde."

Trudy wrapped the towel around her head and went into the bathroom, where she peered at herself in the mirror.

"You've done another wonderful job," she said to Cricket.

"Thanks. If I don't succeed as a psychologist, I should become a beautician. Come to think of it, from what Kiki at the Curl 'n Comb tells me, a lot of beauticians could be psychologists."

"Speaking of psychology, what exactly have you been telling Tim to help him out so much?"

"Tim? I don't know."

"He came into the shop the other day to buy a birthday card for Haggerty, and he said you've gotten his head straighter than it's been in a long time. Maybe he was talking about getting his *hair* straighter. What is it, his head or his hair?"

"His head, I guess. I don't even have a passing acquaintance with his hair."

"I thought you said there wasn't anything between you." Trudy turned on her hair dryer and began to blow her hair dry. Cricket stepped aside so the hot stream of air wouldn't hit her directly in the face.

"There isn't," she said loudly. She thought about it for a moment before deciding to be truthful. "What I mean is, we've kissed a few times, but that's all."

Trudy turned the hair dryer aside and stared at Cricket. Her hair stood out in wet yellow spikes. She looked like Bill the Cat in the Bloom County comic strip.

"Are you saying that you wish that Tim would do more than kiss you?"

"Go ahead and finish drying your hair, Trudy. I can't stand the way it looks. And I don't know what I want Tim to do. That's the problem."

Trudy turned up the heat setting on her hair dryer so her hair would dry faster. They didn't speak until Trudy's hair was almost dry. Then Trudy yanked the plug out of the socket.

"I'm not going to bother with curling the ends under at the moment," she said. "Let's have a talk." She led the way into her living room where Jeremy lay napping in his portable crib. "Come into my bedroom," Trudy whispered, and Cricket tiptoed after her.

"Now," said Trudy once they were sprawled on Trudy's king-size bed like two teenagers enjoying a gab session. "What exactly is going on between you and Tim Vogel?"

"Nothing," Cricket said.

"Explain please."

"He takes me someplace, brings me home, kisses me good-night and disappears into his apartment. Or we watch television at my place, he kisses me good-night and makes fast tracks upstairs. It's almost as though he's afraid of me.''

"You are a very threatening person," observed Trudy with a twinkle, whereupon Cricket tossed a pillow at her head.

"I can't figure it out, Trudy. I mean, he'll open up to me, like the time when he told me about his rift with his family, but then something inside him retreats."

"How does he kiss you?"

"Very pleasantly."

"I mean, does he kiss you as though you're his sister? Or is it a sexy kiss?"

"It's sexy, but not too sexy. As though he doesn't want to get me aroused. I get turned on plenty, though, and that's the trouble."

"So we have here a guy who comes on to you and then disappears when things look like they're going to get interesting," mused Trudy.

"Maybe he's seeing someone else," Cricket said, her heart sinking.

"I haven't heard of his taking anybody out since he came back in January and moved in with you."

"He *didn't* move in with me, Trudy. He lives in the upstairs section of the house where I live, that's all!"

"Well, you know what I mean."

"I've tried to understand what's going on between us. After all, I'm studying psychology. I simply can't figure it."

"The attraction is there when you're together. I've seen it."

"Is it that obvious?"

"Yes, when I saw you at the Susurro concert—"

"I didn't know you were there!"

"I sat seven or eight rows behind you, but even so I detected electricity in his warm blue glances."

"Warm blue glances! Trudy, you've been reading too many romance novels! There wasn't anything like that!"

"You were watching Manuel Susurro, and I was watching Tim watching you. His glances were more than warm, they were superheated!"

Cricket recalled the lingering effect of the languorous music and how it had put her in an erotic mood. She remembered Tim's arousing kiss as he said good-night. Perhaps Trudy had a point.

"If that's true, then apparently I won't have to do anything but bide my time if I want Tim to take our relationship one step further."

"Probably not. But if you want to speed things up, you could float around the kitchen in a see-through nightie," Trudy suggested.

"I don't even own a see-through nightie, and if I did, it wouldn't be practical to wear it. I like pajamas that open down the front. I'm still nursing Jeremy every morning, you know."

"I know," Trudy sighed. "Isn't it about time to stop?"

"Yes. Soon," Cricket said.

"I have a nightgown you could borrow," Trudy said, jumping up and pulling a sheer gown of bright magenta from a dresser drawer.

Cricket stared at it. Not only could she see right through it, but the neckline dipped to the waist and was laced with a narrow ribbon. The straps were embroidered with tiny flowers. The gown was new and still wore its price tag.

Cricket glanced at the price and almost fell off the bed.

"Why, Trudy, that's as much as I make in two weeks from my sandwich route."

"I know it's expensive, but I bought it for this weekend. I found out today that Walt's not going to be able to be here, so you're welcome to wear it if you like."

"It's not exactly my speed, Trudy, but thanks. Anyway, it clashes with my hair. Why isn't Walt coming?"

Trudy made a show of folding the gown and putting it away in the drawer. "He has the flu," she said.

"There's a lot of flu around now," Cricket said, feeling sorry for Trudy. She looked so disappointed.

"He says he'll be here next weekend," Trudy said.

"That's good. Uh-oh, Trudy, I hear Jeremy stirring. I'd better go."

Cricket gathered Jeremy and his belongings and bundled them both up for the short walk home. Trudy accompanied them to the back door.

"Thanks for doing my hair, Crick. Anytime you decide you want to become a blonde, let me know and I'll return the favor."

Cricket laughed at this. "Sure, but do they have a shade called boring blonde?"

"Borrow that nightgown I showed you, and you couldn't be boring," Trudy said.

"No way. Bye, Trudy." Cricket struck out through the crusty snow toward home.

The house was quiet. Although it was Saturday, she hadn't seen Tim. He had been driving away as she returned from running her route in the morning. He left scrambled eggs for her in the frying pan and a note that said, "Have to run errands for Haggerty. See you later." Cricket hadn't known whether "later" meant later that day, later that night or some other "later." Tim hardly ever skipped eating breakfast with her, and she missed him.

Haggerty was certainly keeping Tim busy this week. Tim had scarcely been home at all. Sometimes Cricket heard him creeping in so as not to disturb her late at night, and at such times she usually managed to go back to sleep. When she couldn't sleep, she'd listen to the floorboards creaking overhead, wondering if the noise was made by Tim or by mice.

She put off cooking anything for dinner, hoping that Tim would show up. Finally, at eight o'clock that night, with Jeremy sleeping soundly in his bed, Cricket decided that Tim wasn't coming home in time to eat with her.

"Don't be silly," she said to herself, talking out loud so there'd be some kind of sound in this big old house. "He never made an agreement to eat dinner with you every Saturday night." Still, the loneliness grew until it was a dull ache behind her breastbone. She tried to tell herself that she wasn't missing Tim and that she was merely lonely for adult company.

Around nine o'clock Trudy phoned. Cricket could tell right away by the nasal tone of her voice that Trudy had been crying.

"It's Walt," Trudy said flatly.

"What happened?" Cricket asked.

"His mother called from Florida. He must have mistakenly given her my number as the place where he'd be this weekend. Anyway, do you know what his mother, whom he once described to me as very old and sick, said?"

"I can't imagine," said Cricket.

"She wanted to speak to Walt, and when I explained that he wasn't here, she said she wanted to leave a message. She said that he couldn't call her back after tomorrow since that's when she's leaving to run a senior citizens' marathon on behalf of her condominium recreation association! Very old and sick, my eye!''

"Trudy, I know how upset you must be, but give Walt a chance to explain.''

"I can't even call him. He's laid up with the flu at Rona's house!''

"Maybe you misunderstood Walt when he described his mother.''

"I doubt it. If he's lied about her, how many other lies has he told me?'' Trudy said unhappily.

"Do you want to come over?''

"No, thanks, I'd like to stay home in case Walt gets a chance to phone me. Anyway, I'm not dressed. I'm wearing the bathrobe Walt left here, because it smells like him.''

Cricket sighed. "Okay, Trudy. Call if you need anything.''

"Maybe a fresh box of Kleenex,'' Trudy said before hanging up.

Cricket wished that she had someone to talk to about Trudy. Trudy unloaded her troubles on Cricket, but Cricket had no one to listen to how upsetting Trudy's romantic misadventures were to her.

When Trudy didn't call back, and a glance out the kitchen window showed Trudy's house to be dark, indicating that she'd gone to bed, Cricket made herself a sandwich and sat down to watch *Saturday Night Live*. The show wasn't as funny as usual.

Maybe that was because Cricket's attention was divided. Every time a car rounded the corner, its tires hissing on the damp street, she craned her neck to see out the window. Once when one seemed to hesitate outside the house, she went to the window. The car was an unfamiliar Buick, and it pulled into a driveway down the street. Finally, when it appeared that Tim wasn't coming home soon, she dragged herself to bed where she slept in fits and starts. Later she lurched wide-awake when she thought she heard Tim come in.

It wasn't Tim, though, she realized when she didn't hear the stairs creak. It must be those mice again.

She closed her eyes, and then she heard a rattling in the kitchen. Oh, no! The mice had somehow managed to get into the house. She explored the bottom of the bed with her foot, but she couldn't find the cat. Where was Mungo when she really needed him?

Cricket got up, not knowing what she would do if she confronted a mouse. She rushed into the kitchen without bothering to put on her robe.

When she flipped on the light, she confronted Tim instead, startling him. He appeared to have closed the refrigerator only seconds ago and stood blinking at her while holding a milk carton in his hands.

"Tim! I thought you were a mouse," she said, feeling like an idiot.

"I am no mouse," he said with unusual dignity. "Would you care for a glass of milk?"

"I'm not dressed," she said unnecessarily.

He scoured her with an ironic look. "Obviously," he said.

This would definitely not do. Cricket yanked an old raincoat off a hook beside the back door and pulled it on. One button was missing, but she primly fastened all the rest. Very deliberately, Tim removed a glass from a cupboard and poured milk into it for her.

"What time is it?" Cricket asked, easing herself onto a chair.

"Middle of the night," Tim said.

"In that case, I only have a few more hours of sleep left, but unfortunately I'm wide awake."

He set the glass on the table in front of her. "Drink your milk. It's a wonderful soporific."

"It's what?"

"Makes you sleep. It works, honest." Tim drank a long draft of milk and sat down across from her.

Cricket couldn't figure out whether to say anything or not. She wasn't sure, but she thought Tim might prefer silence. He looked stolid, even grim, sitting across from her. And he watched her in a strange way.

"Cricket," he said.

She merely stared at him, her expression blank.

"Cricket," he said again.

"I'm going to go to bed as soon as I finish my milk," she said. She felt like a stranger in her own house at this moment.

"Cricket, we've got to stop meeting like this," he said heavily.

"Are you trying to be funny?" she asked.

"I am and I am not. Figure that one out."

"Tim, you've been drinking."

"I've had a Scotch or two."

"Whatever your problems are, you won't solve them that way."

"I just decided that. Tonight. I found the answer at the bottom of my glass."

"That's not where most people find answers."

"I don't either, usually. But in this case, it seems appropriate. I cracked up a plane in Florida because I was out drinking the night before, did I tell you that?"

"No," she told him.

"It was dumb. I should have known better than to fly that day."

"I agree."

"But I've decided, and you can be my witness, that I'm going to give up drinking. Maybe a beer now and then, but that's all. I'm going to tread the straight and narrow path."

"I'm glad to hear that. What brought on this resolution?"

"Haggerty. He's going to Arizona on vacation, and he wants me to run his flying service while he's gone. I am about to become a respos-respos-responsible citizen."

"Haggerty must trust you quite a lot to let you handle his flying service."

"You bet. I promised him I'd do a good job. I promised him another thing, too, but you make it mighty hard to live up to it."

This remark unnerved Cricket. "You promised him something to do with me?" she said.

Tim nodded solemnly. "I promised—but you know what I promised."

Cricket shook her head to clear it. She had been prepared to deal with mice when she'd rushed into the kitchen tonight, but she certainly hadn't been prepared to handle Tim when he was in this condition.

"I have absolutely no idea what you promised Haggerty concerning me, but it's most interesting. You can tell me about it in the morning," she said, washing her hands of Tim and his problems. She lifted her glass to her lips, preparing to drain it.

Tim grabbed her wrist and pushed it down to the table. His eyes bore into her, but not in a frightening way. They begged for understanding. *What does this have to do with me?* Cricket wondered.

"I told Haggerty I wouldn't hurt you," he said heavily.

"Hurt me?"

"He said I looked like a heartbreaker to him. He said you've had enough trouble in your life and that you didn't need any more." Tim hadn't released her wrist. Slowly she relaxed her grip on her glass and turned her hand so that it clasped Tim's.

"I never thought—" she began.

"Oh, yes, you did. We've been playing a game of advance and retreat ever since I moved into the upstairs apartment. I'm aware of it, and I'm sure that you are, too. Now the question is, do you want me to advance? Or do you want me to retreat?"

Cricket was speechless. She opened her mouth, but no sound came out except a silent little "oh."

"If you say retreat, I'm going to move out tonight," Tim said, staring at her.

"And if I don't?" She could barely say the words.

"You might get hurt," he said evenly.

"You wouldn't hurt me, Tim," she said, as sure of this as she was of her own name.

"Not intentionally, but women have a way of getting their feelings trampled when they fall in love with a man who won't commit. I've never committed myself to any woman, and frankly, I can't imagine that I ever will. I'm flighty. I don't stick around when the going gets tough."

Cricket felt as though she might burst into tears, and she raised her free hand to her mouth as though to restrain herself. "So exactly what are you trying to tell me?" she asked.

"I'm telling you that I'm as attracted to you as I've ever been to any woman, and maybe even more so. I can't go on without—without knowing you better. I'll leave if you want me to go, but I'm not sure you do. You'll have to tell me what you want, Cricket."

She felt the pulse in his hand. It beat against her thumb in a strong, steady rhythm. She closed her eyes and swallowed, trying to think.

"What happens if I ask you to stay?" she asked, opening her eyes. He was watching her silently, humorlessly, as though waiting for the axe to fall.

"If you do, I'll walk upstairs to my apartment and I'll try to get some sleep. Otherwise, I'll get my gear and leave immediately.''

"If you stay, we can talk tomorrow?''

Tim nodded. His hair shone like spun gold in the overhead light.

She gazed at him, knowing that whether or not she would have a relationship with this man hinged on what she said at this moment. She had grown to like him, to care about him, and she had become extremely curious about him. She desired him. If she asked him to leave, she would never get to know him. He would be merely a stranger who had walked into her life and walked just as rapidly out of it again before they had explored the full potential of their relationship.

Tears clouded her eyes. "I don't want you to leave, Tim,'' she said strongly and firmly. She blinked away her tears to see that Tim was staring at her with tenderness.

"You don't?'' he said. "You really don't?'' His expression lifted and lightened. He looked as though he didn't trust himself to break into a smile even though he wanted to.

"No, I don't want you to go,'' she said.

He reached across the table and took her hand in both of his. "I can't believe it,'' he said. "I was sure you'd ask me to leave. I've never come right out and said to a woman what I've said to you. I thought you'd give me my walking papers. Cricket, are you sure? Do you know what you're saying?''

She stood up. "I'm not making any guarantees, either, Tim.''

He drew a deep breath. "I know that,'' he said.

Cricket pulled the raincoat more tightly around her, although she didn't know why. "I'm going to check on Jeremy, and then I'm going to get some sleep,'' she said.

"So am I,'' he said. He felt sober now. For the first time tonight, he really looked at Cricket. Her hair was rumpled, and her face was so pale that her freckles stood out in stark relief. But she looked like a woman who knew her own mind. For the first time he admitted that she was his type after all.

"See you in the morning,'' said Cricket, pushing her chair under the table and carrying her glass to Mungo's bowl, where she poured the rest of her milk into it.

"Wait,'' he said.

Cricket straightened to find him standing beside her. She stared up at him, transfixed by the intensity of his expression.

Slowly he enfolded her in his arms and pulled her close. His heart beat steadily beneath the rough wool of his sweater, and he lowered his face until it was buried in her hair. Her arms went around him, and she closed her eyes, allowing herself to feel her physical attraction to this man.

"I just want you to know that I don't want to hurt you," he said quietly. "I have a history of hurting people, you know."

"That's in the past," Cricket murmured.

"For a long time, I haven't had a future," he said. He pulled away from her, and his eyes searched her face.

"Things are different now," Cricket said.

Tim thought about running Haggerty's business, and he thought about his life in this house. He felt optimistic on both fronts, but he didn't trust his optimism. Most of all, he didn't trust himself.

"Are you sure you want me to stay?" he said, giving her one more chance to back out.

She nodded slowly. "Yes, Tim," she said solemnly.

He felt as though he were standing on the edge of a precipice, waiting to fall. Even living in the same house with Cricket was a kind of commitment. And yet, it was an exciting one. If he could stay, if he could make something of his relationship with her, his confidence in himself as a worthwhile human being would be restored. His emotional state had been so precarious that he couldn't stay in Curtisville to support his family in their time of need, but maybe he could redeem himself by standing by Cricket in hers.

"You were going to check on Jeremy," he reminded her. As if to punctuate his statement, Jeremy whimpered slightly and was silent.

Cricket slipped away to Jeremy's room, her pulse beating in her ears. Jeremy slept on his stomach and one foot was stuck between the bars of his crib. Cricket gently freed the foot and refastened the crib blanket. Jeremy sighed, and she brushed his short brown hair away from his forehead.

When she returned to the kitchen, Tim was gone. Upstairs she heard noises, as though someone were opening and closing dresser drawers. For one unsettling moment, Cricket thought that perhaps Tim had changed his mind and was planning to leave tonight after all.

The noises subsided, and Cricket went back to bed. She slept fitfully until dawn, and when she awoke she was sure that her conversation with Tim the night before had been nothing but a dream. It wasn't until she saw their two glasses side by side in the kitchen sink that she was convinced that it had really happened.

Chapter Nine

The next day Jeremy seemed out of sorts. He refused the bottle of milk he had been drinking every morning since completing the weaning process, and he only ate a little cereal, most of which he spit out. With severe misgivings, Cricket dressed him in his snowsuit and took him out into her camper, which she had heated beforehand.

When she arrived back at the house after running her route, Jeremy seemed slightly feverish.

"I don't know what's wrong with him," Cricket fretted as she ate the pancakes Tim had prepared. She kept a wary eye on Jeremy, who sat in his high chair rubbing his eyes. It had been a hectic morning, what with her oversleeping. She hoped Jeremy wasn't getting sick.

"Maybe he's just tired," Tim said, trying to be helpful. He knew that after their middle-of-the-night discussion, he was certainly tired, and there were mauve half circles under Cricket's eyes. Neither of them had spoken of last night.

"He acts as though he wants to go to sleep," said Cricket as Jeremy started to whine.

She left her breakfast to put Jeremy in his crib. He fell asleep almost immediately.

"I'd better call Renee to see if she's free to sit with Jeremy," Cricket said with a worried look at the clock.

"I don't have anything to do this morning. I can keep an eye on Jeremy if you'd like," Tim offered. He wanted to make himself as helpful to her as possible in reparation for the way he had acted last night. In retrospect, he realized how crude he had been.

"I couldn't impose, Tim. After all, you have work to do for Haggerty."

"I can go to the airport this afternoon just as well," Tim insisted.

Reluctantly, after consulting her baby health-care book and deciding that Jeremy's symptoms were too general to define, Cricket went to her first class, leaving Jeremy in Tim's care.

"Call the college and have them get me out of class if Jeremy shows any signs of fever," she urged Tim before she left.

"Will I have to take his temperature?" Tim asked in alarm.

"No, I can be home in five minutes to take it if necessary. If he wakens and cries, or if he's flushed and hot, that's how you'll know to call me. And I'll telephone in an hour or so between classes so I can get a progress report. Tim, you don't know how much this means to me."

Tim slid an arm around her shoulder. "Don't worry," he consoled her. "Uncle Tim can handle it."

Cricket managed a smile as she left the house, but she had a hard time keeping her mind on her work in her psychology class. She kept thinking about her conversation the previous night with Tim, and she worried about her baby.

"Where's Jeremy?" several people asked.

"He's at home. I'm afraid he's coming down with something," she answered.

People were sympathetic, but no one was particularly helpful. None of her classmates could understand what the responsibility of taking care of a baby was like. They were all typical college students, much as Cricket had been before she became a mother.

She ran breathlessly to the nearest pay phone after her first class dispersed.

"How's Jeremy?" she asked Tim when he answered.

"Sleeping. I checked on him a few minutes ago, and he's still sacked out. Anything I should do?"

"No, let him sleep. I'll call you again in an hour."

After Cricket's phone call, Tim wandered into Jeremy's room and stood looking down at him. Jeremy was a handsome little tyke, with that fuzzy brown hair and fat cheeks. His eyelashes were long and curled sweetly against his cheek. His chest rose and fell with each breath.

It occurred to Tim that, having promised Cricket he'd look after

Jeremy, he was now the sole person in charge of a defenseless human being. Suddenly he was staggered by the responsibility.

Was this what it was like to be a parent? To know that this child depended on you, only you, for its every need? In the unlikely event that the roof fell in, Tim would be duty bound to save Jeremy at the expense of his own neck. He was so overcome with the dimensions of his responsibility toward Jeremy that he sank down on the rocking chair and stared at the sleeping child through the bars of the crib. The bars seemed like a prison, not for Jeremy, but for his caretaker. Before this, Tim had never comprehended Cricket's life and how confined it was by her love for her son.

After a while, he stood and tiptoed out of the room with a new reverence for what parenthood meant to both child and parent. Thinking it over, he paced the floor until he saw Cricket fairly flying up the front walk.

"Is Jeremy all right?" she asked, bursting through the front door.

"Let's check," Tim said with relief. He was more than ready to return the care of Jeremy to his mother.

They tiptoed into Jeremy's room. Jeremy lay listlessly on his side, absently fingering a stuffed duck.

"Jeremy?" Cricket said.

The baby focused his eyes on her face and grinned, holding his arms out to her. She picked him up, and from the heat radiating from his body, Cricket knew that Jeremy had a fever.

"I'd better take his temperature," she said, looking worried.

Tim wanted to absent himself from this procedure. "Could you eat a sandwich?" he asked, wanting to be of help.

"Maybe later," Cricket said as she shook the mercury down in the thermometer.

Tim repaired to the kitchen and began to rummage through the Tupperware containers holding Cricket's sandwich supplies.

Jeremy's temperature was well above normal. This alarmed Cricket because Jeremy had never been sick before. Cradling Jeremy in one arm and dialing with the other hand, she called the pediatrician.

"Keep an eye on him, and take his temperature frequently," Dr. Moss told her. "There are a lot of viruses around, and possibly he's coming down with one."

Cricket didn't attend her afternoon classes even though Tim insisted that he didn't have to go to work and could watch the baby.

"I want to be with Jeremy if he's getting sick," Cricket said, and at her urging, Tim finally left for the airport.

Jeremy fussed, refused to eat lunch and cried. Cricket tried to distract him by winding up his musical swing and letting it swing him for over an hour. Finally he accepted a bottle of juice, and afterward, Cricket put him to bed. When he woke up, his fever was even higher.

That night, Jeremy's nose began to run, and the next morning Cricket took him to the doctor, who diagnosed a rhinovirus and prescribed medication. The medication helped Jeremy's stuffy nose, and he slept a lot. That in itself was a big help.

"Whenever you're ready to go back to classes, I'll be glad to take care of Jeremy," Tim told her, and Cricket could only thank him. He was so kind to her, helping her make sandwiches every night, watching Jeremy in the mornings while she ran her route.

"I don't know how we'd get along without you," she told him. Tim smiled as though gratified by this statement, but Cricket couldn't help musing that he must be getting impatient. After all, he had told her that he wanted to have a relationship with her, and she had agreed. Then Jeremy had fallen sick, and dealing with his illness sapped all her emotional energy. Cricket couldn't even begin to think about her budding relationship with Tim until her child was healthy.

She and Trudy shared a midweek commiseration by telephone.

"Tim and I have finally decided that we have a relationship," she told Trudy.

"Do you want to borrow that magenta nightgown yet?" Trudy's nose sounded stuffy, and Cricket wondered if Trudy was coming down with a cold or the flu.

"No, thanks," Cricket said. "We've only *decided*, we haven't done anything about it."

"Run that by me again," Trudy said in disbelief.

"What I mean is that we've each admitted our passion, but we haven't consummated it."

"You must have been hitting the books too hard lately, Crick. You sound like a textbook. Why haven't you consummated it?"

"Jeremy's been sick, and taking care of him is running me ragged. Tim, too. He's been wonderful about helping me."

"The way you two carry on a love affair seems backward to me. Most people deal with passion first, responsibility second."

"We're not most people, Trudy. Have you heard from Walt?"

"He called once. I didn't mention his mother."

"Why not?"

"I'm afraid, I guess. If I ask Walt about the lie he told me about his 'old and sick' mother, he might see me as unsupportive and go back to Rona."

This time Cricket lost her temper. "Walt never left Rona, Trudy. And if he told a lie, you might as well confront him. My guess is that none of the women Walt knows ever tell him that they know when he's lying, and that enables him to keep on doing it. He knows from experience that no one will call his bluff."

"What women?" Trudy said frostily.

"Any women in Walt's life. He lied to his mother when he told her he was going to be at your house, he lies to Rona by giving her a false explanation when he's going to see you, and he's lied to you." She closed her eyes, willing her friend to take her observations in the spirit with which they were offered.

Trudy began to sob softly into the telephone. "I love him so much," she said. "I don't want to lose him."

"I understand," Cricket said. She was at a loss to make Trudy see what she didn't want to see.

"Anyway, Cricket, it was only one falsehood. What difference does it make when the rest of our relationship is so good?"

Cricket wasn't about to listen to Trudy make excuses for Walt. "Listen, Trudy, I think I hear Jeremy. I'll talk to you later, okay?" She replaced the receiver in its cradle and went to copy class lecture notes she had borrowed from one of her fellow students.

The whole time she was writing, Cricket seethed at Trudy's insistence on staying blind and deaf to Walt's manipulations. The more Cricket thought about it, the more it seemed as if Trudy were holding on to a little-girl kind of innocence in order to re-assure herself that it wasn't her responsibility to gauge the character of the man before she had an affair with him. Even Trudy's inability to understand the way Tim and Cricket were cautiously establishing their relationship seemed part of the same self-defeating syndrome. As much as Cricket wanted to, there didn't seem to be any easy way to knock sense into her friend. She burrowed into her books, trying to put Trudy and her problems out of her mind.

Tim found Cricket studying at the dining room table when he came home.

"Anything new about Jeremy?" he asked, bending to kiss her cheek as a matter of course.

As his lips brushed her skin, Cricket felt a sudden rush of gratitude toward Tim. He was so different from Walt. He had always been honest with her. He wasn't pushing her for intimacy, nor had he pointed out that taking care of Jeremy put a crimp in their budding relationship. He was, in short, a comfort to her.

Without a warning, she stood and put her arms around his neck.

"Hey, what's this?" he asked, resting his hands on her waist.

"I needed a hug," she said a bit sheepishly, unsure how to explain her exact feelings.

"I like this," Tim said, tightening his arms around her. He wondered what had brought on Cricket's mood, but he wasn't about to question it. He nuzzled her forehead.

She disengaged herself. "I'm glad you like it, but it's time for me to get busy in the kitchen."

"I brought dinner," he said, calling her attention to a foil-wrapped package he had set on the table.

"It smells wonderful. What is it?"

"There's a new gourmet fast-food place called Harry's out by the airport. They had a grand opening today, and I brought lasagna home."

"Oh, Tim! Lasagna is one of my favorite foods."

"I'll get plates and forks," he said.

Cricket dug around in the linen closet and found place mats, which she dimly recognized as a wedding gift she had never used. She arranged them on the table and lit a couple of candles she discovered in a drawer in the breakfront.

"This looks festive," Tim said in approval. He produced a bottle of wine.

"What's the occasion?"

"We're celebrating my running Haggerty's flying service," Tim told her.

"He's gone, then?"

"He left yesterday. My big accomplishment today is that I talked a reluctant farmer out near Elk Rapids into paying his delinquent bill."

"How does it feel to be in charge?" Cricket asked. Tim was smiling and expansive today, looking as though he enjoyed his new role.

"It feels wonderful. I've always been merely an employee, you know, even when I worked on the farm for my father. It's a whole new sensation to realize that the decisions I face can make or break the business."

"Here's to you. And to your future," said Cricket, raising her glass.

Tim leaned back in his chair and watched her. Her hair fluffed out around her small heart-shaped face, and her gaze was warm and accepting. He felt peaceful when he was around her, more so than he'd felt with anyone in a long time. He marveled at that feeling. Not so long ago he had thought he'd never be able to feel anything but pain and guilt.

"Is Jeremy any better?" he asked.

"A little. He's over the worst of it, I think."

"I'm glad." He paused. "Cricket, about the other night," he said.

She stopped eating and lifted her eyes to his.

"In case you haven't guessed, I want the progression of our relationship to be normal and natural."

"I know," she said, as though he was telling her that he thought they ought to take the evening paper instead of the morning one.

"What I mean is, I don't want a quick tumble in bed."

"Better too slow than too fast," Cricket agreed amicably.

He watched her for a while, captivated by the way she took such small bites, chewing them carefully before swallowing.

"I don't think I've ever met a more *sensible* woman," he said.

"Is that a compliment?"

"Of course."

Cricket looked unsettled. "I'm past the stage where I think that going to bed with someone is the best way to get acquainted," she said, thinking of Trudy and Walt.

"Did it ever occur to you that we act like a married couple?" he said.

She smiled at him. Trudy had said as much, but Cricket saw nothing wrong with this. "Lately, yes. We act like some married couples. My marriage wasn't like this in the least."

"What was it like?"

"My husband never wanted to settle down. I was like a millstone around his neck. I was always waiting for him to come home."

"Why did you marry him?"

"Hugh was my first boyfriend. We broke up after we'd gone together for two years, and at that point he left Manitou while I started college. When he came back a year later and wanted me to marry him, I had this crazy idea that I could fix everything that went wrong the first time. Well, it didn't work, which left me with the feeling that I had failed not just once, but twice."

"Maybe he was the one who failed—both times."

"He had a lot to do with it, that's for sure. At the time, I thought it was all my fault." She shrugged and took another sip of wine.

"Where is he now?"

"Who knows? I've only heard from Hugh once since the divorce, and that was when Jeremy was born. He sent a silver rattle, monogrammed with Jeremy's initials. It was obviously not something that Hugh had picked out himself. It looked like the choice of a tasteful but impractical woman. I remember wishing that Hugh had sent a few boxes of disposable diapers instead."

They sat silent for a few moments, lost in their individual reveries.

"How about you, Tim? You never married?"

He shook his head. "I could have, once or twice."

"Were they Curtisville girls? Or was it when you were in the air force?"

"One local girl, who married someone else and has two-point-four kids or whatever the current standard is. I was crazy about a German girl when I was stationed in Europe. I had the sense to know that she wouldn't be happy living in Curtisville, Kansas, for the rest of her life. That's what I was planning to do at the time." His voice rang with bitterness.

"And now you're not going back to Curtisville?"

"There's nothing to go back there for," he said.

"What about your parents?"

Tim shrugged and focused his eyes on the ceiling. "I can't face them or their friends. They hate me for leaving."

"I think you're probably being too harsh on yourself," Cricket said quietly.

Tim pushed his chair back, and the legs scraped on the hardwood floor. He winced at the noise. "Maybe I am. Hey, who's supposed to clean up? If the one who cooks doesn't clean up, who cleans up when neither of us cooks?"

"Not Harry's gourmet food service, that's for sure. I suppose we're both the unlucky ones. Do you want to wash while I dry?" She carried her plate into the kitchen.

Tim was already running water into the sink. He flicked her legs playfully with the end of the dish towel. "I'll wash, you dry, and then it's a toss-up as to who sweeps the floor," he said.

They washed their dishes, then watched the news on Cricket's television set. They forgot about sweeping the floor.

JEREMY WOKE CRICKET by screaming in the middle of the night.

She had moved to the small couch in his room so she could be near him if he cried. She jumped up to find Jeremy flushed and in pain, and he was yelling at the top of his lungs. Cricket didn't know what to do.

"Cricket?" said Tim, roused from his sleep by the noise. He peered around the edge of the door to Jeremy's room, his hair tousled and his eyes puffy from sleep. He wore only a pair of sweatpants.

"Oh, Tim, I don't know what's wrong," Cricket said. She gathered Jeremy into her arms, scared because he was crying so hard. His face screwed up into a furious knot, and his fists flailed against her chest. Once in a while he tugged at his right ear.

"Get the baby book, will you, Tim?" Cricket said over Jeremy's wailing.

Tim found the baby health-care book on the shelf. "What should I look up?" he asked. He didn't know what to make of Jeremy. The baby had been sleeping peacefully when they went to bed around ten.

"I don't know. Try looking under 'Illnesses—Colds,' or something like that."

"Does he have a rash?" Tim asked after a hurried consultation of the book.

Cricket laid the screaming Jeremy on his dressing table. She inspected his chest and back for signs of a rash. Jeremy cried the whole time, and she felt helpless to do anything about it.

"No, I don't see a rash," she said.

"Hmm," Tim said, running his forefinger down the index. "Here it says, 'Colds—complications of,'" he said.

"Look it up. Oh, Tim, what am I going to do? He's in pain!"

"We should call the doctor," Tim said.

Cricket tried her best to soothe her small son, but nothing she did seemed to have any effect.

"Here—how about earache? *Otitis media*—that's a middle ear infection. It's common in babies and children after they have a cold. Fluid builds up behind the eardrum and causes pain and tenderness."

"He keeps touching his ear, so maybe that *is* what's wrong. Here, Tim, will you hold Jeremy while I go call the doctor? He won't be able to hear me on the phone if Jeremy's in the same room." She deposited Jeremy in Tim's arms, kissed the top of the baby's head, and hurried to the telephone in the other room.

Jeremy stopped screaming momentarily, long enough to eye Tim with a certain amount of interest.

"It's okay, fella," Tim said softly. "We're going to take good care of you, your mommy and me."

Jeremy wrinkled up his face and let out another piercing yell. Tim held the baby against his broad, bare chest and patted his back. It was the first time he'd ever held Jeremy, except for that first day when Jeremy had drooled all over his hand.

"There, there," he said comfortingly. He kept patting Jeremy's back because that's what his instinct told him to do. Jeremy's hands clutched at the dark hairs on his chest.

In the other room, Cricket carried on a hurried conversation with Dr. Moss.

"He wants to see Jeremy in his office right away," she said in a rush when she returned. Jeremy was draped over Tim's shoulder, and his crying seemed less frantic.

"*Now?* He wants us to take Jeremy out in this cold?" The weatherman had predicted subzero temperatures.

"You don't have to go, Tim," Cricket said gently.

"Of course I'll go. Someone has to drive, and someone has to hold him. Why don't you get dressed, and then I'll go put on my

sweatshirt and shoes." Cricket dressed herself and Jeremy in rec-
ord time, and Tim drove them to the Manitou Children's Clinic.
Dr. Moss met them there and, with jovial reassurances, gave Jeremy a shot of penicillin and numbing drops for his inflamed ear.
Jeremy quieted almost immediately, and by the time the three of
them had reached home, Jeremy was drowsy and relaxed in
Cricket's arms.

They laid Jeremy in his bed, gave him his stuffed duck to hold
and stood beside his crib until he fell asleep. When at last his
eyelids drifted closed, Cricket and Tim quietly left the room.

Outside in the hall, Tim took Cricket in his arms.

"A rough night, huh?" he said.

"You said it," she replied. Her arms went around him, seeking
his strength. She didn't know how she would have managed without him.

"I never knew how hard it is to have children," he told her.

She managed a laugh, which was muffled against his coat front.
"What a way to find out," she said. "Thanks, Tim."

He brushed the hair off her forehead and kissed her temple. "I
guess I'd better let you get some sleep," he said.

"I suppose so," she said reluctantly. She didn't want to go
back to the narrow couch in Jeremy's room.

They stood, arms around each other, for a while longer.

"Tim," Cricket said in a low voice.

"Mmm?"

"Would you, I mean would you like to—to sleep in my room
tonight?"

His eyes, clear and candid, searched her face. "There's nothing
I'd like better," he said.

"I know we're both tired, but there's no need to be apart,"
she said.

He nodded, and tentatively she touched a finger to his lips. He
kissed it and followed her into her bedroom.

He tossed his coat on the straight-backed chair, and helped her
off with hers.

"I think—I think I'd feel more comfortable if we turned off
the light," she said.

He flicked the switch, and the room was cast in a mellow glow
from the night-light in the foyer. They each disrobed, feeling only

slightly self-conscious at this new intimacy. When Cricket stumbled as she slid out of her jeans, Tim steadied her.

"I sleep in the nude," he told her.

"I wear pajamas," she said.

"Put them on if you like."

"No," she replied, shivering. She climbed into bed and held the covers up so that he could join her.

Her body was warm to his touch. He slid his arms around her and pulled her to him. Her breasts brushed his chest, and her prominent hipbones grazed his stomach. His desire for her was dormant.

She kissed his neck and sighed. She smelled sweet, like honeysuckle. He listened while her breathing lapsed into a regular rhythm. Finally she slept.

What a strange situation this is, he thought wryly to himself. He never could have dreamed that he was capable of lying in bed with an attractive woman without wanting to do anything but hold her. And yet holding her close, listening to her breathing, was all he wanted for the moment.

He slept, and when she stirred, he stirred, and when she murmured his name in the night he kissed her gently and told her to go back to sleep.

Chapter Ten

The next morning Cricket awakened earlier than usual. Carefully she snaked one hand out from under the covers and turned off her clock radio. Her heart warmed to the sound of Tim's steady breathing.

Carefully, so carefully, she eased out from under the comforter and wrapped her bathrobe around her. She padded quietly across the width of the house to Jeremy's room and looked in on him. He was sleeping comfortably, and experience told her that he would awaken soon enough. Silently she hurried back to her bed, where Tim had rolled over with his back to her. She smiled to herself and lay down beside him, settling into the warm imprint his body had left on the sheets. She lapsed into a dozy state of happiness thinking about the transformation Tim Vogel had wrought in her life.

Life was easier with Tim around. He was someone she could count on, and for a long time, Cricket hadn't had anyone like that. He helped her with her sandwich business, and he could be relied upon to take care of Jeremy when necessary. Last night, when they had made their mad rush to the doctor's office, Tim had been wonderful. She simply couldn't have managed without him.

She smiled to herself and snuggled closer to Tim's warmth. He mumbled something, and Cricket fell into a dreamy half sleep. When she awakened, it was twenty minutes later, and the sky outside her window was beginning to come alive with ribbons of light. She slid out of bed again and went to give Jeremy his morning bottle.

Tim was still asleep when she was ready to run her route. She didn't want to take Jeremy with her today, since an icy wind was blowing out of the north, so after a few minutes' thought, she put Jeremy back in his crib and gave him some of his favorite crib toys to play with. She was sure that Jeremy would play quietly in his crib until she returned. If he didn't, she was confident that Tim would know what to do.

She hurried through her sandwich route, anticipating eating breakfast with Tim as usual when she returned. But much to her surprise, Tim wasn't in the kitchen when she walked in. Breakfast wasn't ready, either.

"Tim?" she called uncertainly.

Her voice echoed hollowly, and she heard no answer.

Pulling off her muffler and draping it carelessly over a living room lamp, she hurried through the living room and called upstairs.

"Tim?"

There was no reply.

Puzzled, Cricket bounded up the stairs. The house seemed eerily quiet. She knocked on the door, but Tim didn't answer.

She ran downstairs again. She noticed a note on the foyer table.

"Cricket—had to go to airport about a problem at Haggerty's trailer. See you at dinnertime. Hope Jeremy is feeling better." He had scrawled his initial at the bottom.

"Jeremy!" Cricket gasped, her heart lurching.

With a sharp pang of dread, she ran into Jeremy's room. Jeremy slept, his rump in the air, his hand clutching his stuffed duck.

Cricket collapsed against the doorjamb, her mouth dry, her heart pounding against her chest wall. Tim had left Jeremy here all by himself, and for how long?

She must have made a sound, because Jeremy opened his eyes and murmured a stream of consonants. Thankfully Cricket rushed to his crib and scooped him into her arms.

Jeremy continued babbling and watching her face for a positive reaction. Cricket couldn't respond to him in her normal fashion because she was still overcome with relief.

She felt his arms and legs and diapered him, and then, her heart still pounding, she doctored his ears with the drops the doctor had supplied. As her initial panic subsided, guilt washed over her in waves. She should never have left Jeremy in Tim's care without clearing it with Tim first.

But as her guilt faded, and she saw that Jeremy really had suffered no harm from being alone, her anger at Tim grew. He should have looked to see if Jeremy was in his crib before he left for the airport. Hadn't he been watching Jeremy for her every morning since Jeremy had come down with a cold?

As she was snapping Jeremy into his corduroy playsuit, she heard Tim's car draw up to the curb outside. Hoisting Jeremy on her hip, she rushed into the foyer.

Tim blew in on a blast of icy air. "Brr!" he said. "I think I'll put on another sweater. Hi, Cricket." He casually reached out to pull her closer.

Cricket was so angry by this time that she saw red spots in front of her eyes. "How could you, Tim? How could you leave without checking to see if I'd taken Jeremy with me this morning?"

Tim pulled a blank expression. "Jeremy?"

"Yes, Jeremy. You left him here by himself. Anything could have happened to him. Anything!"

"I didn't think about it. Did I say I'd watch him for you?"

"We didn't discuss it, but I assumed that you would. You've baby-sat him while I ran my route every other day since he's been sick."

"I know, but—"

"I left him in his crib, thinking that if he woke up crying, you'd be here. Then I came home and you were gone. I panicked."

"Cricket, I'm sorry. I didn't know. Did you leave me a note?"

"No, I didn't think about it. I thought you'd *know*."

"How would I know? Am I supposed to be psychic? I'm used to coming and going as I please."

"When you're responsible for taking care of a baby—"

"I didn't know I was Jeremy's keeper today. You never mentioned it."

"His keeper! Do you think of him as a kind of—of zoo animal?" She glared at him over Jeremy's fuzzy head.

Tim clapped his hand to his head. All this was moving too fast for him. He warned himself to slow down, to explain.

"I had a call from an airport security guard, who saw the door to Haggerty's trailer flapping in the wind and wanted me to check to make sure that no one had broken in. I left in a hurry. Jeremy never occurred to me," he said in a calmer voice.

"I know I've kept you from work during the past week, and I apologize for that," Cricket said. Tears began to stream down her face, and she dipped her head to wipe her wet cheek on the shoulder of her sweater.

Tim shook his head to clear it. He heaved a big sigh. "There's no need to apologize, but if you want me to do something, you'll have to ask me. I can't possibly *know* everything you're thinking by some kind of ESP," he said. He resented that she was using her tears to unfair advantage.

"There's no harm done," Cricket said stiffly as she comprehended Tim's disengagement from the argument.

Tim touched Jeremy's hand, and Jeremy grinned and kicked his feet against Cricket's stomach. Cricket winced. Tim thought she grimaced out of anger.

"I came home to get an extra sweater. I have to go back to the airport," Tim said heavily. He took the stairs to his apartment two at a time. He was gone for only a moment, and he sidestepped Cricket and Jeremy when he came back down.

He shifted awkwardly from one foot to the other. "Like I said, Cricket, I really am sorry," he said.

"I should have left a note," Cricket said. Her voice had a flat sound to it, probably because of her crying.

"Yeah, that would have been a good idea," he said, and the words were sarcastic. He avoided her eyes as he left.

When the door closed firmly behind him, Tim interpreted it as a slam. He jumped in his car and drove away as fast as the icy streets would allow. All the way out to the airport, past fields white with new-fallen snow, he thought about what had happened.

Should he have checked to see if Jeremy was in his crib before he left? And if Jeremy was there, was Tim supposed to tell the airport security guard who had called about the problem with the trailer door that he couldn't come to the trailer right away? Should he have gone to the airport, taking Jeremy with him? If he had taken Jeremy out in the cold to the airport after last night's bout with earache, might not Cricket have been just as furious about that?

What it amounted to, he thought unhappily, was that he had landed right in a can of worms.

He wasn't adept at human relationships, and he was the first one to admit it. He was likable; people had told him that. He had a winning personality. But things always went wrong somewhere along the line, requiring more of him than he was capable of giving.

His usual solution was to give up on the problem, whatever it was. He had almost never seen a problem through to a satisfactory solution because he usually ran away. That way it saved everyone a lot of trouble, especially him.

He could do that now. He could turn around on this highway, drive back to the house, pack up his things and move to the trailer. Haggerty kept a bed there in case he wanted to take a nap on slow afternoons.

Tim pictured Cricket, red eyed, red nosed and accusing him with her eyes as he walked out the door. She was acting the part of aggrieved spouse even though they were not married. He reminded himself that Cricket wasn't usually like that. She had always been, to his knowledge, upbeat, optimistic and cheerful even in the worst of circumstances.

It was her mother instinct that was aroused in this instance. She might be unflappable in other situations, but when her child was threatened, she acted for all the world like a feisty mother hen. He smiled at the analogy because, back on the farm, he had once seen a mother banty hen take on Old Mose, his father's crack hunting dog who was threatening her chicks. The mother hen had squawked and pecked at the dog's nose and heels until he ran howling, and Old Mose had never ventured near the chicken house again.

Last night, Cricket had nestled close to him under the covers. She had been trusting and sweet, and he had wanted to protect her against every trouble and hardship. Maybe that was the way Cricket felt about Jeremy. No wonder she had been angry with him.

Her small body beside his in the bed had aroused him this morning, although he had turned away so she wouldn't know. He had savored his desire for her, had lived inside it for a while, experiencing it. It was something with which he wanted to be utterly familiar before he offered it to her.

If he left now, that would never happen. He would never press against her in the night, urging her on with his ardor. He wouldn't taste the warmth and wetness of her lips, nor would he expand his body into hers and touch her afterward with damp and knowing fingertips. He would never love her.

That seemed like too great a price to pay for this morning's thoughtlessness. He pulled his car to a stop outside the trailer, and the sunlight on the snow in the field beyond dazzled his eyes. He thought about Cricket and her red nose and red eyes, and that vision disappeared and was replaced by a new Cricket image, this one clear-eyed and smiling with a radiance that seemed well-nigh unreachable.

He wanted to reach that special radiance of hers, to touch it, to draw it inside himself until he was filled with it. The amazing thing was that he wanted all of this more than he wanted to run.

It was then that he knew for certain that he would go home to her before it was dark.

WHEN TIM WALKED OUT the door that morning, Cricket thought she might throw up.

How could she have attacked him about a circumstance that was mostly her fault? It had been stupid and presumptuous of her to assume that Tim would automatically look after Jeremy.

Limp and distraught from their confrontation, she managed to quell her nausea long enough to call Renee to come over to stay with Jeremy, and she played with him until Renee arrived. Jeremy was in good spirits, laughing and cooing, and she felt comfortable about leaving him this morning. This was fortunate, because it was almost time for midterm exams at the college, and she had a lot of catching up to do after her recent absences. Her nausea subsided into a nervous ache in the pit of her stomach.

When Renee came, Cricket took a few minutes to change her sweater, which smelled like Jeremy's ear drops. Her eyes fell on her new silk blouse as soon as she opened the door of her closet.

She hadn't bought that blouse to wear to class. Still she fingered the delicate fabric, appreciating the sensory aspects of it. She was like that—she liked to match fabric to mood. The winter after Hugh left, she was sure that she owed her sanity to an old red fleece warm-up suit she had worn almost every day. The soft fabric had seemed to enfold her, to cuddle her when there was no one around to provide that comfort.

She slipped her arms into the sleeves of the blouse and tucked the tails into her wool slacks. It *did* look nice. Best of all, wearing it definitely made her feel better. And she wasn't taking Jeremy to class, so there was no danger that he would spit up on it or tear the delicate lace with his fingernails. That was what finally decided her. She threw her coat on over the blouse and hurriedly called a goodbye to Renee.

The day dragged on slowly, dulled by a lowering sky. When Cricket finally arrived home at three o'clock, Renee informed her that the weather service was predicting snow for the afternoon. Cricket had arrived just in time to put Jeremy to bed for his nap, and she did. She invited Renee to stay and drink a cup of tea with her, but Renee had to hurry home to meet her boyfriend. Cricket felt at loose ends.

She studied, finding it hard to concentrate. She called Trudy at the card shop, but according to Mary Sue, Trudy had driven to Eau Claire to pick up an order of stationery and wouldn't be back until later.

Cricket went into her bedroom and straightened the bed covers. She wondered what Tim was doing. She deeply regretted the way she had acted this morning. She reminded herself of an old fishwife, haranguing Tim so that he'd fled for his life. She wouldn't blame him if he never came back.

That was an awful thought! What if he didn't come back? What if she never saw him again? Fear made her knees weak. Life without Tim was unimaginable.

Was she telling herself that she couldn't live without him? As she was pondering this possibility, she heard the familiar sound of his car rounding the corner.

"Tim!" she said involuntarily. From her window she saw him get out of the Mustang and slam the door. She thought that the set of his shoulders seemed unduly apprehensive.

Time stopped, and it seemed to Cricket that time had been slowing down ever since she first met Tim. Minutes, hours, days used to speed by, but now they had slowed to a pace that made her feel every part of every minute. There was never a second when she wasn't fully aware of how she felt, both emotionally and physically, and she wasn't used to this awareness of herself. Maybe she never would be.

Tim walked with long strides up the cement path to the house, and he reminded her of a young, healthy colt, long-legged and strong. The sight of him made her hold her breath, and something tightened inside her head, cutting off consciousness of everything but him.

He inserted his key into the front door lock, turned it, and Cricket froze. He walked into the house as he usually did. She found herself thinking involuntarily, *Don't wake Jeremy*, and she knew that she wanted Jeremy to stay asleep more for her sake than his own.

Tim didn't call her name. He moved quietly to the door of her room and saw her standing at the window. He knew then that she had watched him since he got out of his car.

She lifted her hand as if in supplication, but then it strayed to the curve of her breast. She left it there, unaware of the poignancy of the gesture.

He didn't speak, but he didn't have to. His pupils darkened and the color of his irises deepened, and she thought that if she wanted to, she could see straight into his soul. He stepped toward her, and she met him halfway.

The alertness of her body surprised him. She had looked so soft and pliable before he took her in his arms, but she was as tense as though she was poised to run. He stroked her back, much as he had stroked Jeremy's last night. She relaxed slightly. He continued to move his hands up and down the silky fabric, caressing her into tranquility.

She would not, despite his tender ministrations, become tranquil. Instead she reared back and examined his face with wary eyes. Her eyes softened to a mossy, sensuous green, and she said, "Tim, I—"

He said, "Shh, I don't want to hear it," and silenced her with his lips.

She sighed softly and raised her arms, folding them behind him until they overlapped. He stopped caressing her back and slid his hands to her waist where he pulled her blouse out of her slacks. Underneath, her skin had the dewy softness of rose petals. She twisted her body against him, seeking the proper fit.

She helped him out of his coat, and he tossed it on the chair.

The buttons of her blouse were round fabric-covered knobs and very small. He couldn't force them through their loops.

She sensed the problem and tried to help. Their hands met. Hers fluttered against his, and he dropped his hands to her hips. She wasn't fast enough with the buttons, however, so he tried again. Cricket was afraid that he would rip the delicate silk. Again their hands fought, and this time Cricket parted the buttons from their loops. The blouse fell away and fluttered to the floor like a fallen butterfly. She tried to see the falling motion through Tim's eyes. She hoped he found it graceful; she hoped he found *her* exquisite. She didn't want to appear awkward to him in any way.

When they stood unclothed before each other, it seemed like the first time, although they both knew that it wasn't. It only seemed like the first time, because the time before had been devoid of desire.

The shade at the window of Cricket's room was raised, and the only thing that concealed them from passersby was the sheer curtain. It was gray and cloudy outside, and a light snow was beginning to fall. Cricket's bright hair glowed like a flame in the dusky bluish light.

A lump formed in Tim's throat as he gazed upon her. She returned his gaze levelly and with curiosity. Tentatively she reached out a hand and touched the mat of hair on his chest. It was surprisingly dark for such a blond man.

Her touch energized him, and he pulled her into his arms. The time for tenderness was over. This was a time for the slaking of their long-denied hunger. In a sudden rush of heat their passion burst through, and they both wondered how they had managed to postpone this inevitable moment for so long.

His tongue found hers, and her mouth opened wider to accommodate it. She directed his touch, arching to meet it, experiencing her reawakening to the sexual urge with a sudden, piercing joy.

She discovered that his hands and mouth knew her better than she knew herself. He found all the places that cried out for touching, for kissing. She clutched him to her, and suddenly he swung her into his arms, rendering her dizzy and weightless. And then they were on the bed, tumbling the sheets she had so recently smoothed, finding new ways to pleasure one another. Cricket felt as though she had left her own body and been replaced by another more sexual being. She was a passionate distillation of herself.

He held himself apart for a moment, committing her face to memory so that he would never forget how she looked at that moment. She was flushed and breathing hard, and in the depths of her eyes he read her need for him. There was more, too, but for the moment he pushed the existence of her other emotions from his mind. For now it was enough that she needed him so much.

When at last they joined, it was with a sense that this was something special in their lives. Her chin found the hollow beneath his shoulder and her stomach molded to the curve of his. Her pleasure was full of astonishment. She had not known that it was possible for a man to give so much of himself to lovemaking. His knowledge of her made her think that he must have made love to her many times before in his thoughts. His wonder told her that it was even better than he had imagined. Finally she cried out for him to finish, unwilling to deprive either of them any longer.

Afterward they lay spent in each other's arms, reluctant to break the silence that wrapped them in such loving intimacy. Whatever the questions had been before, whatever fears had been stirred by their earlier misunderstanding, all was forgotten and forgiven. Here in their cozy bed, locked together in a warm embrace, they gloried in their new knowledge of each other.

Outside, the snow fell like drifting feathers, enveloping them in a soft white world, sparkling fresh and new.

Chapter Eleven

"Does this look all right?" Tim asked anxiously, tugging at the knot of his tie.

"It looks perfect," Cricket told him. She had never seen Tim wearing anything as formal as a suit. He had put on a dark blue one, the only one he owned, and the effect was stunning.

"I don't know why Trudy insists on getting dressed up for this thing," Tim said.

Cricket flitted into her bathroom. "This thing is a dinner party to introduce us to Walt," she called over her shoulder. "Trudy has been planning it for two weeks."

Tim followed Cricket into her bathroom. It was a place that he didn't normally invade, women's bathrooms being what they were. There was usually powder in the air to make him sneeze, and women were always washing things in their bathroom sinks. This bathroom, with its dangling panty hose, drying sweaters and soggy underwear, was a veritable hanging garden of Cricket's delights. Tim willingly climbed the stairs every morning to shave in his own apartment.

"Don't kiss me now," Cricket warned, critically applying lip gloss. "You'll get all sticky. Watch out, I'm going to spray," and she pointed the nozzle of a can of hair spray at him.

"I think I'll go get Kimberly," he said.

"Good idea." Cricket set her hair spray on the sink and whirled around. She danced over to him and hugged him.

"I thought you said no kissing," he said.

"Hugging is okay," she said.

"I agree with that, anyway," he said as he returned her hug.

Cricket hummed as she straightened the living room after Tim left. Jeremy played in his playpen, and she stopped to check his diaper. Miraculously it was still dry.

In a few minutes, Tim and Kimberly came laughing into the foyer. Tim took Cricket's coat out of the closet and held it for her. She turned her back to slip her arms into it.

"Ready?" he said, smiling down at her.

"Ready," she replied as she returned his smile.

Ragged patches of fog hid the hedge behind Trudy's house. Bitter cold surrounded them as they made their way through the shrouded bare trees in the backyard.

They climbed the stairs to Trudy's porch and rang the bell. Tim put an arm around Cricket's shoulders as they waited for Trudy to answer. He had taken pleasure in the invitation to Trudy's dinner party. This invitation was an acknowledgment that they were now a couple. Trudy and Walt would be there, and so would Mary Sue and Talbot, Trudy's brother.

Trudy stood in the warm rectangle of light in the doorway and welcomed them inside. She introduced Tim to Walt, who wore a professorial herringbone tweed jacket with worn suede patches at the elbows. A glowing crumb of a cigarette clung to Walt's lower lip. It was replaced by a more scholarly looking pipe when they settled in the living room with their drinks.

Trudy was a vivacious hostess. She fluttered here and there, hanging up coats, offering drinks and occasionally letting her hand rest briefly and possessively on Walt's shoulder or arm in silent affirmation that he was hers.

"So what do you do for a living, Tim?" Walt asked without much interest. He blinked his sad eyes and waited.

"I fly," Tim said, unwilling to give more information than that. He had already decided, from Walt's limp handshake, that Cricket's assessment of the man had been more than kind.

"Is that so?" Walt said. "What kind of flying?"

"Aerial applicating," Tim said.

Walt sent up a smoke signal from his pipe, and Trudy, nervously listening from her perch on the arm of the couch, stood and walked to Walt's chair.

"Tim first visited Manitou last summer, when he helped spray the crops," she said, placing placating fingers at the base of

Walt's neck. Walt sent up two more puffs of smoke, nearly asphyxiating her.

Trudy ran to get the tray of appetizers.

"Here, Tim," she said much too gaily. "You must try these stuffed mushrooms."

Tim, who considered mushrooms a taste one had to be born with, took one to be polite.

Cricket's eyes sought Tim's over the brim of her glass. A sympathetic spark flashed between them, binding them together in this company of people whom they thought of as "others." At this point in their relationship, they were so caught up in each other that anyone else was superfluous.

Finally, mercifully, Trudy called them to the dinner table. Cricket, to her dismay, was seated beside Walt. Tim, who was left-handed, found himself seated to the right of Mary Sue so that their elbows bumped when he picked up his water goblet. Talbot, observing that things weren't going well, clammed up entirely and answered every conversational foray with a monosyllable.

During the soup course, Walt took a sip of his sherried-crab bisque and pronounced it too cold to eat.

"I'll warm it for you," Trudy said, hopping up from her chair.

"No, no, it's all right," Walt said sourly, and he kept eating.

"It'll only take a minute in the microwave," Trudy said, clearly torn between snatching the bisque out from under Walt's spoon or sitting back down again.

"I said it's all right," Walt repeated testily, clattering his spoon down on the plate and glaring at her.

Trudy was cowed by his behavior, but nevertheless, she slid the soup out from under Walt's glare and retreated to the kitchen.

"I said it was all right, didn't I?" Walt said challengingly as he swept his glance over the other dinner guests. Cricket stared down at her soup, mortified for Trudy's sake. Her appetite had diminished considerably.

By the time they were halfway through the main course, Tim and Cricket were telegraphing messages with subtly raised eyebrows and slight lifts of the shoulder, so that there might have been no distance between them. The messages all said, *I can't wait to get back to our own house, can you?*

They suffered Walt's pompous assessment of William Blake's poetry—"As if anyone at that table cared," Tim was to say scornfully afterward—and Walt's insufferable explanation of how to solve the problem of illegal aliens. It wasn't until Walt began discoursing on the farm crisis that Tim got really annoyed.

"Actually," Walt said as they were finishing Trudy's pièce de résistance, a strawberry cheesecake, "it's the farmers' own fault that they're in so much trouble. Why, if they hadn't been so gullible when bankers were offering them loans at high interest rates, they wouldn't be going bankrupt now."

Tim pushed his chair away from the table, and Cricket watched helplessly as a deep furrow formed between his lowered eyebrows. He gripped the edge of the tabletop with white knuckles.

"Surely that's not all there is to the problem," trilled Trudy with a worried glance at Tim. She bit her lip, and just as Tim was about to say something, Trudy said prematurely, "Let's all go in the living room for coffee."

Cricket stood, knocking a small dish of nuts to the floor. The dish spun and landed face down on the oriental rug.

Cricket poured out an apology and stooped to pick up the nuts. They kept slipping out of her fingers, hopping around on the rug like giant fleas. The rug was so intricately patterned and the light was so dim that she could hardly see to pick them up. Tim, whose face was flushed an angry red by now, knelt to help her. He had not spoken a word since Walt had made his outrageous statement about farmers.

When they had replaced the nuts in the dish, Cricket said quietly, "Let's go in the kitchen." Tim stood slowly and, with a thunderous look at Walt's back, followed Cricket.

"I can't let him talk garbage like that," he said to Cricket when they were alone. A vein pulsed at his temple.

"Please, Tim, this isn't the time to make a scene," Cricket begged.

"If I have to go into that living room with him, I'll punch him. I'm leaving."

"Tim," Cricket said.

"I'll see you when you get home," he said, heading for the back door.

"At least let me make our excuses," she hissed as his hand reached for the doorknob.

He hesitated. She looked distraught. Cricket was Trudy's loyal friend, and he couldn't blame her for that. Trudy had enough problems without his adding any more to them. And Cricket would be left to pick up the pieces if he stormed out of here.

"All right," Tim said wearily, his anger fading in the face of Cricket's embarrassment. "Say whatever you want."

"I'll say I called home and that Jeremy has another earache," Cricket decided in desperation. She went back through the dining room door and rushed to the living room, where she began to explain as quickly as she could. Much to her surprise, Tim appeared at her elbow.

Trudy expressed dismay that they were leaving, although Cricket was sure that she detected shades of relief. Walt merely stared at them with a saturnine expression that he probably considered scholarly, and Mary Sue and Talbot made sounds of regret. Finally, Cricket and Tim escaped into the freezing night air.

It was so cold that Cricket could feel particles of ice in the air that she breathed. Nevertheless, she breathed deeply. It was such a relief to be free of the evening and of the people.

Tim took her gloved hand in his as they walked. "I apologize," he said. "I just couldn't stand it anymore. If there's anything I know about firsthand, it's the farm crisis. I can't bear it when some two-bit authority like Walt starts to sound off."

"You could have tried to convert him to your way of thinking," Cricket reminded him gently.

He focused troubled eyes on her. "I can't even talk about it," he said in a quiet voice.

She squeezed his hand. "I'm sorry, Tim. But you can't live in a world where no one ever mentions the problems of the farmers. Why, they're in the news all the time."

Tim sighed. "You're right. I *am* supersensitive about it. I'll try to do better."

"It *was* an awkward evening," Cricket said. She had discerned something disturbing in Walt's attitude toward Trudy. Despite her adoration, he had belittled Trudy in many ways. The more Walt found fault, the harder Trudy worked to make him happy. Cricket was afraid that this state of affairs boded ill for her friend.

"Even aside from Walt's stupid talk about farmers, that was one of the worst evenings I've ever spent," Tim said as they stamped the snow off their boots on their own porch.

"I agree," Cricket said wholeheartedly. "Isn't Walt awful?"

"Worse," said Tim, making a face, and they both laughed.

Tim slid an arm around Cricket's shoulders and pulled her close so that the contours of her body fit his. "I can't believe how good it feels to get home. It seems as though we've been gone for years," he said fervently, as the warmth of their home enveloped them.

Tim took the sitter home, and Cricket waited for him at the door. Somehow the rocky moments of the last few hours made her feel closer to Tim than ever. She appreciated him. Compared to Walt, he was a prince.

When Tim came in, she was waiting at the door, aquiver with impatience. Her eyes glowing, she lifted her hands up to cup his cold cheeks, and he placed his hands over them. He immediately sensed her expectation. He felt a rush of gratitude that Cricket was always waiting for him when he came home. He kissed her once, and then, as eager as she was, he enveloped her in a big bear hug. Finally, laughing, excited at the prospect of the long night stretching before them in its infinite possibilities, they fell into bed and made love into the wee small hours of the morning.

"WAS IT SO BAD?" Trudy asked anxiously while bouncing Jeremy on her knee as his mother prepared to leave.

Cricket paused in front of Trudy's back door. She had brought Jeremy to Trudy's house because Trudy had volunteered to baby-sit. She didn't want to get involved in a long, drawn-out discussion of Trudy's dinner party now.

"The food was wonderful," she said warmly. Trudy brightened at this.

"I don't mean the food," Trudy said after her smile faded. "I mean Walt. He was in a bad mood that night, Cricket, or he would have been more sociable. He had a fight with Rona before he left her house."

"That's too bad," Cricket said.

"And that's why Walt can't be with me this weekend. He has to calm Rona down, he says, before he tells her it's over between them."

Jeremy began to whimper, a welcome diversion. "Here's Jeremy's teething ring," Cricket said, pulling it out of her pocket. "I keep it in the refrigerator so it will be cold. The cold feels good on his gums, doesn't it, Jeremy?"

Jeremy laughed obligingly as Cricket put the gel-filled ring in his hand. "I guess I'd better go before he starts to fuss again, or Tim and I will never make it to the ice rink. Bye, Trudy. We won't stay too long." Cricket headed for the door.

"Stay as long as you like, Crick. If Walt can't come to see me, at least I have Jeremy." Trudy nuzzled Jeremy's cheek, and he giggled. Cricket left the two of them in Trudy's sunny kitchen playing pat-a-cake.

The sky was a bright blazing blue, and a new snowfall frosted the spruce trees in the backyard. Cricket found Tim in her kitchen, untangling the tangled laces of his borrowed ice skates.

"Do they fit?" Cricket wanted to know.

"They sure do. Kimberly's father and I wear exactly the same size shoe. Are you ready?"

Cricket swung her skates up from the floor beside the back door. "As ready as I'll ever be," she said.

They walked toward the college campus, where there was a small oval rink. Cricket hadn't been there in a couple of years, although she was entitled to use it by way of her student activities card. Tim had accidentally found her forgotten skates under the stairs when he was setting traps for their peripatetic mice.

"Hey!" he'd exclaimed. "I didn't know you could skate!"

"Of course I can skate! How could a person grow up in Wisconsin without learning to skate or ski?"

"You know how to ski?"

"Of course," Cricket had said. Her expression clouded momentarily. "Not that I get to do it very often these days," she amended.

"We'll have to remedy that," Tim had said with a grin, and then he invited her to go skating this morning.

Cricket felt like a kid again, swinging down the street holding hands with Tim. Someone had built a snowman in a front yard, and its hat had fallen off. Cricket stopped and jammed the hat back on the snowman's head. A little boy inside the house tapped on the window and mouthed "Thank you" through the glass.

The rink wasn't especially crowded for such a nice day, perhaps because many students were home studying for tests.

"Why aren't you studying today?" Tim asked as they sat on the wooden bench in the warming hut lacing up their boots.

"Because I'm skating with you," Cricket said, smiling at him.

"You're not jeopardizing your grades, are you?" he asked.

"No. I'll study tomorrow. And anyway, I start my internship at the community mental health center after exams. I can afford to let up a little now that I'm so close to getting my degree."

They clattered down the scarred wooden ramp to the ice.

"Tell me about the internship," Tim said.

"I've been looking forward to it ever since I declared my major. It'll give me a chance to observe mental health professionals at work and to help people, I hope. The mental health center has offered me a job after I graduate, so this internship serves as on-the-job training for me."

"That sounds made-to-order for you," Tim said as they began to glide around the edge of the rink.

"It is."

The snow on the side of the rink was piled so high that they couldn't see over it. Above the mounded snow, birches spread leafless arms. Sounds were magnified out on the ice, and they took on crystalline overtones. Being outdoors seemed to increase the dimensions of their relationship. Today it felt vast and encompassing. Skating beside Tim, Cricket felt invulnerable. She smiled at him expansively, hoping he shared her feelings. He smiled back at her. Their joy in each other's company was a silent pact between them.

When they were pleasantly tired, they went into the warming hut, where the air seemed as steamy as a sauna after the cold crispness of the outdoors. There they drank cups of cocoa vended by college students. Finally when the winter's chill had seeped through to their bones, they pulled their boots back on and began to walk home.

"Did you ever skate in Kansas, Tim?" Cricket asked.

"Not much. I went in for a lot of winter sports when I was stationed in Europe with the air force."

"I suppose there was no skiing in Kansas."

"I liked to ski cross-country. My friend Sarah and I used to do that a lot. That was when her husband, James, was alive, of course. Remind me to call Sarah sometime, Cricket."

"Call her when we get home today," Cricket suggested.

Tim walked several paces without speaking. "I'd like to, but I don't feel comfortable about it yet."

"Because you're ashamed of running away?" Cricket ventured softly.

Tim nodded. "Sarah's the one who would know how my parents are getting along. Our families are close."

"Are you afraid she'll be angry with you?"

"She might be, but Sarah doesn't hold a grudge. She'd be delighted to hear from me, I know."

"Call her, Tim."

By this time, they were at their back door.

"I don't know. Some things are too hard to face," he said, resting one hand on the porch railing and staring down at his boots.

"Tim," said Cricket, touching his arm. "You have to get over it sometime. You'll have to reestablish contact with your family before you can begin to heal."

Tim managed a grin. "Am I still so broken?" he asked in a joshing tone.

"You won't be able to bury the past until you face up to it," she said seriously.

He didn't speak but gazed off into the distance as though considering this.

"I'm going over to Trudy's to get Jeremy," Cricket told him, leaving him alone to think his thoughts in private. Maybe if she wasn't in the house he really would pick up her telephone and call Sarah. If he did, she'd know that he was beginning to gather together the pieces of the life that had been shattered by the sale of his family's farm.

Cricket knew, as soon as she returned with Jeremy in her arms, that Tim was talking on the phone with Sarah. He spoke in a falsely hearty voice, one that she suspected he had adopted to hide his hurt.

"And Ma—what does she do with her time? Is that right? Well, I'm glad to hear it. She always was a good seamstress."

Cricket hushed Jeremy and handed him a teething biscuit. While Tim talked she busied herself with nipping dead leaves off the philodendron in the kitchen window. Finally she heard Tim say, "You too, Sarah. And again, tell Cliff I said he's a lucky guy. Write soon."

In a moment, Tim appeared in the kitchen doorway. "Is it all right if I let Mungo out?" he asked. Cricket looked at him. He seemed none the worse for his conversation with Sarah.

Cricket nodded, and he opened the door for the cat, watching Mungo as he jumped off the porch.

"Mungo," he said. "Funny name for a cat."

"It's Gaelic. It means lovable."

"Interesting," Tim said, but he wasn't thinking about the cat. "Is there any of that Jell-O left?" he asked.

"Bottom shelf," Cricket said, pointing to the refrigerator. Tim took the Jell-O out of the refrigerator and stood eating it directly from the bowl. Cricket waited for him to speak first.

"Sarah married Cliff Oenbrink. This is the first time I heard about it," he said finally.

"Who is Cliff Oenbrink?"

"A professional farm manager. He came to Curtisville last summer and helped Sarah keep her farm productive after a big hail storm destroyed her wheat. She sounds happy."

"That's good," said Cricket.

"And Pa has a part-time job repairing machinery at a farm equipment place. Sarah says that Ma has fixed their trailer up really nice. I can't imagine my parents living in a trailer. They've always had the farmhouse," he said with a downcast expression.

"What else did Sarah tell you about them?" Cricket asked.

"Sarah's going to write me a long letter, she says. She's going to look in on Ma tomorrow. Ma has been sewing for other people. Sarah says that Ma's making a bridal gown this week."

"That's wonderful, Tim," Cricket said. She paused. "Do you feel better now that you've called Sarah?" she asked.

Tim took a while to answer. "I suppose so," he said at last. "I'm worried about Pa—Sarah said he's had back trouble. And Ma works so hard, I imagine that she's wearing herself out doing all that sewing. I wonder—" But he stopped talking abruptly and set the Jell-O bowl down on the counter.

"You wonder what?"

"I wonder how they are, how they *really* are," he said in a low voice before turning on his heel and disappearing upstairs, where he seldom went anymore unless he wanted to be alone.

Sighing, Cricket checked her sandwich-making supplies and started a grocery list. She knew better than to invade Tim's privacy while his conversation with Sarah was so fresh in his mind.

That night when they lay in bed and she was tickling Tim's

stomach the way he loved her to do, Cricket said lazily, "Have you thought about paying a visit to Curtisville lately, Tim?"

He stiffened, then relaxed. "Some," he said.

She stroked his stomach some more. "Maybe it would be a good time to go when Haggerty gets back from Arizona at the end of the month," she said.

"Maybe," he conceded reluctantly.

"I can't imagine being separated from Jeremy in anger the way you and your parents are separated now," she murmured, and then she fell silent.

Tim stared at the ceiling, lulled by Cricket's gentle stroking. Her speaking of Jeremy brought unbidden thoughts to his mind. He recalled the way he had felt about the baby the first time he'd ever baby-sat for him—the overwhelming feeling of responsibility for a helpless child. His own parents had felt that for him once. It was hard to imagine himself as small and as dependent as Jeremy, but he had once been a baby and they had cared for him. He owed them.

Cricket stopped stroking gradually, and Tim moved to take her in his arms. He held her close long into the night, wide-awake and reliving the painful memories that he longed to bury forever in the past.

Chapter Twelve

The next weekend, after exams, Tim announced that he and Cricket were going to Wintermont to ski.

"We'll go Saturday morning, stay Saturday and Sunday nights, and we won't drive back until early Monday, since that's a school holiday," he told her. His eyes glinted with enthusiasm.

"Jeremy, too?"

"No," Tim said, slipping his arms around her from behind. "I've already made arrangements for Trudy to take care of Jeremy all weekend. She'll be delighted to move in here while we're gone."

"Trudy! But I can't impose on her for a whole weekend! Anyway, what about Walt?" Cricket turned in the circle of Tim's arms and stared up at him.

"Walt isn't planning to show up this weekend. He gave Trudy a long song and dance about having to take one of Rona's kids to a Scout get-together. She told me about it when I stopped by the Card Boutique the other day. Since she wasn't going to be seeing Walt, Trudy was looking for something meaningful to do this weekend."

"The most meaningful thing for Trudy to do would be to break up with that creep," Cricket said darkly.

Tim laughed and said, "It just so happens that I couldn't agree with you more."

Cricket made arrangements for Renee and her boyfriend to assemble her sandwiches and run her sandwich route on the mornings when she would be gone. She looked forward to the ski weekend at Wintermont the way a child looks forward to Christmas. She had never been away from Jeremy for more than a few hours.

After more preparation than Hannibal made when he crossed the Alps, according to Cricket, she and Tim departed for the ski resort on Saturday morning as scheduled.

"You'll be sure to give Jeremy his vitamins tomorrow," Cricket reminded Trudy before they left.

"Don't worry, I'll take good care of him. I'm thrilled to have Jeremy to myself for the whole weekend. This will show me what I'm getting myself into if I decide to have a baby."

"Trudy is thinking about having a baby?" Tim asked as the two of them pulled away from the front curb a few minutes later in his Mustang.

"If she marries Walt," Cricket told him in an exasperated tone.

Neither of them was willing to let thoughts of Walt dominate their day. During the hour-and-a-half ride to Wintermont, it was heaven to be together without interruptions.

"Where are we staying at Wintermont?" Cricket asked casually.

Tim shot her a teasing grin. "I wanted to surprise you."

"You surprised me enough when you presented me with this whole preplanned package," she said wryly.

He laughed and reached for her hand. He held it loosely on his knee. "I'm glad you were surprised," he said.

"That still doesn't answer my question," she said.

"What question was that?" he asked, his expression all innocence.

"About where we're staying!" she said.

"There are cottages scattered in the woods surrounding the Wintermont Lodge. I rented one."

"Oh, Tim, that sounds lovely."

"And private," he said with a meaningful look.

She lifted his hand and pressed her cheek against it. Then she turned her face and kissed each of his fingertips one by one. He stroked her hair briefly before returning his attention to the highway.

Cricket rested her head on the back of the seat and enjoyed the sensation of someone else's being in charge. Tim's car passed those of other weekend skiers, their skis fastened in ski racks atop their cars, heading for the same place that Cricket and Tim were going. Cricket realized with a jolt that there was a whole world out here, and it was full of people who went places and had a good time. For too long she hadn't been one of them.

The Wintermont Inn was a modern hotel, well managed and catering to a weekend ski crowd. Tim and Cricket checked in at the front desk where they were given the key to their cottage, and after leaving the inn, they drove along a winding road through deep snowy woods.

"It's so beautiful here," Cricket said as they slid out of the car beside a cottage styled like a Swiss chalet. A balcony hung from the upper floor, its railing carved with hearts.

The cottage was luxurious, with a loft on the second floor. On the first floor, a king-size bed occupied a dais before a bank of picture windows overlooking the ski slopes in the distance. A huge fireplace occupied one wall of the living area, which included a small kitchenette. Outside on a rear deck, a hot tub steamed invitingly.

"Let's go rent our skis, and then we'll eat lunch," Tim suggested. They changed into their ski clothes. Cricket had borrowed hers from Trudy.

"I'd rather lend you my magenta nightgown," Trudy had said when Cricket stopped by to pick up the ski outfit.

"Oh, Trudy," Cricket had demurred.

"Take it along anyway," Trudy insisted, stuffing it into the same bag with the ski wear. The magenta nightgown tumbled out now, and Cricket shoved it in the back of her suitcase.

"Ready?" asked Tim, smiling and offering his hand.

"Ready," Cricket said, smiling back.

They rented their skis at the Wintermont Lodge, and deciding to skip lunch, they headed for the slopes.

Tim was a superb athlete, Cricket observed as she followed him down the slope. Halfway down, he pointed his skis straight downhill and tucked the poles close to his body. He sped down the hill, ending in a spray of snow at the bottom.

He was waiting for her when she, skiing more conservatively, reached the end of the run.

"Do you want to check out the Big Chill?" In his eyes she saw the light of challenge and daring.

The Big Chill was a more expert trail, but Cricket, easily keeping up with Tim, reveled in the sensation of swooping over moguls and flying through the flats. They played "follow-the-leader," first with Tim in the lead, then Cricket. They swooped and dipped along the trails as gracefully as sea gulls.

"Wow," said Tim with admiration when they reached the bottom. "That was something!"

"Yes," Cricket said, pushing her goggles up. "Let's do it again!"

When they felt themselves tiring, they slowed down. They managed one more run on the Wintermont Special, the most scenic trail, before long violet shadows creeping across the landscape told them that it was time to quit.

They stowed their skis in a locker at the lodge and walked slowly through the twilit woods to their cottage. There, pleasantly exhausted, they pulled off their parkas and boots and bib overalls, their thick wool socks and long underwear, and jumped laughing into the hot tub.

"You are some hot-dog skier, Cricket Erling," Tim said admiringly.

Cricket threw her head back and laughed. "I haven't skied in so long that my muscles are sure to be sore tomorrow," she said.

"That's why we have this hot tub," Tim said. "So that you can soak away your aches and pains." He pulled a bottle of brandy out of the swirling steam on the deck and carefully poured two glasses. They leaned against each other and cradled the brandy snifters in their hands.

"I don't feel like us," Cricket said dreamily.

"What does that mean?" Tim's voice sounded deep and relaxed.

"It means that we're like two other people. I'm not concerned about Jeremy's waking up, and you're not worrying about the airport security guard calling you about Haggerty's trailer, and there aren't any mice scratching overhead."

"Cricket, I have news for you," he said, deliberately relieving her of the snifter and setting it with his on the edge of the tub. "We're not two other people, we're ourselves."

She looked at him, and her eyes sparkled. "Prove it," she whispered, and he swept her into his arms and carried her into the house where he wrapped them both in a big bath sheet provided by the hotel management. And then, more slowly, he unwrapped them and took her, rosy and warm, to bed.

Later they dressed to go to dinner in the inn dining room, although they briefly considered ordering dinner delivered to the cottage. Surprisingly it was Tim who decided in favor of going to the inn.

"Look at it this way," said Tim as he knotted his tie. "We hardly ever get to go out to dinner together. Why not enjoy it while we can?"

Cricket, who wore a dress of mauve silk retained from some forgotten occasion in her past, paused while brushing her hair to kiss him. "Why not?" she said.

The dining room at the inn was softly lighted, and there were fresh flowers on each table. A group of musicians wandered the dining room, serenading the guests.

"What shall we ask them to play?" Tim said.

"I don't know," Cricket replied. She was warm with love and with wine, and she thought Tim was the most handsome man in the dining room.

"They could play our song," Tim said.

"But we don't have a song," Cricket said.

"We should. Think of one."

Cricket racked her brain. Outside the window, a bank of evergreen trees was illuminated by a spotlight. "Oh, how about 'Evergreen'?" she said off the top of her head.

"'Evergreen' it is," Tim said, and when the musicians arrived at their table, he asked them to play it.

"What a funny way to choose our song," murmured Cricket when the last strains of the beautiful love song had faded, and the musicians had gone to the next table.

Tim smiled and rested his hand on hers. "But an original way," he told her.

"You're supposed to fit the song to your feelings, not your feelings to the song," Cricket admonished playfully.

Tim became suddenly serious. "Who says I don't feel that way?" he said.

The waiter brought the main course, and when he had left, Cricket focused her eyes on two people standing in the doorway waiting to be seated.

"What's wrong?" Tim asked, noting Cricket's narrowed eyes.

She nodded toward the entrance. "That," she said. "Don't turn around," she cautioned quickly. "Wait until they pass our table."

The couple Cricket was watching followed the hostess to a table in a secluded corner, but both Cricket and Tim got a look at the man.

"That's Walt, isn't it?" Tim said.

Cricket nodded and tried not to think about Trudy back in Manitou with no one for company but Jeremy.

"And Walt's supposed to be back in La Crosse, taking Rona's child to a Scout function?"

Cricket nodded again.

"Well, well," Tim said softly. "Walt may bore *us*, but he certainly doesn't have that effect on women, does he?"

"Do you suppose that's Rona?" Cricket said, sneaking a look. The woman was a redhead, and she and Walt were leaning toward each other in a manner that could best be described as intimate.

"Rona? No, I doubt it. This one looks too young to have two school-age children. My guess is that this is Walt's girlfriend number three."

"Meaning that Walt not only has Rona, but also Trudy and this redhead on a string?" Cricket asked incredulously.

"Exactly."

They ate quietly. Cricket was thinking.

"Do you suppose Walt saw us?"

"I think he's spotted us now. Look, he's turning his chair so that his face is hidden in the shadows."

"I'd love to walk up to Walt now and start a conversation," Cricket said through tight lips.

"But you won't, because we're going to finish our dinner, have a nice after-dinner drink and go happily back to our cottage."

"Is that all?" asked Cricket with an inviting smile.

"Not quite," said Tim.

"WHAT'S THAT?" Tim asked.

"This?" said Cricket, lifting the magenta nightgown out of her suitcase.

"Yes. Have I ever seen that before?"

"I hope not. It's Trudy's nightgown."

"Why is it in your suitcase?"

"She insisted on my borrowing it. Apparently this nightgown is the ultimate in romance for a weekend tryst."

"Not in my opinion," Tim said, parting Cricket's undergarment so he could see more of what he considered the ultimate.

"Dear Tim, why won't you let me be sexy?" she said, letting the magenta nightgown fall to the floor in a heap.

"You already are."

"Mmm, Tim, wait," she said, struggling to shed her shoes.

"Waiting is not something that I'm prepared to do."

"Tim!"

"You've got the name right," he assured her, bending her backward onto the bed.

"Tim...."

"Mmm-hmm, do that again, and don't stab me with your high heel."

"Tim, oh Tim...."

And then there was silence.

"WOULD YOU LIKE ME BETTER as a blonde?" Cricket said the next morning.

"Blondes don't appeal to me much anymore."

"Since when?" Cricket said with interest. She was arrayed across his chest with her head pressed against his opposite shoulder. They had slept late, and the sun shafting through the wide picture window glinted off his hair.

"Since I met you," he said, turning toward her and kissing her so deeply that Cricket disengaged herself momentarily to close the drapery for privacy.

"WHAT I CAN'T FIGURE OUT about Walt is, how does he keep all his women from finding out about each other?" Cricket said as she stepped out of the shower shrouded in a terry-cloth towel.

"Why do you care?" Tim asked. He had been standing at the window wrapped in his own bath towel as he watched skiers skimming down the trails.

"Because Trudy is my friend," Cricket said unhappily.

"My guess is that Walt isn't going to be able to keep Trudy from finding out about him for long, and that right now he's sweating it out, wondering if you're going to tell her."

"I wish I knew if I should," Cricket sighed as her towel fell away.

"What I'd like to know is if we're ever going to make it to

the ski slopes today," Tim said, slowly dropping his own towel on the bed.

"Wet bath towels on the bed won't go over too well with the management," Cricket warned as Tim crooked his leg behind her so that she fell over it backward onto a cozy window seat.

"Hang the management," Tim said.

ON SUNDAY NIGHT THEY LAY before a roaring fire in the fireplace, reclining on a purple wool throw. Cricket ran her fingers through Tim's hair. She liked doing this. It seemed like a particularly intimate contact.

"I'm having a wonderful time," Tim said. She had curved her torso around the pillow supporting his head, and his hand clasped her ankle.

"So am I. I can't recall ever enjoying anything more," Cricket said.

A log fell in the fireplace, crackling and spitting and sending a flare of flame up so that his face was momentarily brightened. He stroked her ankle beneath the slacks she wore.

"What if," he ventured carefully, "what if I thought I was falling in love with you?"

Cricket's heart stilled. "That's a very big if," she replied evenly.

"But what if?" he insisted, craning his neck to look at her.

Cricket stopped threading her fingers in and out of the shiny blond strands. She sat up, looking steadfastly into the fire. It was so hot that her cheeks began to burn.

"Well?" he asked.

"Then I suppose I'd have to decide if I am falling in love with you," she said finally.

"And then?"

"I don't know," she admitted.

They were silent for a long time, staring at the flames. The air around them seemed to flicker with anticipation. He reached out and lay his hand along her inner thigh.

"You make me happy, Cricket," he said quietly.

She wondered if she really made him happy, or if she had merely filled the vacuum inside him. Not wanting to face the answer, she dipped her head and kissed him on the lips.

"Ah, Cricket," he said when their lips parted. He regarded her with an intent half smile. "My little Cricket on the hearth."

She slid down on the rough purple fabric, and he began to peel away her clothes. At last they lay beside one another, their skin made rosy in the glow of the fire. Her longing was intense and as hot as the flames in the grate.

Her legs wrapped around him, binding him to her. Their climax was swift and simultaneous, and it left them gasping in surprise.

Now it was his turn to wind his fingers in her hair. He kissed her breasts, and he lay his head against her chest and listened to the slowing rhythm of her heartbeat.

"I do, you know," he said so softly that she might have missed it.

"What?"

"I do love you," he said as he held her in his arms and proved to her once more exactly how much.

Chapter Thirteen

On Monday morning, Trudy went to work at the Card Boutique and took Jeremy with her. After they arrived home from Wintermont, Cricket and Tim stopped by the shop to pick Jeremy up and take him home.

Cricket rushed inside the shop, eager to be reunited with her son after their first separation. Jeremy was sitting in his windup swing, and his eyes grew wide at the sound of his mother's voice. He broke into a giant grin.

"He was so much fun, Cricket. I loved taking care of him," Trudy said as Cricket hugged Jeremy to her. Cricket could hardly speak because of the lump in her throat. She hadn't realized that she missed Jeremy so much.

"Hey," Tim said softly when Trudy had gone to get Jeremy's diaper bag. "You're not having any regrets about having gone to Wintermont with me, are you?"

Her eyes met his. "No," she said emphatically, and they exchanged a look that said it all.

At home, Cricket fed Jeremy his lunch, and then she sat with him in her lap, stroking his hair and marveling over him as she hadn't since the day he was born. Everything seemed new to her: his big brown eyes, his jack-o'-lantern grin, his shell-pink fingernails and toenails. Had she ever really appreciated the wonder of him? She had to admit that having a baby had complicated her life, but she wouldn't have traded him for anything.

She knew that she wouldn't want to do anything for the rest of the day but play with her baby. She spread a blanket and laid him on the floor. Jeremy laughed up at her when she dangled a toy mirror just out of his reach.

"So how's the reunion going?" Tim asked, coming downstairs after a brief trip up to his room.

"Great. He missed me, Tim."

"I'm sure he did. Cricket, unless you need me, I'm going to run out to the airport and see if there's any work I need to do."

Cricket smiled up at him. *Unless you need me,* he had said. How could she tell him that she *did* need him, but not for anything inconsequential? She needed him for his affection, his caring, his help, his admiration. But all she said at the moment was, "That's fine, Tim."

"Would you like me to bring something from Harry's for dinner?"

"How about lasagna? I've been keeping a bottle of red wine in the kitchen, and I've been thinking that it's about time to get rid of it."

"That's something I'd be happy to help you do," he said. He bent to kiss the top of her head before leaving.

While Jeremy was napping, Cricket threw away a lot of old notes and test papers from the last academic quarter and then found herself at loose ends. For once in her busy life, there seemed to be nothing that absolutely needed to be done. She sat in the dining room bay window, stared out at a flock of juncos searching the ground around the bird feeder for seeds and thought about the time she had spent at Wintermont with Tim.

It was, Cricket decided in a flash of certainty, the best vacation she'd ever had in her whole life. Tim had been so easy to be around. He was unfailingly good-natured and pleasant. Try as she might, she couldn't find anything wrong with him. Except, of course, his tendency to leave, either emotionally or physically, when he found himself beyond his depth.

While Cricket watched, Mungo crept stealthily out from under Trudy's hedge. He crouched motionless, watching the juncos. His eyes darted back and forth as the birds hopped around the pole on which the bird feeder rested. Cricket stood, thinking she would go to the door and shoo Mungo away.

But the cat was too quick. Before she could move, he pounced. Frightened, the birds fluttered up and away. Mungo sat down and contemplated his failed maneuver, staring unblinkingly at the remnants of the flock as they sat twittering on the limb of a nearby tree.

"Come in here, Mungo," Cricket called at the back door. A disgruntled Mungo bounded across the snow and ran into the kitchen, sitting down suddenly in the middle of the floor to administer a few quick licks to his cold fur.

Cricket stood at the door watching as the birds settled again around the pole of the bird feeder, chirping among themselves as though nothing untoward had happened.

From the standpoint of a bird, Mungo's stalking and pouncing was not so unusual. Birds were used to having to fly away at the first threat of danger. They were conditioned to that response.

And Tim had also conditioned himself to fly away when he was in trouble. Fright or flight: it was one of the human animal's basic defenses. The question in Tim's case was whether he could learn another response. Could he learn to face his fears?

His behavior at the dinner party when he had wanted to leave because of Walt's comments but had then appeared in the living room when Cricket was making their excuses made her think that perhaps he could. With time, and the feeling of security brought about by a strong, consistent relationship, perhaps Tim would no longer find it necessary to fly away when threatened.

Cricket could only wait and see.

"THERE'S A LETTER on the hall table for you, Tim," Cricket called as soon as she heard Tim's footsteps in the foyer when he came in from work one night that week.

Tim stood in the hall reading it. He walked to the kitchen door. "It's from Sarah," he announced.

"Oh? How are your parents?"

"Pa went to the chiropractor, and his back is better. Ma has finished the bride's dress and is working on a dress for the maid-of-honor in the same wedding. Ma looked tired when she saw her, Sarah says." He paused and frowned, reading that passage again.

"Anything else?"

"Bernie's wife, Liz, is going to have another baby. Their third," he said with obvious pleasure.

"What children do they already have?"

"Two boys. I hope this one's a girl," Tim replied. He had

never been particularly interested in his nieces and nephews before, but now, knowing Jeremy, he understood what it meant to be having a baby. He had an irrational notion to tell Bernie and Liz about this new comprehension of his, even though telling them was a silly idea. He'd certainly never said anything so personal to either of them before.

"And Sarah—how's she?"

"She says that Ben, her ten-year-old son, won some kind of medal from the 4-H Club for the lambs he raised. He's a neat kid. I'd like to see that medal. I was there when he brought those lambs home, and they looked puny. He must have done a great job with them."

"You could go home and see Ben's medal," Cricket said softly.

Tim shook his head. "I don't know, Cricket," he said. He thought about Curtisville often, but he couldn't see himself going back there for any reason. The fact was that he still couldn't bear the thought of walking into his parents' little trailer and facing them after running away. Driving up to it, getting out of the car, comparing the trailer to their big farmhouse with land spread out in all directions—no, it would be too much.

"I think you're ready to go back," Cricket said stubbornly.

"Cricket, can you imagine how it would be if I did? I'd have to face Ma and Pa alone, and those first awkward moments would be more than I could stand. Unless," he said slowly as a new idea occurred to him, "unless you could be persuaded to go to Curtisville with me."

"And leave Jeremy? Oh, Tim, I couldn't. Isn't this something you have to face on your own?"

Tim swallowed, his mouth suddenly dry. "I wouldn't *have* to do it alone. Cricket, please think it over. Jeremy would go with us. I'd like my parents to meet both of you."

The air seemed to rush from Cricket's lungs. "I—I'm not sure I'm ready for that," she said with a self-conscious laugh.

He walked across the kitchen and grasped her by the shoulders. There was no way to avoid looking into his eyes. They shone with sincerity and hope. "Please, Cricket," he said.

It was hard to deny Tim anything when he looked at her that way. She knew what going back to Curtisville would mean to

Tim. It was a way to bury the past so that he could get on with the future. Did he think that his future could include her?

"When would we go?" she asked.

"At Easter during the college's spring break. Didn't you tell me that you have two weeks off then?"

Cricket nodded.

"Then you'll think about it?" His voice was urgent.

"I didn't say that," she said, attempting to twist away from him. She couldn't imagine meeting all those vague people from Tim's past—his parents, his brothers, the much-admired Sarah. The thought was overwhelming.

"But you will think about it," Tim said, pulling her unresisting body into his arms and kissing her, and Cricket knew that she would consider accompanying Tim to Curtisville, although she still believed deep inside that this was something that Tim should do on his own.

CRICKET AND JEREMY came in from her internship at the mental health center one evening about five o'clock. Cricket deposited Jeremy in his playpen, heaved a weary sigh, and said, "It's impossible."

Tim, who was reading the directions for yet another mousetrap to replace the unsuccessful ones they had been using, said, "What's impossible?"

"Taking Jeremy to the mental health center with me while I work. It's all right with the director as long as he isn't disruptive, and I thought he'd just sit quietly in a corner and play in his playpen. I can forget about that. Today during a group therapy session I was auditing, Jeremy talked so much that I had to get up and take him out in the hall."

"He talked?"

"He learned how to say mama this morning, and he must have said it a million times in that one group session," she said, plunking Jeremy down on the floor where he immediately pulled himself up by hanging onto the couch. Tim smiled, set aside the mousetrap directions and pulled Jeremy up into his arms.

"Did you make trouble for Mama, Jeremy? Shame on you," Tim chided, and Jeremy laughed and bounced up and down in Tim's lap.

"I'll have to get a regular daytime baby-sitter," Cricket said, looking harried as she sank down onto an armchair. "There's a lady over on Tenth Street who keeps several babies Jeremy's age. I'll call her and see if she could manage one more."

"Cricket, you can't afford it," Tim said.

"I'm getting paid to work at the mental health center," she pointed out.

"It's not much," Tim said.

"Well, it doesn't matter. Even if I have to pay all of my salary to a baby-sitter, at least I'll know that Jeremy is being well taken care of."

"But how well? I've heard about that lady on Tenth Street. Somebody told me that a number of the children she watches have chicken pox. There's no telling what Jeremy might pick up there. That's an important consideration for a baby under a year old."

"You sound like my pediatrician," Cricket said in exasperation. "That's something Dr. Moss would say." She got up and went into the kitchen to set a pan of water on the stove to boil eggs for egg salad.

Tim followed her, carrying Jeremy. Jeremy reached out and twisted Tim's nose, but Tim only laughed and brushed the tiny insistent hands away.

"Cricket, we could solve this problem together. Haggerty will be back at the end of the week, and I won't have to go to the airport as often as I do now. I could do the bookkeeping for the business and make phone calls right here at home. I could watch Jeremy for you."

"Every day?" Cricket asked in surprise.

"Every day while you're at work."

Cricket's heart melted toward him. Tears sprang to her eyes. "I didn't expect—I mean, I wasn't hinting," she said.

"I know," Tim said gently. He came over to where she stood. "I'd like to spend time with Jeremy. He's kind of fun, actually."

"What can I ever do to repay you?" Cricket asked, looking up at him and thinking that his eyes had never been so blue or so earnest.

"Come to Curtisville with me at Easter," he said coaxingly.

"Oh, Tim," she said. She realized too late that he had backed her into a corner.

"You might even enjoy it," he said, trying to sound as optimistic as possible.

Cricket smiled a rueful smile. "All right, Tim," she said. "I'll go to Curtisville with you."

He grinned his familiar quirky grin, but she knew he was deeply grateful and also relieved.

"Let's hug on it," Tim said. "You, me and Jeremy."

Cricket held out her arms and wrapped them around Tim and her son. It was a warm feeling, and Tim said unexpectedly, "Our first family hug."

Cricket caught her breath. Is that the way Tim thought of the three of them? As a family? She didn't know what to think.

CRICKET SLIPPED THROUGH the back hedge to Trudy's house to tell her about her plans to go to Curtisville with Tim and heard Trudy sobbing before she even knocked on the door.

"Come in," Trudy said when she saw that it was Cricket.

"Trudy, what's wrong?" Cricket asked in concern. She was pretty sure she knew, but Trudy would have to tell her before she could comment.

"I could kill that jerk," Trudy said.

"Walt?"

"Do I know any other jerks?" Trudy said bitterly. "No, wait, don't answer that. Come into the living room, we'll talk."

They settled themselves on Trudy's living room couch and Trudy said, "Walt has somebody else."

Cricket had never told Trudy that she and Tim had seen Walt with the redhead at Wintermont. Now that Trudy knew, it seemed pointless to keep the secret any longer. "I know," she said.

"You know?"

"Tim and I saw Walt with a redhead when we went skiing last weekend. I wanted to tell you. I was waiting for the right time."

"There's no right time to tell someone that the love of her life is two-timing her," Trudy said.

"I can't disagree," Cricket sighed. "How did you find out?"

"My brother, Talbot, told me. He heard some of the other professors at the university talking about Walt and how cleverly he was juggling three women. Talbot figured out that I was one of them. He knew about Rona, of course, but it didn't take much investigating to find out that Walt was also carrying on with a twenty-two-year-old computer programmer from Chippewa Falls." Trudy began to sob.

"Walt really wasn't good enough for you," Cricket consoled, patting Trudy's shoulder.

"Don't you think I know that after this?" Trudy sobbed.

"Have you told him it's over?"

Trudy's sobs subsided. She reached for a Kleenex from the box beside her. "Not yet," she said evasively.

"You can't possibly be thinking that you want to keep him," Cricket said, shocked.

"I love him," Trudy insisted through her tears.

"Trudy!"

"I don't know how to get in touch with him to break it off. I called his office at the university and got some student who didn't know if he was in class or when he would be back. And if I call his home, I'll get Rona."

"You could ask Rona to take a message, such as, 'Walt—you're an SOB and we're through. Signed, Trudy.' That would make for interesting conversation around their dinner table tonight, I'll bet!"

"How can you possibly joke when my heart is broken?" Trudy asked.

"Oh, Trudy. Look, I'm really sorry. But hasn't it occurred to you that this happens to you over and over again?"

"Men are all jerks."

"Wait a minute, I'm not buying that," Cricket said firmly.

"What do you mean?"

"There are a lot of nice men out there," she said, thinking of Tim.

"Just because you found one, doesn't mean they're all like that," Trudy sniffed.

"That's not my point. You choose the wrong guys, Trudy. You might as well face it."

"Choose them? They choose me!" Trudy exploded indignantly.

"Back up and think about how you started going out with Walt," Cricket suggested.

"As you very well know, my brother brought him to spend the semester break here. Walt asked me out, and I fell in love with him. That's how it started."

"Talbot brought Walt when Walt wanted to apply for a job at Manitou College. You came over right away to ask me to go with you, Talbot and Walt for dinner, and you already had stars in your eyes. You had allowed yourself to fall in love with Walt before you even found out much about him." Cricket sat back and waited for Trudy's reaction.

"Well, Walt and I knew we liked each other from the start," Trudy said.

"Is that so? That's what you thought, but my guess is that Walt wasn't thinking that way at all."

"Who knows what men think?" Trudy said, lapsing into sobs again.

"We're supposed to be able to judge men according to our past experiences," Cricket said.

"I'm certainly flunking that course," Trudy said. "I keep re-living my mistakes over and over."

"Right!" Cricket exclaimed triumphantly. This was exactly what she had wanted Trudy to realize.

Trudy raised troubled eyes to Cricket's. "Do you mean that you think it's a pattern?"

"I certainly do," Cricket told her.

Trudy thought for a moment, wadding her Kleenex into a sodden ball.

"Maybe you're right," she said at last, with dawning conviction.

"Think about Dennis," Cricket urged, naming a man Trudy had broken off with two years ago.

"You mean Fatman," Trudy said. Since she never referred to her ex-boyfriends by name after she broke up with them, she had named Dennis, Fatman because of the roll of fat around his waist.

"Fatman," agreed Cricket.

"Fatman and I fell madly in love, and then I found out he hadn't really divorced his wife," Trudy recalled.

"Yes, but you didn't want to believe it when people said they saw his car outside her house at all hours of the day and night when he was supposed to be seeing only you."

"You're right," Trudy said glumly.

"Does that romance fit the pattern?"

"I'm afraid so."

"And what about Irvin? I mean King Kong."

"He swore to me that he never drank a drop, and I believed him until I came home and found him throwing the antiques I inherited from my Aunt Edith against the wall in a drunken rage."

"Mary Sue heard that Irvin went on binges every so often from a friend of hers."

"I told her she must be mistaken, even though I suspected something strange about him from the first."

"Don't forget Charlie," Cricket reminded her.

"Con Juan," Trudy said. "He was a con man through and through."

Charlie had been renamed Con Juan because he had been running around with several other women, including one of the students in the high school geography class he taught.

"I flipped head over heels for Con Juan because he had a line of patter," Trudy said.

"He used to tell you how wonderful and beautiful and smart you were, and in the same breath he'd tell you what a rotten person he was," Cricket reminded her.

"And I would believe all the great stuff he told me about myself, and I would insist that he wasn't as rotten as he thought he was. He ate it up."

"Was he as rotten as he thought he was?"

"You bet!" Trudy said, managing a smile.

"You never see the bad in people, Trudy. That's a good trait, but where men are concerned, you're going to have to learn to discriminate. To find out if the man is suitable for you before you fall in love with him."

"I can't exactly put a detective on the trail of any guy I go out with," Trudy said.

"You could keep yourself emotionally intact until you figure out if he's likely to have any other loves, old or new, that would keep him from getting serious about you. You could wait to see if there are any serious problems before handing over your heart."

"It sounds easy enough, but when you're in the throes of love, it's hard to pay attention to your head. Other parts of your body seem to take charge."

Cricket laughed. "Maybe you'll be wiser now," she said.

"Perhaps," said Trudy, although she looked doubtful. As if she couldn't help herself, she started to laugh.

"What's so funny?"

"What I'm going to do to Walt. Can you imagine what Rona is going to say when I call and leave a message for Walt that I'm breaking up with him?"

"I was only joking when I suggested that. Surely you're not going to—"

"Oh, yes, I am! It's perfect." Trudy's eyes revealed a diabolical gleam.

"Trudy," Cricket began.

"Never mind the lecture. I feel better already, just thinking about Rona putting Walt on the spot when he walks in their front door."

Cricket sighed. "I'm glad you feel better, I suppose. Trudy, I came over to tell you that Jeremy and I will be going to Curtisville, Kansas, for two weeks at Easter. Do you think you could feed Mungo for me?"

"Of course I'll take care of Mungo. With Walt out of my life and no other man on the horizon, it's not as though I'm going to be too busy. So you're going with Tim to meet his family. That's terrific."

"I'm looking forward to it now, although I was nervous about it at first. Tim's been so encouraging that I want to help him through this. It's shaping up as a major crisis in his life. He hasn't spoke to any member of his family since he ran out on them when they were on the verge of losing their farm."

"Cricket, you absolutely glow when you speak of Tim. Are you in love with him?"

Cricket flushed and smiled. "I think so," she admitted.

"I'm happy for you," said Trudy, and she hugged her friend.

When Cricket got up to leave, Trudy said affectionately, "I simply don't understand how you managed to find a good man so easily. I went to bat many times and always struck out. You went to bat once, and you've hit a home run. It doesn't seem fair, especially since you've been married once already."

Cricket returned Trudy's hug. "Don't worry, Trudy, you'll find the right guy someday. This is a whole new ball game for you," she said. When Cricket left, Trudy was waving out the window and wearing a tearful but determined smile.

"Well, that gets rid of Wonderful Walt," Cricket muttered under her breath.

She could hardly wait to find out what Trudy's nickname for Walt would be.

SHE AND TIM WERE LYING in bed that night after the lights were out when Cricket thought to tell him about Trudy and Walt.

"So Trudy finally found out what Wonderful Walt was up to," he mused.

"Yes, and I think I've made her see the mistakes she's made every time she's fallen in love."

Tim chuckled. "How did you do that?"

"I showed her how she's ignored the signals with each man."

"Signals?"

"You know, the signs that were there all the time, and that she convinced herself were unimportant or didn't exist."

"But she loved them," Tim said, mimicking Trudy's voice.

"Tim," she said, raising herself on her elbows. "Don't you have compassion for poor Trudy?"

"Yes," he said honestly. "I wish her luck in love forever after."

Cricket lay back down again. They were quiet for a while.

"I wish that everyone could be lucky in love forever after," Tim said when Cricket had almost fallen asleep.

"What does that mean?" she asked sleepily.

"It has something to do with you and me," he said.

Cricket, mindful that her visit to Curtisville was coming up in a couple of weeks, said nothing. But inside she felt a warm, romantic glow. He loved her, and he was talking about forever after.

As in, *happily forever after.*

Cautiously loving him, she slid her hand into his and fell asleep.

Chapter Fourteen

The Windrush Valley landscape stretched out below them endlessly, its checkerboard fields stripped brown and raw by the harsh extremes of the Kansas winter. Here and there a gaunt windmill cast a crooked shadow on the land or an idle oil rig reared like a rusted praying mantis.

"The land doesn't look good for much from up here," Tim shouted over the roar of the single-engine Beechcraft. "You have to see it in summer when the crops are growing to realize how fertile it is."

Cricket peered out the window of the airplane as they spiraled downward toward the landing strip at the tiny Curtisville airport. Tim landed the plane smoothly, without a bump. In the back seat, Jeremy sucked on his bottle, which Cricket had given him so that he'd have something to swallow to equalize the pressure in his ears while the plane lost altitude. As the plane slowed on the tarmac, Jeremy tossed the bottle into the front seat and said, "Babababababa!"

"I think this kid's a born air traveler," Tim said with a grin as he helped them both out of the plane.

Cricket looked around her with interest. Someone was shouting and waving at them from a shack at the other end of the field.

"It's Sarah," Tim said, and carrying Jeremy, he hurried to meet her.

Sarah, her blond hair flowing behind her, ran to greet them and hugged them both. Tears shone in her eyes as she held Tim at arm's length. "Tim! You look wonderful, and you've gained weight!"

She turned to Cricket and, linking an arm through hers, said, "I'm so glad to meet you, Cricket. I'm delighted that you could come with Tim."

"So am I," Cricket said with a glance at Tim. He was looking down at her proudly, as though he liked showing her off to Sarah. Cricket took heart from this and slid her other arm through his. They walked to the parking area in a tight little group.

Once they were in Sarah's station wagon, Sarah drove slowly toward town.

"Your parents are expecting you and Cricket sometime after supper," Sarah said to Tim.

"That's good. I'm glad you didn't arrange for us to go there straight from the airport."

"I wasn't sure if you'd want to sit down across the table from them and eat a meal before you've had a chance to visit with them a bit," Sarah said.

"You mean, before I've had a chance to repair some of the damage I've done to my relationship with them," Tim said.

"That, too," Sarah replied.

"How do they feel toward me?" Tim asked hesitantly.

"They love you, Tim."

"But do they talk about what I did? About my running away?"

"I've never heard your father mention it. Your mother talks about it occasionally. She speaks of it the same way she does about your sister, Norrie, and how she disappeared and never came back. Your mother feels so relieved that you've come home to Curtisville, Tim."

Tim didn't reply, and so Sarah turned her attention to Cricket. "I've readied my parents' old room at my farmhouse for you and Jeremy, Cricket. It has a private bath," she said.

"I can't tell you how much I appreciate your having me," Cricket said.

"Oh, it's our pleasure. My two children will love having Jeremy around. My daughter Lucy is seven, and she adores babies."

"Do you think it will be inconvenient for my parents to have me staying in their trailer with them for two weeks?" Tim asked.

"Your mother has cleared off the bed for you in the second bedroom where she does her sewing. She's thrilled that you're staying with them, Tim."

"What about my father?"

"Your father never talks much," Sarah said.

"I know," Tim said with a sigh.

It was not lost on Tim that Sarah had taken a route that wouldn't require them to pass his family's farm. He looked out the window, suddenly overcome with sadness for what used to be.

The wide fields, some of them being readied for planting, sped by. Here and there land sprouted with winter wheat which, after slumbering in the soil throughout the long winter, was reaching toward the sky in preparation for a summer harvest. The growing wheat didn't provoke any stirrings in him, which was a surprise. As a farmer's son who had been expected to become a farmer himself, Tim had thought he would feel more emotional about the land he had known and loved.

In order to distract himself from the memories, Tim switched on the radio. The afternoon cattle market report was playing. It was followed by a commercial jingle extolling the virtues of eggs. Tim laughed at this.

"What's so funny?" Sarah asked.

"I had forgotten the sounds of Kansas," he said as the egg jingle faded, and the air waves vibrated with the strains of a Dolly Parton song.

Soon Sarah turned off the highway down a winding farm road that straightened before climbing a hill. Sarah shot an amused look at Tim, accelerated at the top of the hill and lifted her foot from the brake as they sped down it. As the car swooped downward, Sarah and Tim laughed at the reckless roller-coaster sensation.

"That's the way we've always gone over this hill. My son, Ben, calls it Mr. Toad's Wild Ride in honor of the ride at Disneyland," Sarah explained as she parked the station wagon beside the corrugated metal barn.

"It's Tim! It's Tim!" cried the two blond whirlwinds who erupted from Sarah and Cliff's big white farmhouse.

"I knew you'd come home, Tim! I just knew it!" Lucy exclaimed. Tim swung her in his arms and strode with her into the house. Lucy had always been a special favorite of his.

"You two had better get back inside before you turn into icicles," Tim warned. It was a nippy March afternoon.

"Icicles? It's spring," Ben said as he galloped along behind him.

Once inside, out of the wind, Tim introduced Cricket to Cliff, Sarah's husband, and to the two children.

Cliff was a tall, smiling man with dark hair. "We're glad you're here," he told Cricket.

"Does Jeremy like peas?" Lucy asked, tugging at Cricket's jacket sleeve.

"Not much," Cricket said.

"Good," Lucy said. "I don't, either."

"Why don't you?" Tim asked.

"When I was little, Mom told me never to put anything green and slimy in my mouth," was Lucy's explanation before running away to find the toys she had been saving for Jeremy to play with. They all laughed at Lucy, and Cricket felt right at home.

Sarah and Cliff had collaborated on a wonderful supper complete with vegetables that Sarah's mother, Charlotte, had canned last summer.

"In spite of my growing fondness for Harry's gourmet take-outs back in Manitou, country cooking is always the best," Tim said when he had eaten his fill.

"That's what my father says," Sarah said.

"How is your father? And how is Charlotte?"

"Pop's doing fine after a slight heart attack last summer. And my mother enjoys living in town. She plays cards with her friends once or twice a week. Mama and Pop come out here for Sunday dinner a couple of Sundays a month. They've adjusted to moving off the farm pretty well, considering that they didn't want to leave it at first."

"And what are you going to plant this year, Sarah?" Tim admired Sarah for taking over her family's farm when her father had to retire because of ill health.

"I'll be planting sorghum again, and I'll probably allot some acreage to lespedeza and alfalfa," Sarah said.

"She's thinking about buying a herd of cattle. They could graze on the sorghum stalks in the fields after harvest," Cliff said. Cliff was a farm manager for Agritex, a large farm management firm headquartered in Minneapolis.

"Cattle? Pa talked about doing that," Tim said.

Sarah started carrying plates into the kitchen.

"I know it was hard to go against your father's advice to diversify your crops," Tim said as he followed her. Before Sarah took over Windrush Valley Farm, the only crop ever planted was Turkey Red wheat.

"It certainly was, but I'm glad I did," Sarah replied. She sent him an unobtrusive sideways glance. "Tell me, Tim, have you thought about getting into farming again?" she asked.

"I don't know, Sarah. What happened to our family farm still hurts too much for me to think about it."

"Farming is more than a job to me. It's a way of life. I don't understand how you can turn your back on that," Sarah said.

"There's no security in farming," Tim said.

"Is there security in anything these days?" Sarah countered.

"Who knows?"

"How is your job working out?" Sarah asked. In the dining room, they heard Cricket and Cliff clearing the table.

Tim scraped a plateful of chicken bones into the garbage can. "Pretty well. I like working for Haggerty. We get along well, and the Manitou airport is a nice one."

"You always did hang around the airport here, from the time you were a little kid," Sarah said fondly.

"I've always felt as though an airplane hangar is my second home," he said.

"Is there any chance that your job with Haggerty is permanent?"

"He hasn't said anything about that."

"But you'd like to stay with him, isn't that right?"

"You're awfully inquisitive, Sarah," Tim said. His eyes twinkled at her.

"I'm as fond of you as if you were my brother, Tim. Goodness knows, I worried myself nearly to pieces when you left home without a word to any of us. I'd like to know that you're okay."

"I'm okay," he said.

"You look more settled than you've ever been," Sarah conceded.

Tim considered this. "I suppose I am," he said.

"I like Cricket. She's been good for you."

"I thank my lucky stars that I met her," Tim said fervently.

"Is it serious, Tim?"

He thought about this while he stacked plates beside the dishwasher. "I think so," he said quietly. "I love her."

"I'm so glad," said Sarah, smiling gently.

"And things are good for you and Cliff?" Tim asked.

Sarah nodded.

"Then I'm happy for both of us," Tim said, and he squeezed his old friend's hand.

"I WANT YOU AND JEREMY to go with me to visit my parents," Tim said to Cricket after supper.

"I think your first meeting with them should be private," Cricket said.

In his mind's eye, Tim saw Mina and Frank as they had looked on the television screen during the ABC special report. It was the only way he ever pictured them now—sad, depressed and down-and-out.

If his parents really looked that way, he didn't know how he would be able to stand it. He desperately wanted Mina to be round-faced and smiling, the way she'd always been. He wanted Frank to act hale and hearty. He found it hard to absorb the fact that the loss of their farm had changed his parents forever. Or maybe he was learning to accept the change, but didn't want the change to show.

"Ma loves babies. Jeremy would help break the ice," he said, beginning to feel desperate. He couldn't imagine going to his parents' trailer alone.

"Jeremy might fuss and make things harder."

"He hardly ever fusses. Please, Cricket, it would be easier with you and Jeremy there."

Finally the pleading in Tim's eyes convinced her, and Cricket went to dress Jeremy for the visit.

They borrowed Sarah's station wagon, and Tim drove into Curtisville, which, with its two thousand people, was a good deal smaller than Manitou. On the outskirts of town, Tim turned the station wagon at a weather-beaten sign that said Sunflower Mobile Home Park. There were no sunflowers in sight, not even a picture of one.

"Well, here we are," Tim said heavily. He stopped the station wagon, and Cricket glanced at his face as he surveyed the motley collection of trailers. His face was ashen.

A cluster of mobile homes huddled close together on a single road that made a circle. This arrangement reminded Tim of covered wagons circled around a campfire for their own protection when they stopped at night while traversing the wide and dangerous prairie. He gritted his teeth and eased the station wagon over a speed bump. He didn't like the bleak appearance of the Sunflower Mobile Home Park; he never had.

"Are you all right, Tim?" Cricket asked anxiously.

"I—I didn't expect this closed-in feeling. I'm sorry, Cricket. I can't believe my parents live in a place like this. I can't imagine their living anywhere but on Vogel land."

Cricket's hand reached across the gap between them and clasped Tim's. The car idled down the row of trailers.

"Here it is," Tim said.

Frank and Mina's new home was one of the smallest trailers in the park. He noticed with a pang that his parents had mounted the old brass ship's bell, the one his father had brought home from the navy, outside the trailer.

The bell brought back memories. His mother had called her children for dinner with that bell, and upon hearing it, they would drop whatever they were doing wherever they happened to be on the wide reaches of the Vogel farm. The bell was now mounted on a stanchion to one side of the trailer's front door, its surface brightly polished. It was a defiant reminder that Vogels, wherever they lived, took pride in their home.

Tim stepped out of the station wagon, opened the back door and lifted Jeremy out of his car seat. When he straightened, his mother was standing in the doorway of the trailer, smiling.

"Tim!" she said, clattering down the metal steps to meet him. She held out her arms. "It's so good to have you home again!"

Tim handed Jeremy to Cricket, and then he was enveloped in his mother's soft, warm embrace. She smelled the way his mother had always smelled, like fresh-baked yeast bread, and he hugged her back, fighting the lump in his throat.

"Come in, all of you!" Mina cried. They hurried inside the trailer, and Tim was surprised to see his brother Leonard there. After Leonard's hearty handshake, it was easy for Tim to inquire after Leonard's wife Terri and their children.

"Terri and the kids are fine, Tim, just fine."

Tim looked around for his other brother, but he wasn't there. "How's Bernie doing?" Tim asked.

"Bernie has a cold," Leonard replied too quickly, thus leading Tim to understand that Bernie had been invited tonight, but hadn't wanted to see him. Tim shot an involuntary glance toward the closed door on the other side of the room. He assumed that it led to one of the two bedrooms. Was his father in there?

No one mentioned Frank Vogel. Tim looked around uneasily. His mother saw his inquiring glances, but she tightened her lips and said nothing.

When they had all sat down, Tim averted his eyes from the cheap paneling of the tiny living room and ignored the ugly brown carpet. Instead he focused on the bright, cheery curtains Mina had hung at the windows. He was touched to see a bouquet of flowers, the kind you could buy at the Supermart for $3.99 a bunch. He suspected that his mother had splurged on them because he was coming home.

"Sarah told me that you're a college student," Leonard said to Cricket.

Cricket warmed to Leonard, who was a big bear of a man and considerably older than Tim. "I'll graduate in June," she told him.

"Cricket's already interning at the community mental health center in Manitou," Tim said. His pride in her was evident in his warm gaze.

"And you, Tim—are you going to do crop dusting this summer?" Leonard asked.

"I think so," Tim said cautiously.

"We're hoping you'll come back to Curtisville," his mother said gently.

"Oh, Ma. I wish you wouldn't start in on that," Tim said.

"Maybe you're right. There'll be time enough to talk about it later. How about a piece of your favorite pistachio cake?"

"*That* I'm ready to talk about," Tim said affectionately. His mother bustled into the adjacent kitchen and began to set out plates and forks.

"Leonard, where's Pa?" Tim asked in an undertone.

"He went out," Leonard said with a shake of his head.

"He knew I was coming, didn't he?"

"He knew, all right." The corners of Leonard's mouth turned down.

"I'm staying with the folks, Leonard. If there's any reason why Pa doesn't want to see me, I'll bunk at Sarah's place instead."

"That would disappoint Ma," Leonard said. "Don't worry, Pa will come around. I think he needed a few minutes to pull himself together, that's all." Leonard cautioned both Cricket and Tim with a warning look as Mina reappeared carrying a tray.

They ate cake and coffee, and Mina took Cricket into the bedroom where Tim would sleep to show her the sewing she had been doing. Cricket marveled at the lacy perfection of Mina's current project, a flower-girl's dress in jonquil-yellow.

"I designed it," Mina told her.

"It's gorgeous," Cricket said, fingering the hand-sewn pearls on the fitted bodice.

"I've always loved to sew," Mina said. "I used to sew a lot for my daughter. Tim told you about Norrie and how she went away, didn't he?"

Cricket nodded.

"I thought I'd never see Tim again when he disappeared," Mina said with a catch in her voice.

"I suppose Tim has had many things to work out," Cricket said carefully.

Mina blinked the tears from her eyes. "You've helped him," she said. "I can see that."

"I hope so," Cricket said.

"Poor Tim. When the bankruptcy proceedings began, Tim became a different person. Almost overnight he became angry and confused."

"And lost," Cricket whispered.

"Yes. You found him, Cricket. Thank you for taking care of him."

"He found himself, Mrs. Vogel," Cricket said.

Mina shook her head. "Please call me Mina. I have an idea that we're going to get to know one another much better."

Cricket smiled. She liked Tim's mother.

Frank, Tim's father, never did show up. Finally, around nine o'clock when Jeremy began to get cranky, they left so that Tim could drive Cricket and Jeremy back to Sarah's house.

"What do you think of my family?" Tim asked when they were on their way out of the mobile home park.

"Your mother's lovely," Cricket said.

"And Leonard?"

"Nice. You don't look much like him, though."

"He looks like my father. I don't look much like either my mother or my father. I look like some guy named—oh, what was his name. Mark something-or-other." He thought about the odd encounter with Amethyst in the bar in Florida. It wasn't the first time he'd been told he was a dead ringer for somebody else.

"Mark?"

"Yeah, this girl I met in Florida thought I was some guy she was crazy about. And when I was in the service, I kept hearing about another guy who looked just like me. Even in Germany, people used to walk up to me on the street and call me by his name."

"That's unusual," Cricket said.

"I'm used to looking like somebody else after twenty-six years of hearing the same thing. Why, when I was a kid and Sarah used to take me downtown, people used to think that we were brother and sister. I look more like her than I look like my own brothers."

"You're right, now that I think about it."

"Sarah and I have joked that we spent so much time together when I was growing up that we finally started to look alike. Even though she's eight years older than I am, we've always gotten along very well. But then, Sarah gets along with everyone. She's one of the few people who can jolly my father out of a bad mood."

"I wonder where your father was tonight," Cricket said.

"That's a good question."

"Your mother never mentioned him, did you notice?"

"She was embarrassed."

He shot Cricket a glance. Her face was blue in the glow of the lights from the dash.

"I was embarrassed for her," Cricket said.

Tim drew his lips into a tight line. "In some ways, I wish I'd never brought you here. I'm afraid you'll get mixed up in the bad feelings between me and my family, and—"

"I didn't sense any bad feelings tonight," Cricket said.

"My father and Bernie weren't even there," Tim said bitterly.

"But your mother and your eldest brother were," Cricket pointed out.

"I wonder what Pa's planning to do," mused Tim. "I'll be living at their trailer the whole time we're here. It's going to be unpleasant if he refuses to come home when I'm around. I have a good mind to call Ma from Sarah's house and tell her I'm sleeping there."

"Don't, Tim. Give your father a chance. Maybe he'll be home when you get back."

"Maybe," said Tim, although he didn't believe it.

Cricket smiled and gripped his arm encouragingly. Tim felt a wave of tenderness toward her. He was glad she was beside him, cheering him on in her own inimitable way.

He left Cricket at Sarah's after he helped her put Jeremy to bed in Lucy's old crib in the downstairs bedroom.

Sarah and her family were watching TV in the living room nearby. Cricket would watch television with them for a while, she said.

"I'll come over in the morning," Tim promised. "I'll take you to lunch, show you around Curtisville, introduce you to some of the people I know."

"Okay," Cricket said.

They held each other close for a brief moment, and when Tim left her, he felt as though he were leaving a piece of his heart. Even though this was his hometown, he felt very alone without her.

He drove back to the Sunflower Mobile Home Park, and it didn't look any better to him the second time. His mother was glad to see him, but there was still no sign of his father.

He and Mina sat up and talked until eleven o'clock or so, and he told her how much he liked Manitou and about his work for Haggerty. Although they both kept their ears tuned for the sound of Frank's car, they avoided mentioning the crisis that had divided their family.

Finally when Mina couldn't keep her eyes open any longer, they both went to bed. Tim heard his father come in about midnight, and he held his breath as his father's cautious footsteps paused outside his bedroom door. Then his father walked to the other end of the trailer and went into the room he shared with Mina. Tim heard the door close softly after him.

At last, worn out from the emotions of coming home again, Tim fell asleep.

In the morning when Tim got up, his mother was in the kitchen frying bacon, and there was no sign of his father.

"Where's Pa?" he asked Mina.

Mina paid undue attention to the sizzling bacon. "He's gone," she said.

"I heard him come in late last night," Tim said.

Mina didn't answer.

Tim poured himself a glass of tomato juice from a container in the refrigerator and sat down at the kitchen table.

"Is it going to be like this during my whole visit, Ma?" he asked softly. "Is Pa going to avoid me?"

Mina's hands shook as she set a plate of eggs and bacon in front of her son.

"It's hard for your father, son," she said.

"I know I shouldn't have left the way I did, Ma, and I can honestly say that I'm sorry. I won't get a chance to apologize to Pa if I never see him."

Mina sat across from Tim. "You hurt your father," she said slowly. "It will take him a while to get over it."

"Ma, the reason I came back to Curtisville in the first place was to apologize. I want to be forgiven for running away when you needed me. If I can't have your forgiveness, tell me now. It would be best if I left right away."

Mina paled, but she kept her composure. "I forgave you long ago," she said in a low tone.

"That means a lot to me."

"With your Pa, it's a little harder."

"How about Bernie?"

"Bernie loves you, Tim. I think he feels closer to you than to any of us. That's why he took it so hard when you left."

Tim hadn't eaten a mouthful of his breakfast. He picked up a piece of bacon and bit into it. It tasted like sawdust in his mouth. He had always known the enormity of his actions. He wished he could turn back the clock and do everything differently, but it was too late for that.

Mina spoke, seeming to choose her words carefully. "Your father and I have a new life now. It's different, but it's not a bad life. Frank likes his job. I've found a lot of creative satisfaction in my sewing. Both your Pa and I have tried to find the silver lining in our particular dark cloud. Losing the farm seemed like the end of the world at the time, Tim. But now we know that we're going to be all right.''

"That's good, Ma."

"How about you, Tim?"

"I'm getting on with my life," he said. He pushed his chair back from the table.

"Aren't you going to eat your breakfast?"

"Sorry, I'm not very hungry. Coming back home hasn't been easy, you know."

Mina smiled shakily. "I understand that. I'll give the bacon and eggs to the dog next door. He'll love it."

"They let you keep dogs here?"

"As long as they're small ones. Your father and I are thinking of getting a puppy. Bernie took old Patsy, you know." Patsy had been the Vogels' big Labrador retriever, and Bernie's children were attached to her.

"I'm going to go over to Sarah's to pick up Cricket and take her and Jeremy to lunch in town. Would you like to go with us?"

"Not this time, son. I have to finish the dress I'm working on." Mina got up and slid her chair under the table.

"Next time, then. You and Sarah and I are going to lunch together before I leave."

"I like Cricket, Tim. She's very sweet."

Tim grinned. "I know." He bent to kiss Mina's cheek, went back into the bedroom to get his car keys and told his mother goodbye. She watched him from the window as he drove away. She looked very much like her old self, and that made Tim glad. At that moment he was happy that he had come back to Curtisville, if only for his mother's sake.

Tim headed his car down the highway toward Sarah's farm. A wild and blustery March wind tore across the prairie. He drove slowly, taking in the familiar sights. Ed Wilson's dog sitting by the mailbox, waiting patiently for the mailman. The dog only sat there Monday through Saturday, somehow knowing through that sixth sense that dogs seem to have, when it was Sunday and the mailman wouldn't come. John Falgren waving at him from behind the wheel of his ancient red pickup truck; John was undoubtedly on the way to the Chatterbox in town, where he would sit and chew the fat with all the other farmers who frequented the place.

Curtisville was the same as it had always been, but the eyes though which Tim saw the town were different. His eyes were used to Manitou, with its larger population and its newly renovated Main Street lined with fine shops; with its college bell tower and the war memorial in front of the town hall. Curtisville and the surrounding area seemed smaller now and more insignificant in his life. He wondered when the town had ceased to be important to him.

Tim slowed the station wagon at the road that led to Sarah's farm, but something made him keep driving past it. A certain dread fascination made him do it. He wanted to see his family's farm one last time.

He crossed the ridge and there it was, spread out before him. The Vogel land. His forefathers had fought for that land, wresting it from the wilderness with their primitive plows and axes. They had broken the sod and planted wheat, living in a sod shanty until they could build a decent house. He and his family had continued the tradition. Then they had lost it. Vogels lived here no more. Tim wondered who occupied the house now.

He drove down the familiar driveway. The rural mailbox had been vandalized, ripped right off its post and tossed broken into a ditch. When Tim saw it there, he stopped and got out of the station wagon. He picked up the mailbox and stared at it, brushing the dirt off the red flag that they always used to put up when they wanted the letter carrier to stop and pick up their mail. The flag was bent and rusty, and the mailbox was so twisted that the door wouldn't shut. Like a lot of other things, it was broken beyond repair.

Tim tossed the mailbox back in the ditch. Then he got back in the station wagon and drove to the house.

As he stepped out of the car, he was overcome by a sense of déjà vu. When this was his home, it had been his custom to park in front of the house in just this way, then to jump out of the car, run up on the porch and call out to his mother in the special tone of voice he reserved for coming home. Mina would always carol an answer and run to meet him, no matter where she was working in the big limestone house. Today's homecoming was different: the only thing rushing to meet him was remembrance.

He stood uncertainly in front of the house, alone with his memories. No one seemed to be living here; the place had an abandoned look about it. Weeds grew where Mina's bright flowers once danced in the breeze, and sodden leaves blanketed the front walk. It made him sad to see such a loving house standing so unloved.

His gaze fell on the whirligig toy he'd made for Mina in his high school shop class. His father had mounted that toy on a pole in her garden, and there it had stayed ever since. It spun furiously in the wind, the only moving thing on the landscape. Tim had thought that the old keepsake would be sold along with the rest of their belongings at the auction.

With a shock like a splash of icy cold water, Tim realized that someone was standing amid the rank growth of weeds in his mother's flower garden. He strained to see who it was.

The figure stepped out from behind a bank of lilac bushes and stopped. Tim waited, his vision blocked by a big elm tree.

And then the figure moved slowly around the tree, coming into full view, and Tim realized with heart-stopping dismay that the person was his father.

Chapter Fifteen

His father looked thinner than Tim remembered him. Frank walked toward him, his steps slow and deliberate. *Why, Pa's turned into an old man!* Tim thought with a shock. His father's hair, once dark brown with gray at the temples, was almost entirely gray now, and there were deep lines in his face that hadn't been there before. His father's face was like granite: strong and seemingly impervious to emotion. Nervously Tim stepped forward.

His father paused, and Tim realized in that instant of indecision that Frank Vogel was as uneasy and apprehensive as he was about this meeting. Frank's control was not absolute. For a moment, the mask slipped, and Tim glimpsed the tender, caring man who had shown him how to carve animals out of soap bars and taught him how to ride a bike.

"Pa," he said, almost moved to tears to see his father again.

"I knew you would come here," his father said. "I don't know how I knew, but I did."

"I had to see it," Tim replied in a choked voice.

"An international company bought the place," his father said, looking off into the distance. "German people. I don't know what they'll do with the house. They might tear it down."

Tim stared up at the limestone house. "Maybe that would be best," he said.

"They don't mind if I come out here and look around once in a while," Frank said, moving on. Tim understood that his father wanted him to walk with him, and he fell into step beside him.

They strolled in the side yard, past the plum trees, their bare limbs knobbed with tiny furled blossoms.

"I can't imagine Ma without her flower garden," Tim said when they rounded the lilac bushes. It was hard to make casual conversation.

"Your Ma is getting together a garden committee at the Sunflower Mobile Home Park," Frank said with the hint of a smile. "They're going to plant sunflowers around the sign in front."

"Good for her," Tim said.

"She's taking everything pretty well," Frank said.

"She always has. How about you, Pa?"

"I'm fair to middling, I'd say," Frank said.

"How's your back?"

"Better. I can't figure it out. I did all kinds of strenuous work on the farm, and I worked hard all my life. I never had back trouble then. Now all I do is fix machinery, and I have back problems. It doesn't make sense."

They walked on. Crocuses bloomed in the distance where the woods started. They were a reminder that this was spring.

Tim cleared his throat. "I'm sorry for what I did, Pa. I wish I hadn't run away."

Frank blinked rapidly and stared into the distance. "So do I, son."

"I can't ever make it up to you, I know, but—"

"I don't want to talk about it." His father walked a little faster, making Tim take longer strides to keep up.

"You haven't forgiven me, then."

"It's a hard thing to forgive after what your sister Norrie put us through. We never thought we'd have to live the same problem over again."

Tim sighed. His father was going to be stubborn and withhold his forgiveness. Well, Frank was speaking to him, at least. He wasn't giving Tim the cold shoulder. Tim thought maybe he'd better leave before his father got angry and they both said something they'd regret.

"I told Cricket I'd take her to lunch," Tim said, turning toward the station wagon.

"This Cricket—who is she?"

"Somebody I met in Manitou," Tim said.

"Your mother likes her."

"Most people do. Cricket is special, Pa."

Frank nodded. They stood awkwardly beside the station wagon, neither of them knowing how to take their leave.

"Well," Tim said. "I guess I'd better go."

"Tim," said his father, and Tim saw that his throat was working and that it was hard for him to talk.

"Pa?"

"Son," Frank said, and in that moment, looking into each other's eyes, they both knew that to prolong the rift between them would be to perpetuate their family's anguish over something that they all needed to put behind them. Before either of them knew what was happening, Frank had clasped his arms around his son, and the breach was healed.

"Welcome home, Tim," Frank said, and when Tim looked, he saw that his father's eyes were filled with tears.

WORD SPREAD THROUGH Curtisville like wildfire. Tim Vogel had not only come home, but he had brought a woman and a baby with him.

"Is it his baby?" Ida Rae, the waitress at the Chatterbox, asked Sarah.

"The baby is only ten months old. Tim's only been gone for eight. You can add better than that, Ida Rae," Sarah told her.

"Well, I was only wondering," Ida Rae replied huffily.

Sarah relayed this story to Tim because she thought it would make him laugh. Surprisingly it didn't.

"I don't want people to talk about Cricket that way," he said in annoyance.

"I don't think Ida Rae was maligning Cricket. She was gossiping about you," Sarah said. Gossiping about him, Tim realized, had probably been a favorite Curtisville pastime ever since his mysterious middle-of-the-night disappearance.

"Still, I don't like it," Tim said. He had never stopped to think about what the community gossips would make of his sudden reappearance with Cricket and Jeremy in tow.

The three of them were certainly visible around Curtisville. They ate lunch at the Chatterbox, and they stopped to look at the big unfinished mural on the building nearby. Tim took Cricket to church with him on Easter Sunday, where they withstood the stares of many members of the congregation. They walked in the park one day when the weather was warm. In short, they left themselves wide open to speculation by the town busybodies.

Cricket bore it with her usual good humor. As time went on, Tim became impatient with the people of Curtisville for talking about him behind his back.

One day Tim, Cricket and Jeremy volunteered to stop at the Supermart to pick up a few grocery items for Sarah. They ran into the town's mayor, who was also the local veterinarian. Janice Booth wasn't a gossip, but she was an influential person in this town. Tim introduced Cricket to her and was pleased that the two women took to each other immediately.

"What do you think of Curtisville?" Janice Booth asked Cricket as they strolled down the produce aisle.

"It's a beautiful small town," Cricket replied.

"I'm glad she could come back to Curtisville with me," Tim said, putting his arm around her so that Janice would know that their relationship was a close one. He hoped she'd pass that information along to anyone who linked his name with Cricket's. After they had chatted for a while, Janice smiled and moved on, but at that moment, Tim wished that Cricket had more tangible proof of his love for her. He wanted her to wear his engagement ring.

There was little time to discuss this possibility with Cricket because they seldom had privacy. Not only that, but there were so many things for Tim to do during their brief visit. Lucy asked him to visit her tree house down by Oley's Creek with her because she was afraid that a winter storm had damaged it. There was no damage, but after their excursion to the tree house, Ben demanded equal time, and Tim drove Ben into Salina to see a Spielberg movie that they both wanted to see.

Tim spent a day with Cliff, getting reacquainted and accompanying him on his rounds as Cliff visited farmers who employed Agritex's services.

"How is the farming situation around here, Cliff?" Tim asked as they rode along a lonely gray ribbon of highway in Cliff's company car.

"It's about the same. Some farmers around here are going to go under this year, just as they did last year."

"Anybody in particular?" Tim asked.

"I can't say right now," Cliff said.

"Is Sarah's farm safe?"

"Windrush Valley Farm is in great shape, thanks to Sarah's business sense. Last year's decision to diversify her crops paid off. She got a good price for last year's sorghum, and she's ready to install a pivot irrigation system. Sarah's farm is one of the soundest in this area."

"Good," said Tim, who knew that he couldn't bear to go through another farm failure with anyone he knew and loved.

Tim took his mother and Sarah to lunch, and as he lived these two weeks with his parents in the trailer, he began to mend his fences. Frank was overly cautious in getting close to Tim, almost as though he feared that Tim was going to disappear from his life again.

"I'm not planning to fly away again the way I did last time. If I go, Pa, you and Ma will know about it beforehand. You'll have my address."

Frank looked up from the intricate hummingbird he was carving from a block of wood, and nodded. "I hope so," he said. He whittled silently for a while and then said, "What is it that you plan to do with your life, son?"

"I'm not sure. I like Manitou. Maybe I'll stay there."

"I wonder if—" Frank said, stopping in mid-sentence.

"You wonder what?"

"If you wouldn't still be living in Curtisville close to your Ma and me if we hadn't lost the farm."

"That's hard to say. I'd been to Manitou last summer when I was crop dusting, and I always liked it."

"Your Ma sets great store in having her children close by," Frank said.

"She still has Leonard and Bernie," Tim said.

"That's not enough for your Ma," Frank said, shaking his head. "Ever since Norrie left, she likes her kids to be within hollering distance."

There was nothing Tim could say in reply to this. He knew his mother was gradually getting used to the fact that he might not ever live in Curtisville again. It was just another one of the realities she was having to accept in the aftermath of losing the farm, and she bore it stoically and with her unfailing good humor.

Tim's brother Bernie was the hardest member of his family to approach. When Bernie repeatedly failed to show up at family gatherings at the trailer, Tim took the initiative and invited Bernie and his wife, Liz, to dinner with him and Cricket one evening.

Cricket sparkled that night, exchanging hints on babies with Liz, who was pregnant with her third child. Tim was proud of Cricket, both because she knew how to handle a touchy social situation with just the right light touch, and also because she belonged to him. He watched her across the table, her gray-green eyes shining with light, her coppery hair bright in the glow from the candle on their table.

I love you, Cricket, he said to himself, and when she caught him watching her so intently and with such pleasure on his face, he knew that she understood.

When they parted in the restaurant parking lot after dinner, Bernie unexpectedly clasped Tim's hand. "I'll never understand how you could leave like you did, Tim, but now I know why you didn't come back sooner. That Cricket of yours is a stunner."

Tim watched Cricket as she talked animatedly with Liz. His heart swelled with happiness.

"Thanks, Bernie," he said. Mostly because of Cricket, he and his brother parted friends.

One night, he and Cricket baby-sat with Ben and Lucy while Sarah and Cliff went to a Grange banquet in Hutchinson. They sat in the farmhouse's commodious living room, pleased to have the whole big house to themselves. Ever since they had come to Curtisville, privacy had been at a premium.

They turned off the television set and held hands as they sat on the couch. Because he knew that she'd get a kick out of it, Tim told Cricket what Sarah's father, Elm, had said about her.

"Elm said, 'As soon as Cricket walks into a room, she's the principal thing in it.'"

Cricket laughed. "And what did you say?"

"I said, 'That's what happened as soon as Cricket walked into my life—she became the principal thing in it!'"

Cricket's expression softened, and she shifted her position so that she could look directly into his eyes.

"Is that true, Tim?"

"Very true," he said. "I had nothing to live for at that point—no home, no family, no job. I was looking for something, and although I didn't know what it was, I was sure I didn't deserve anything good."

"You had been through some hard times," she said.

"All my goals had become obsolete with the bankruptcy of our farm. I had to find new goals," he said.

"What are they, Tim?"

"I'll give you a hint—you figure prominently," he said with his familiar quirky grin.

Cricket bit her lip, unsure of what he meant.

"I want us to be together, Cricket," he said. "You, me and Jeremy."

"Here? In Curtisville?" she asked.

"I doubt it."

"In Manitou?"

"Possibly. I like Manitou, Cricket. There's more going on there than in Curtisville, and I've been wondering what it would be like to live in Manitou permanently. At this point, it's pure speculation. I'm not entirely sure that I won't want to move back to Curtisville sometime in the future."

"Because of your parents, you mean?"

"Yes, and there are other considerations. I used to get so angry when some of our best young people left Curtisville because of lack of opportunity. And then I was caught in the crunch myself, and what did I do? I left. I don't feel good about that."

"You had no choice, Tim. Once the farm was gone, there was nothing here for you."

"That's what I figured at the time. I knew I had to play the game of life with the hand I'd been dealt, and it had dealt me out of Curtisville, that's for sure," he said ruefully.

"I'm proud of how you're getting along," Cricket said softly, touching a finger to his cheek.

"I have a few more decisions to make, Cricket. One is whether to come back to Curtisville or remain in Manitou. You're the main thing that keeps me in Manitou, in case you don't know that."

"Before you decide what you're going to do, I think you should see what your brother Leonard is going to suggest to you tomorrow when you meet him for lunch at the Chatterbox," Cricket said. Leonard's wife Terri had confided in her about the opportunity Leonard was going to present to Tim. Cricket thought that Tim might be interested. If so, he might want to rearrange his plans. For the moment, she couldn't think about Tim's moving back to Curtisville in terms of what such a move would do to their relationship. The important thing was Tim and what would be best for him.

"What do you know that I don't?" Tim asked.

"Only that I love you very much," Cricket said, looking into his eyes with great tenderness.

Enough to let you go, if that's what it would take to make you happy, she thought to herself, steeling herself to accept this train of events if it actually came about.

"I love you, too," Tim said, but Cricket wondered, *How much?*

"IT'S LIKE THIS," Leonard said the next day when Tim sat across from him at one of the booths in the Chatterbox. "There are these ladies outside Marquette who have been left good farmland by their father. Neither one of them has ever married, and they both teach school in McPherson."

"So they want someone to farm their acreage for them, right?" Tim said. From the excited gleam in his brother's eyes, Tim had already divined the reason for this meeting.

Leonard nodded. "They need somebody who knows how to do it, and the rent is reasonable. Why, I could move my family into the house on the farm, and we could put a trailer out back for you. Together we could make a go of this thing, Tim. What do you say?"

Tim rubbed the back of his neck and tried to think around the pain that had surfaced right between his eyes. Leonard was talking about going into farming again. That might be all right for Leonard, but Tim couldn't imagine himself doing it.

"How much land is it?" he asked. He was stalling for time while his thoughts, some of them dark and dire, marched double-time through his head.

"It's about eight hundred acres, give or take a few. They've got an irrigation system for row crops, and the last guy who farmed it made out pretty well."

"What happened to him?"

"He went back to college full-time. He and his wife got a divorce, and he decided he wanted to be a lawyer. There's no figuring some people, is there?"

"No, I suppose not. Leonard, I can't imagine farming again after what happened to our own family farm."

"I couldn't either, at first. Then I heard about this opportunity, and I thought about how much I miss tramping around the fields in the early morning with the meadowlarks singing and the sun peeping up over the horizon, and I thought, 'How can I spend the rest of my life at a boring desk job?' Farming is in my blood. It's in your blood, too."

"Maybe it is, but I don't feel it," Tim said.

"Tim, it would be a chance to start over," pleaded Leonard.

"I *have* a chance to start over," Tim said stubbornly. "In Manitou, Wisconsin."

"Crop dusting! Why, you'd have to travel all over the country and become one of those gypsies again to make any money at it!"

"I'd have Cricket," Tim said. "I'd like to marry her."

"You can't haul a wife and a child all over creation," Leonard warned.

Tim thought about this. Leonard was right. Cricket already had a job lined up at the Manitou Community Mental Health Center. Jeremy was at an age where he was about to start walking. No, it wouldn't be fair to expect Cricket and Jeremy to wander with him in his travels.

"I see what you mean," he said heavily. The pain in his head burgeoned into a full-blown headache.

"Think over what I've said. It could be the opportunity you need," Leonard said as he reached for their check.

A few minutes ago, Tim would never have thought it over. He had wanted to get as far away from farming as he possibly could. And yet, maybe farming was the only way, if he wanted to marry Cricket. He drove back to Sarah's house slowly, trying to straighten everything out in his mind. Only one thing stood out: he wanted to talk privately with Cricket.

Cricket was outside the farmhouse with Ben, helping him untangle a kite string.

"There, Ben, I think we've got all the knots out," she said, handing the string to him as Tim drove up.

"I'll get something to make a tail for the kite," Ben said, hurrying into the house.

"Well?" Cricket said, smiling up at Tim. The stiff March wind blew pinkish-gold fluffs of hair around her face. His headache suddenly disappeared. Cricket's presence always seemed to make everything right for him.

"Leonard suggested that he and I farm a place he's found over near Marquette. I told him I would think it over. Are you free to take a ride with me?"

From the look of him, Cricket knew that he wanted to discuss this serious topic right away.

"Ben and Lucy's grandfather is here helping Ben make a kite. Jeremy is napping. Let me run inside for a minute and ask them to listen for Jeremy. Would we be gone long?"

"Twenty minutes or so," Tim told her.

Cricket disappeared momentarily and returned. They climbed in the station wagon.

"Where are we going?" Cricket asked.

"I need to talk with you. I thought I'd show you my family farm."

"Are you sure you want to go back there?" Cricket asked, wrinkling her forehead into a knot of concern.

"I've been back once already," he said. "It was the morning after we arrived. I saw my father there." He hadn't told Cricket about that incident. It was something he had felt too emotional about to mention.

"Did it—did it hurt a lot when you went back?"

"Yes, but I talked with my father and found out that he's not still angry with me. He's hurt, but I know he'll get over it in time. Making myself come back to Curtisville was the best thing I could have done."

"I told you so," Cricket said.

"Thank you for insisting that this was what I needed to do. And thanks for coming with me. It's been easier with you here."

"I've had a wonderful time, Tim. I love your parents, and Sarah and I are becoming great friends."

"I knew you would." Tim drove up in front of the old Vogel farmhouse.

Cricket stared up at the honey-colored limestone walls curiously. The house was bigger than she had expected. It seemed solid and substantial. It didn't look like the kind of house that could be auctioned off in a bankruptcy sale. Suddenly she understood the enormity of Tim's crisis. She couldn't have borne to lose this place, either.

Tim got out of the station wagon and opened the door on Cricket's side. He took her hand and led her to the rock wall surrounding the house. The front yard still looked wintry bare, and the wind raced and galloped around them like a frisky colt.

"Today when Leonard suggested farming, my first reaction was negative," Tim said slowly. He was still trying to get a grip on his feelings.

"And then?" Cricket prompted.

"I thought about what I do for a living. I'm a crop duster, Cricket. I fly airplanes, and I have to go where the crops are. Sometimes I have to be away from home for weeks at a time. In fact, it's better to have no home because of the way I have to live."

"What are you getting at?" Cricket asked, her heart sinking.

"What I'm getting at, dear, is that even though I want us to be together in the future, it wouldn't be fair to ask you to follow me wherever I have to go when I'm working. In fact, I'm sure you wouldn't like a roaming kind of life. You couldn't leave Jeremy to come with me, and there's no room for a baby in a gypsy life-style."

"What are you saying, Tim?" Cricket couldn't figure out if he was talking about getting married, or if he was thinking of their continuing to live together. Or maybe he wanted to break off their relationship entirely. She could think of no tactful way to ask. She swallowed and waited for the other shoe to drop.

"Cricket, I don't see how you and I can have any kind of a life together unless I go into farming with Leonard. Even then, we'd have to move to Curtisville. And what would that be like for you? There's no mental health center in this town. I don't know what the job opportunities are for a psychologist who happens to live here."

"I can't imagine abandoning my goal when I'm so close to it," Cricket whispered with a stricken look in her eyes. She added to herself, *Especially if we weren't married.*

"I know you can't give up your career. You've worked so hard that I wouldn't even expect you to."

Cricket gathered herself together and plunged on. "How do you feel about farming now, Tim?" she asked.

Tim was silent for a long time. "I hate the idea of being a

farmer. Seeing our old home place reminds me how unhappy I was when we were making our last stand," he said at last.

Cricket moved closer to him and slid her arm through his. She leaned her cheek against his shoulder. "I don't think you should go into farming unless you really want to do it," she said.

"I agree. I don't know anything else but flying, Cricket. I almost wish I did."

"I love you, Tim," Cricket said, and when she looked up at him like that, with both stars and sorrow in her eyes, he thought that he couldn't live without her.

"And I love you," he said. "We'll work it out."

"Look," Cricket said in order to provide a diversion. "The plum trees are beginning to bloom."

Sure enough, alongside the house, the plum trees wore their new spring wardrobe half-unfolded.

"If only we could renew our lives every spring, like trees," Tim said wistfully.

Cricket smiled and swallowed the lump in her throat. "Maybe we can. It's up to us."

He hugged her and kissed her on the lips, and he realized again how special she was. Optimism rose in him once more as it so often did when he was with her. Whatever it took, they would work something out.

"First thing tomorrow, I'm going to tell Leonard I won't be able to take him up on his offer."

"And after that?"

"After that, we're going to attend Ma's big family dinner. She's going to cook it at Sarah's house, and my whole family and Sarah's family will be there. And the next day, the three of us will go back to Manitou."

Cricket felt the happy tears welling in her eyes. Only then did she realize how much she had feared that Tim would accept Leonard's offer. That this discussion might be for the purpose of breaking the news that he was sending her and Jeremy back to Manitou by themselves.

She turned to him blindly and clasped him to her, and although he at first seemed surprised by the fierceness of her embrace, he kissed her tenderly and told her he loved her before driving them back to Sarah's house.

When are seen in Curtisville. Tim said he wanted nothing more than to get back to our home in Manitou so that the three of us could be together. They are not here, and he acted disturbed in some mumbmable way. Whether it be real, say, given no reference as a way of life, or not almost a new mind.

"He'll come around. Maybe it will help that Jeggerty is back from Mexico.

"Mary," said Haggerty, his been leaving 24 minutes of missing fill be here tomorrow. Hello! said.

"Haggerty's come home to stay," Cricket said. "They brought him.

"I thought Tim? working for Haggerty but now Tim not

Chapter Sixteen

"I thought Tim decided that Curtisville and farming weren't for him," Trudy said as she and Cricket walked along a sidewalk skirted by melting snow.

"So did I," Cricket said, edging Jeremy's stroller around a puddle.

"I told you that there's no understanding men," Trudy said darkly.

"The peculiar thing is Tim's suggestion that I might want to work in Curtisville as a school psychologist, especially since it comes right on the heels of Tim's visit to the admissions office at Manitou College. He talked with the admissions officer and brought home a college catalog. He even circled the courses in the catalog that he thought he wanted to take next year. He seems to be casting in all directions, trying to find something that fits."

"Do you think that Tim has eliminated college from his list of possibilities?"

"Apparently. He called his brother, Leonard, yesterday, and they talked for an hour about the advantages of planting wheat over corn. Can you imagine?"

"Tim sounds confused," Trudy said.

"He isn't the only one," Cricket replied. "I don't know what Tim's thinking anymore."

"Maybe you shouldn't have gone back to Curtisville with him," Trudy said.

"We had a wonderful time. Anyway it wasn't until we got back home that things started to get crazy."

"Crazy!" Trudy exclaimed. "What do you mean?"

"When we were in Curtisville, Tim said he wanted nothing more than to get back to our house in Manitou so that the three of us could be together. Then we got here, and he acted dissatisfied in some undefinable way. I wonder if he really has given up on farming as a way of life, or if he's changed his mind."

"He'll come around. Maybe it will help that Haggerty is back from Arizona."

"Tim says that Haggerty has been leaving all aspects of running the business to him," Cricket said.

"Haggerty hasn't been well. I would imagine that he needs Tim."

"I thought Tim liked working for Haggerty, but now I'm not even sure about that anymore. Oh, Trudy, there's the first robin of springtime!"

The bird hopped along the curb and flew away. Jeremy clapped his hands and laughed.

"That's a robin, Jeremy, can you say robin?" Cricket said.

"Bye-bye," Jeremy said, fluttering his fingers at the bird.

"Isn't he clever? He learned to say bye-bye while we were in Kansas."

"At least the trip was good for something else besides getting Tim stirred up. Sometimes I wonder if it was such a great idea for you to insist that he go back."

"All of my ideas aren't wonderful," Cricket agreed with a wry laugh. "Especially the one about your calling Rona and leaving a message for Walt that you didn't want to see him again."

"It backfired, all right," Trudy agreed. "You should have heard her. She complained about him for twenty minutes, then started telling me how much she loved him."

"What I like is the part where you packed up the dirty socks and underwear he left at your house and mailed them to her."

"I wouldn't have done that if Rona hadn't sounded so bored when she told me that I was the second woman to call and break up with Walt that week. Talk about rubbing it in!"

"Good grief! How many women do you suppose the guy has stashed here and there?"

"As many as will put up with his lying," Trudy sighed.

"He must use Rona only as a housekeeper, laundress and cook," Cricket said.

"No, sex between them is terrific. She told me so, and in detail," Trudy said.

They both laughed.

"Well, it *was* one of his strong points," Trudy insisted.

"Trudy, we're starting a group therapy session at the mental health center for people who repeatedly fall in love with the wrong person. It's on Thursday nights. Why don't you go?"

"To the mental health center? Would that mean I'm wacko?"

"Of course not. It's called the mental health center because we try to keep people mentally healthy. I've met some of the people who will be in the group. I think you'd like them."

"Any men?"

"A few."

"Who?"

"You'll find out Thursday night if you go," said Cricket, turning the men into a carrot to dangle on the end of the stick.

"Hmm. Maybe I will. Will you be there?"

"No, I'm not qualified to conduct group therapy sessions by myself yet."

"You like your job, though, don't you?"

"I love it. I can't imagine leaving it." Cricket frowned at that thought, because despite Tim's assertions to the contrary, she was beginning to worry that this was exactly what he would ask her to do.

"Then don't leave it under any circumstances," Trudy advised.

"The only reason I would leave is so that I could be with Tim. But do you know, Trudy, he hasn't mentioned getting married."

"Most of them don't," Trudy said.

"Tim and I are different."

Trudy focused on Cricket with a hard stare. "Are you, Cricket?" she asked.

"I thought we were," Cricket replied unhappily.

"Just don't become qualified to attend that group therapy session with me," Trudy said, and Cricket had to admit to herself that Trudy had a good point.

"I WAS THINKING," Tim said as he peeled a banana to give to Jeremy, "that I could do aerial applicating in the summer months and get a job here in Manitou in the winter months."

"Doing what?" Cricket asked.

"Oh, anything. I could clerk at the hardware store. I could help Haggerty. I could fix plumbing for young mothers who don't happen to have husbands." He dropped a kiss on Cricket's up-turned nose.

"Tim, sometimes I wonder about you. I heard you talking on the phone with Leonard about farming, and it sounded to me as if you wished you'd decided to rent that farm with him. You were talking about going to college last week, but I haven't heard a word about that lately."

"It's just that there are so many possibilities in the world, and I have to figure out what they are," he said reasonably.

"It's about time you narrowed it down," Cricket said.

"Oh, Cricket, give me a break. I've been through hell since we lost the farm."

"It's just that you seem to fly in all directions at once."

"So you think I should have a sense of purpose, huh?"

"That's part of it," Cricket said.

He wrapped his arms around her and kissed her cheek. "I have one, all right. I'm trying to figure out a way that you and me and Jeremy can live happily ever after." His tone was cajoling, but for once it annoyed her.

"I hope so," she said.

Sensing her aggravation, Tim let her go and lifted his jacket off the hook beside the door. "I have to run out to the airport," he said. "I'll be back later."

"In time to eat dinner together?" Cricket called after him, but he must not have heard her because he didn't answer.

In fact, Tim didn't come back until after she'd eaten a sandwich and was watching a PBS special about caterpillar mandibles on TV. He wanted to make love.

"Wait a minute, this is pretty good," Cricket objected as the camera moved in for a close-up of a fuzzy caterpillar munching on a leaf.

"Not as good as this," he said, nibbling on her earlobe.

"I haven't made my sandwiches for tomorrow," Cricket objected as Tim moved her toward the bedroom, but finally, swept away by his desire for her, she gave in.

Afterward when she lay in his arms, she wondered how she could have been reluctant. As usual, lovemaking was wonderful with him. He was thoughtful, perceptive and considerate. Gratitude washed over her, and she whispered, "Tim?"

"Mmm-hmm," he said sleepily.

"I love you so much," she said.

"I love you, too."

"How much?"

"Enough to help you make those doggoned sandwiches of yours tonight," he said fondly.

Cricket glanced at the clock. Its luminous hands showed her that it was almost eleven o'clock.

"We'd better get started," she said.

"Just a minute," he said, his fingertips teasing her body like so many soft feathers.

"Only a minute?" she said, smiling up at him in the darkness.

His eyes were bright. "Maybe three," he conceded before sliding his body over hers.

"TIM, I NEED TO TALK to you," Haggerty said in greeting the next morning when Tim arrived at the trailer at the airport wearing a T-shirt that had taken his fancy at a shop near the campus last week. It said: Give Me Chastity or Continence, but Not Yet…St. Augustine.

Tim had bought the shirt on the spot. He didn't know much about St. Augustine, but it seemed to him that the guy must have felt the same way Tim had been feeling lately.

Tim was surprised to see Haggerty in the office so early in the morning. "Is anything wrong?" he asked.

"No, but I have a little business deal I want to talk over with you," he said.

Tim sat down across the desk from Haggerty, and Haggerty got up and stumped to the window, where he stared out at the nearby airplane hangar.

"I had a lot of time to think while I was in Arizona," Haggerty said suddenly. "I decided to retire."

"That's a big decision," Tim said. He was aware that Haggerty had been reluctant to stop working. The man had built his flying service from scratch, and it was his very life.

"Nevertheless, I have to do it. I'm getting old, Tim, and I'm tired. My health improved so much while I was in Phoenix that I want to spend my remaining years living in Arizona. These cold

Wisconsin winters are more than I can take." Haggerty coughed as if to punctuate this remark.

"I suppose I can understand that," Tim said. He was curious about Haggerty's purpose. He'd thought when he first sat down that Haggerty was going to tell him that his job here was over, but he sensed from the light of excitement in Haggerty's eyes that there was more to it than that.

"I want to sell the business," Haggerty said abruptly.

"I guess that means I'd better look for another job," Tim said.

"No, wait until you hear me out. I want to sell the business to you, Tim."

Tim stared at the older man. "I don't have any money," he said.

Haggerty waved a careless hand. "The money isn't important. I'm on the board of directors at Manitou First National Bank, and I'm sure I can get you a loan."

"Haggerty, I don't know," Tim said, his head reeling. He'd never thought that he'd have a chance to own a good, profitable business like this one.

"Let me tell you what I have in mind," Haggerty said, pulling a chair next to Tim's. For the next half hour, Haggerty outlined his plan.

In short, Haggerty wanted to sell his business to no one but Tim, and he was willing to take a low price so that Tim could own it.

"You're the only person I know who loves flying as much as I do," he told Tim. "You've got a good head on your shoulders, and you've proved that you can handle the customers. You've worked as a crop-dusting gypsy, and you know how to deal with the fly-boys you'll need to hire in the summer. You're the only heir apparent I've got, Tim."

"This is all more than I ever expected," Tim said slowly.

"Take some time to think it over. But I know you're the man for this job, Tim."

When Tim left the trailer that afternoon, he drove around Manitou aimlessly, down Main Street with its neat row of shops, past the city hall with its war memorial in front, past the college bell tower. He tried to imagine himself staying here for the rest of his life. He tried to imagine himself married and settled down.

He'd be a stepfather if he married Cricket. Fatherhood was

another responsibility Tim had never been eager to assume. He thought about his father and how their relationship had so recently gone off the track. It was just now getting back on it, but the road to this point had been a hard one. If he were Jeremy's stepfather, he'd be the one in charge. The one Jeremy would look up to and admire. Was he worth that kind of admiration?

And marriage. He wanted to marry Cricket, but that would mean accountability to yet another person in his life. He loved her, and he'd meant what he'd said to her about working things out so that they could be together forever. But forever didn't mean until next month or next year. It meant for all time.

All of a sudden he was going to have to make two major decisions at once. He was going to have to figure out whether he wanted to accept Haggerty's magnanimous offer, and he was going to have to make up his mind what to do about Cricket.

He drove to a lake outside town and got out of his Mustang. Pebbles on the lakeshore crunched beneath his boots, and the air was filled with the pungent scent of pine. He walked and he thought, and as he thought, an airplane droned past, framed by tree branches outlined against the silvery sky.

He squinted at the airplane and watched as it dissolved into the distance. When he could no longer see or hear it, he kept gazing into the faraway clouds.

It would be so easy to get in an airplane and go. If he did, there would be no decisions to make. If he made no decisions, his choices in the future would be as open as they were on this day in the twenty-seventh year of his life.

If he flew away again, he would be as free as a bird.

TIM SLEPT LATE the next morning. It was a Saturday, and he woke as he always did when Cricket got up to run her route. He only rolled over into the warm spot she left and mumbled when she said something about taking Jeremy to have his picture taken when she got back.

"Don't bother about breakfast," she said, patting him lightly on his shoulder as she glided past. "Jeremy and I will have breakfast after we have his picture taken."

He heard her return from her route, and he listened to her talking happily to Jeremy as she dressed him for his sitting.

Then she left, and the house was quiet. Tim turned on his back and stared up at the ceiling, waiting for the familiar tinny chatter of Cricket's camper engine.

He heard a few grinds of the starter, and then nothing. In a moment, Cricket rushed into the bedroom.

"My camper won't start," she said with exasperation.

"Use my car," he said. "The keys are on the dresser."

"Come with us, Tim," she said.

"I'm not up yet," he objected.

"It only takes you a few minutes to shower and shave. Please, Tim," she coaxed. "I'll buy you breakfast."

She hardly ever asked him to do anything, and for some reason she seemed to want his company. He swung his feet over the side of the bed, unwilling to deny her this small favor. "I'll be ready in a few minutes," he said, and she broke into a sunny smile.

They left twenty minutes later, with Cricket sitting beside him and Jeremy in his car seat in the back.

"It's a nice day, isn't it?" Cricket observed. The sky arched over them with uncommon blueness, and people running their Saturday morning errands seemed to have shaken the tail days of winter and donned optimistic springtime smiles. Cricket hummed a little tune as Tim drove up and down rows of cars at Kmart searching for a parking space.

When they got out of the car, Jeremy held his arms out to Tim.

"Oh, all right," Tim said playfully. "I'll carry you. Say, Cricket, when is this little guy going to learn to walk?"

"He's already pulling himself along the edge of the coffee table," she said.

"In that case, it'll only be a few weeks before he's running all over the place," Tim said.

Jeremy chortled and buried his face in the collar of Tim's jacket.

Inside the store, many other young couples were with children, spruced up in their new spring outfits.

"But I don't wanna have my picture taken," one vociferous four-year-old complained, and his mother shushed him and dampened his stubborn cowlick with hair spray.

Tim and Cricket edged past a blue-light special in the accessories department and took their place in line. It was only a short wait before it was Jeremy's turn with the photographer.

Cricket gave Jeremy's brown fuzz a precautionary lick with her comb and sat him on the platform in front of the camera.

"Look at the doggie," the photographer, a smiling young woman, said. She waved a plastic squeaking dog in the air and prepared to snap Jeremy's picture.

At the first squeak of the dog, Jeremy puckered up his face and yelled, "Waaah!"

The flashbulb went off anyway, and the photographer, determined to remain good-humored, rushed to pacify Jeremy. Cricket hovered nearby. "He almost never cries," Cricket said truthfully.

"A lot of them are frightened by the strangeness of all the people in the store," the photographer said.

Jeremy was distracted by Tim, who stood behind the registration desk and waggled his eyebrows. Nevertheless, the next time the flash went off, Jeremy squeezed his eyes shut and prepared to let out another howl.

"Come up here, Daddy," the photographer said to Tim. Tim looked around uncertainly. He wasn't sure she meant him.

"Yes, you," she said, taking him by the arm and positioning him next to her. "When I get ready to take your son's picture, make that face you were making."

"Like this?" Tim asked, waggling his eyebrows again.

"Just exactly like that. You know, I can sure see the resemblance in you two guys. Your little boy is going to look just like you when he grows up."

"But he's not—" Cricket began, only to be interrupted by the photographer.

"You stand over here, Mommy," she said, moving Cricket until she stood on the other side of her.

"Jeremy," called the photographer.

Jeremy looked interested.

"That's right, Jeremy, turn your head toward Daddy."

Jeremy brightened.

"Good. Jeremy, you're such a handsome little boy. You look just like your Daddy. Can you say Daddy?"

"Dada," said Jeremy, favoring Tim with a beatific smile.

"Wonderful! Let's get another shot. Look over here at Mommy, Jeremy," the photographer said. Jeremy grinned at Cricket, and the flash went off.

"Those are good shots," said the photographer as she checked off a box on a form. She glanced up at Tim. "I can tell that you and Jeremy have a really special father-son relationship," she said.

"I don't know," Tim said. He was embarrassed by the photographer's assumption that he was Jeremy's father, but he didn't know how to correct her. He glanced at Cricket, who was holding Jeremy. Her cheeks were pink with embarrassment.

"You'll receive your proofs in about two weeks. Jeremy, you're a cute boy. Don't break any hearts before you come back and see me, all right?"

Jeremy grinned, and Cricket began to push her way through the waiting crowd around the photo registration desk.

"I'm sorry about that," Cricket said when she and Tim were clear of the people.

"It's all right," Tim answered, striding along beside her.

"I should have said something right away," she said. "I should never have let her think that you are Jeremy's father."

"I said it's okay," Tim repeated.

"It's not all right," Cricket said vehemently. She slowed and waited for him so that they could leave the store together.

"It's only natural that people should mistake us for a family group. Heck, sometimes *I* mistake us for a family," Tim said.

Cricket nailed him with a look. "What is that supposed to mean?"

"It means—it means that you've been my family ever since I came to Manitou. It means that I think of us as a threesome."

Cricket was silent, trudging beside him to the car. He opened the door for her and helped her fasten Jeremy in his car seat.

"Where would you like to go for breakfast?" Tim asked a bit too brightly before he started the engine.

Cricket stared out the window, acting moody and distracted.

"Breakfast?" She looked at him as though she'd never heard the word before.

"You said you wanted to go out for breakfast. In fact, you promised you'd treat me," he said. He waited. Her eyes, gray-green and troubled, were as unfathomable as the sea.

"I forgot," she said.

"How about the new snack shop downtown? I've been wanting to try it. I'm going to hold you to your promise of food. I'm starved.'' He smiled at her, trying to spark a light in her eyes. He failed utterly.

''The snack shop is fine,'' she said before staring out the window again.

They ate an excellent breakfast at the new place, and it was uneventful except for Cricket's lack of response to virtually anything Tim said. He began to wish that he could be as successful with her as he had been with Jeremy back at Kmart. Just to see if he could be, he waggled his eyebrows at her, but the only person who laughed was the waitress who caught him at it. Cricket only withered him with a look, and Tim decided that Cricket thought he was flirting with the waitress.

He despaired of explaining, and he wondered why he should have to. When they got home, he told her he was going to the airport, but instead he rode to Eau Claire and spent the afternoon wandering around a shopping mall, trying to figure out what he was going to do with his life.

He bought Cricket a gold bracelet in a store where he went, mostly out of curiosity, to price engagement rings. If he decided not to stay in Manitou, he'd give her the bracelet as a farewell gift. It might help her to think well of him after he'd gone.

Chapter Seventeen

Cricket and Jeremy went to Kroger that afternoon to buy sandwich supplies, and she ran into Haggerty at the lunch-meat counter. Haggerty greeted her with profound relief.

"Cricket, if anyone would know, you would. My wife sent me to buy bologna, and I don't know the difference between all-beef bologna and the regular kind. Do they taste different?" he asked.

"Not much. I always buy the plain, old, ordinary, regular kind. I suspect Gracie does, too," she said.

"That's what I'll get, then," Haggerty said, lifting a packet of bologna off its hook. He stopped to take in Jeremy, who was leaning over the handle of the shopping cart and fingering the toggle buttons on Cricket's coat. "My, the little fellow is really getting big, isn't he?"

"He's almost a year old now," Cricket said proudly. Jeremy made a grab for Haggerty's bologna, and Cricket moved the shopping cart so that Jeremy couldn't reach it.

"Did Tim tell you that I'm planning to retire to Arizona?" Haggerty asked.

Cricket tried to recall if Tim had mentioned this. She was sure she would remember it if he had, but at the moment, all she could offer was a blank look.

"Well, anyway," Haggerty went on, "I'm planning to leave as soon as possible. Right after I get the sale of my business to Tim squared away, that is. When is he going to make up his mind? He wants it, doesn't he?"

"I don't know. You can reach him at the airport today," Cricket replied uncertainly. Haggerty's question had caught her by surprise. She knew that Tim hadn't said anything about buying Haggerty's business.

"I just came from the airport, and Tim hasn't been there all day," Haggerty said with a frown.

"I *thought* he said he was going there," Cricket said, her voice trailing away because this wasn't strictly true. She *knew* that this was what Tim had said.

"Well, don't worry about it, I'll catch up with Tim sooner or later. Let me know when Jeremy's birthday comes up. My Gracie would love to bake him a cake. That's her hobby, you know—baking cakes. Why she's already figuring out a way to set up a home cake-baking business in our condominium apartment in Phoenix. See you later, Cricket," Haggerty said as he ambled off toward the cash registers.

Cricket clung to the handle of her shopping cart, her emotions in a ferment. It was a shock to find out that Tim clearly hadn't been sharing everything in his life with her.

When had Haggerty told Tim that he'd be willing to sell his business to him? Before she and Tim went to Curtisville? After they got home? Why hadn't Tim mentioned it to her? With all the discussions they'd had about Tim's future, why had he never mentioned this all-important fact?

Numbly she gathered her supplies and passed through the checkout. She drove home in a kind of stupor. There could only be one reason why Tim hadn't told her about his opportunity to buy Haggerty's flying service, Cricket decided by the time she was home putting the groceries away. Tim didn't want her to know anything about it. All his talk about wanting to be with her and Jeremy, about their being his family, meant nothing. He had a chance to remain here if he wanted to, and apparently he didn't want her to know. That could only mean that he wasn't being honest with her.

Jeremy went to bed early that night, and Cricket fidgeted, unable to stay at any task for long. She dreaded Tim's footstep on the front porch. She knew that for her own peace of mind, she would have to confront him. His vacillation translated to the simple question: *Does he want me, or doesn't he?* After Hugh, she and Jeremy needed a man who was settled.

It was eight o'clock before Tim drove up. She waited in the darkened living room like a prisoner awaiting the arrival of the executioner. She hadn't eaten anything since breakfast, and her stomach felt as though it was occupied by a nest of horned lizards.

"Cricket?" Tim called as soon as he opened the front door.

She remained silent, gathering her strength for the coming ordeal.

"Oh, there you are. Why are you sitting in the dark? Let's turn on some lights." Shedding his coat, Tim strode to the lamp.

"No, don't turn it on," Cricket said.

"Why?"

"I'd rather you didn't. Tim, I need to talk with you."

Something changed in him, as though her tone of voice caused a shift in his mental axis. He walked lightly to the couch where she sat and eyed her with a wary inquisitiveness.

"Sit down," she said.

"Is something wrong?" he asked, peering at her in the dim half-light.

"I assume so. Tim, I ran into Haggerty today. He told me that he wants you to buy his business. Why haven't you ever mentioned that to me?"

"I was thinking it over, trying to put it in the proper scheme of things," he said after a slight pause.

"Proper scheme of things?" Cricket said. She was unable to keep a certain caustic quality out of her voice.

"I've been trying to figure out what to do with my life. You know that. We've discussed it many times."

"You never mentioned that one of your options is to buy Haggerty's business. You were talking about returning to Curtisville. You mentioned going to Manitou College."

"I know," Tim sighed. "I should have told you about this opportunity, I suppose, but I wanted to chew it over in my own mind before I dragged anyone else into my decision-making process."

"Dragged? You led me to believe that you wanted me and Jeremy to be part of your life. You wouldn't have had to drag me into making any part of your decision, Tim." Her eyes were as hard as gray agates.

"Cricket, you misunderstand. For somebody like me, settling down in one place is a major decision. Getting married is another major decision—not just for me, but for anyone."

"You never mentioned getting married," Cricket said with a catch in her throat.

Tim stared. "What do you think we've been talking about all this time?"

Cricket shrugged. "I couldn't assume you were talking about marriage when you never mentioned the word," Cricket pointed out. "I thought you meant that we'd just go on living together."

"Why do you think I would take you all the way to Curtisville, Kansas, to meet my family if I didn't want to marry you?"

"I thought you wanted me along for moral support."

"No. I mean, yes. Your help was very important to me, Cricket. I couldn't have done it without you." He moved toward her as if to take her in his arms, but she dodged out of his way. His look tore at her heart.

She had to press on. She had to find out if he was playing games with her mind.

"Haggerty said you hadn't been at the airport all day," she said quietly.

Tim shifted uncomfortably and seemed to find something fascinating about the rug. "I was going there, but I changed my mind. I drove to Eau Claire instead. I've been spending a lot of time by myself, Cricket. Thinking."

"Thinking," she parroted.

"You don't know what it's like, trying to make up my mind. First I'll decide that I want to take Haggerty up on his offer. Then I think that if I do, my days of traveling wherever I want are over. All the decisions I have to make look like doors. Every time I open one door, I'll close another. It's frightening, Cricket. Maybe you don't understand." His eyes pleaded for acceptance.

"I think I do," Cricket said firmly and with a steely glint in her eyes. "You need to grow up, Tim."

"Hey, I don't think—"

"Listen to me. Some of us have to grow up fast, like I did when I found out I was pregnant with Jeremy. I had to make a lot of quick decisions, and I had no one to help me. But I made them, and I've done my best. That's all any of us can do, Tim."

"I'm sorry about what happened to you, Cricket, but I don't see what that has to do with me."

"It doesn't have anything to do with you unless you want it to," Cricket said pointedly.

"What are you saying?"

"I guess that what I'm saying is, make up your mind. Because I can't put my life on hold while you dillydally from one thing to another. If you want to farm, go ahead. If you want to buy Haggerty's business, go ahead. Maybe I'll be here when you get through being wishy-washy, and maybe I won't." In spite of her hard line, she had a shameless urge to touch the sprigs of hair peeking over his shirt.

"Cricket, aren't you being unfair?"

"I don't think so. You have a fear of things to which other people make commitments."

"I love you, Cricket. I want to marry you."

For the first time since they began this discussion the anger in her eyes disappeared, and tears took its place.

"Well? Will you?" He put out a hand and slid it under her hair. The gap between them narrowed.

She blinked, and the tears began a slow slide down her cheeks.

"I don't want to talk about it until you make up your mind about what you're going to do," she said.

He kissed her lips, and her tears flavored them with salt.

He moved away from her, and the pain in her expression made his stomach contract. "I guess I'd better move out of the house," he said slowly. "We need time and space between us right now." He hoped she would ask him to stay.

She didn't. "Where will you go?" she asked. Her lips were very pale, but she held her chin up. In her hurt, she called on a majesty he never knew she had.

"I can stay at Haggerty's trailer at the airport," he said.

Cricket nodded slowly, and he removed his hands from her arms. She swayed slightly, sitting there on the couch, and he said with concern, "Are you all right?"

"More or less," she said. Then, "Mostly less," she amended.

He massaged her shoulder where it had become rigid, hoping to convey his silent understanding, and then he left her in the darkened living room. She heard him throwing his belongings out of the upstairs closet as he packed.

He came downstairs slowly and stood in the foyer. His blond hair dipped over his forehead, which was wrinkled in concern.

"This isn't goodbye," he said. "I'll be in touch."

He shimmered through the mist of tears in her eyes.

"You can reach me at the airport," he said with his hand on the doorknob. "Tell Jeremy—" he said, but he couldn't go on.

He closed the door softly when he left, and it was such a long time before he started the Mustang's engine that Cricket thought he had changed his mind.

But then the engine roared to life, and the car idled slowly up the street, taking Tim wherever he wanted to go and possibly out of her life.

CRICKET WAS SO DISCONSOLATE over Tim's moving out that Trudy invited her to attend a daylong trade show in Minneapolis with her three weeks later. Renee was engaged to stay with Jeremy, and Trudy and Cricket set off early on a Saturday morning.

By the end of the day, as Trudy headed her car back across the Mississippi River and east toward Manitou, Cricket admitted to herself that she had been no help to Trudy whatsoever. Trudy was driving, and suddenly Cricket realized that Trudy was waiting for her to reply to something she had said.

"I'm sorry, Trudy," Cricket apologized. "I can't keep my mind on anything."

Trudy nodded understandingly and waited until a Mack truck passed them on the left before edging over into the left lane of the interstate. "I know how it is. I'm not over Walt yet, either."

"There's more to it than that, I'm afraid," Cricket sighed.

"What do you mean?"

"I think I'm pregnant, Trudy."

Trudy drove in stunned silence. Then she braked the car and pulled into the slow lane.

"You're lucky I didn't run the car into the median strip," Trudy said shakily.

"I can't seem to do anything right lately," Cricket said. She sank down into the seat and put a hand over her eyes.

"Have you told Tim?"

"No. Don't you tell him, either."

"He has a right to know."

"Not until I'm sure."

"When will that be?"

"After I go to the doctor. I already used one of those home pregnancy-test kits. It came out positive."

"Those kits aren't always reliable, you know."

Cricket sighed. "I know," she said.

Trudy drove on in silence. "I can't believe that after what happened with Hugh, after you got pregnant with Jeremy during that reconciliation attempt, you'd be dumb enough to let it happen again."

"I'm extremely irregular, Trudy. That's how I got pregnant the first time—I had no idea that there was any chance of it. And this time—well—my body hasn't returned to normal yet."

"Unless normal for you is pregnant."

"Don't tell Tim, Trudy. Promise?"

"Would I tell the enemy?"

"He isn't the enemy," Cricket said.

"All men are the enemy," Trudy insisted.

"Just because of Walt—"

"His name is no longer Walt. The name I've coined for him is Shiversplints. His legs are thin and white, and they get goose bumps on them after he takes a shower."

"You never told me *that*," Cricket said, interested in spite of herself.

"I don't believe in telling *all* the intimate details," Trudy said.

"You told me quite a few," Cricket said.

"That's all over. Shiversplints is passé. He's out of my life. Why, I wouldn't have the guy on a silver platter." Trudy focused intently on the car ahead of her. "Well, maybe certain *parts* of him," she amended, and both she and Cricket convulsed in laughter, the best antidote to depression that either of them could think of at the moment.

When she got home, Cricket stared at herself in the mirror. She'd always hoped that Jeremy would have a brother or sister someday, but not under these circumstances.

She turned sideways and assessed her profile. She didn't look pregnant. But then, who did in the first few weeks?

TIM HAD CALLED HER a few times since he'd moved to the trailer, but during their brief conversations, Cricket fathomed that he was no closer to knowing what he wanted to do with his life than he had been in the beginning. She tried so hard not to pressure him in any way during these phone calls that she came across as noncommittal and unenthusiastic. She was afraid that if she talked to him for any length of time, she'd tell him everything.

He probably thinks I don't love him, she thought miserably to herself.

Nothing could have been further from the truth. She thought about Tim constantly, and never did she think of him without a deep twinge of pain. She moved through the days and nights as though there were weights strapped to her arms and legs. She felt heavy with loss. Things seemed to have sharp edges to them: people's voices, Jeremy's demands, the objects she touched. Five pounds melted from her already-slender frame in the first week that Tim was gone because she had no appetite. When she tried to eat, sometimes she couldn't force the food down. Her stomach seemed to be filled with lead.

She missed Tim terribly, and so did Jeremy.

From Trudy she heard that Tim hung out at the Rathskeller. Trudy had seen him leaving once with a college girl. Cricket made discreet inquiries and discovered that her name was Adria, that she lived off campus in an apartment and that she had long brown hair streaked with artificial blond highlights. She was a cello player.

Cricket had nightmares about an enraptured Tim watching Adria play the cello as her long gleaming hair fell forward over her face and instrument. There was absolutely no evidence to support this awful vision; nevertheless, Cricket shed tears over it. She couldn't bear to think that Tim found any other woman attractive.

She had to admit that someone named Adria who had long highlighted hair and who played the cello had a certain cachet. Certainly such a girl was much more desirable than a divorced mother with the name of an insect.

Cricket had her troubles, but Trudy, meanwhile, was learning a lot about her problems in her group therapy at the mental health center. Trudy began to talk cautiously about dating other men.

"The trouble is that there just aren't that many good men around," she moaned to Cricket.

"Oh, yes, there are," Cricket replied before she thought about it.

"You mean Tim," Trudy said.

"Yes. There aren't many bad things about him. It would be easier if there were."

"He wasn't completely honest with you," Trudy pointed out. She was still smarting over Walt's many deceits.

"It's not as though I can't understand why Tim didn't tell me he had the opportunity to take over the flying service," Cricket argued in his defense.

"What do you mean?"

"If you knew the soul-searching Tim has endured since his family lost the farm, you'd understand, too," Cricket said.

"He sounds like just another commitment-phobic man to me," Trudy said with asperity, but Cricket wasn't so sure. He had said he wanted to marry her, after all.

On one of the long nights when Cricket lay awake in bed, adding new dark circles to the ones already rimming her lower eyelids, she forced herself to think about Tim in detail.

He was good with Jeremy. He helped her with everything she did. She liked his family and friends. He got along well with Trudy. They enjoyed doing things together. Their sexual relationship was unparalleled.

Tim was wonderful, he was perfect, and he was gone.

Overhead the mice scrabbled. Tim might be ideal, but one thing he hadn't been able to do was eradicate their colony of mice. She'd better reset the trap under the stairs.

The baby. What if there really was a baby? How would she ever tell Tim she was pregnant?

She rolled over on her stomach and fell asleep. Tomorrow she was going to the doctor. Then she would know for sure.

TIM SPENT THE WEEK after he moved out of the house he shared with Cricket in a fog. He felt as though he was fighting a thick, obscuring mist. It kept him from seeing things in their proper perspective. It caused him to head in the wrong direction, then double back on himself. It made him light-headed and disoriented.

The trailer at the airport was cramped and uncomfortable, and all Haggerty said when Tim revealed that he wanted to sleep there for a while was, "Humph." Tim wasn't sure what Haggerty knew about his breakup with Cricket. He hoped he knew nothing. Tim well remembered Haggerty's threat when he found out that Tim was seeing her.

Haggerty had called Tim a heartbreaker then. Tim had vowed never to hurt Cricket, and yet he had hurt her after all.

"What else could I have done?" Tim asked himself out loud

more than once. It had never been in his nature to be able to face decisions, to face anything he didn't want to face.

He tried to become part of Manitou's social structure, but after the tranquil domesticity of the life he had shared with Cricket, it was impossible. The Rathskeller with its miasma of stale beer and cigarette smoke seemed particularly inhospitable, and Nickelodeon's, with its memories of their first dinner together, only made him sad.

He met a girl named Adria, but she wasn't as interesting as Cricket. He knocked around Manitou like a lost soul, wondering how he could have entertained the notion of living there permanently.

Of course, it had been Cricket who had been the main attraction in Manitou. Not the airport or the college or the social life, but Cricket.

Haggerty asked him on a Friday three weeks after he'd moved out of the house when he was going to get around to making a decision about buying the flying service.

"If you aren't interested, I should start advertising for another buyer. A fellow in St. Paul expressed an interest in buying if I ever wanted to sell," Haggerty said gently.

"Haggerty, I—"

"Before you get started, let me show you something," Haggerty said. He pulled open a desk drawer and drew out a sheaf of papers.

"Here it is," he told Tim.

"What is it?" Tim asked.

"Everything we need to get the deal started. Here's the paperwork from the bank. See, I've already got preliminary approval on the loan."

Tim stared at the papers. Somehow seeing his name, Timothy F. Vogel, typewritten on the top line of the loan application made the idea so much more real. As he read the convoluted legal language on the document, he felt a sense of accomplishment. Haggerty had faith in him, and the bank had faith in him. Now all he needed to become a successful businessman like Haggerty was faith in himself.

Did he have that kind of faith? Could he become the kind of solid, respectable citizen bespoken by these signed papers? He searched his heart for the answer.

"It's a fine life, Tim," Haggerty said quietly. "I never regretted being the owner of this business. Oh, the pilots give you trouble by not showing up where or when they're supposed to, and there's always new equipment to buy, but I've been involved in aviation. For me, that was important. I love flying, and this was a way to be part of it."

Tim loved flying, too. Ever since he was a kid hanging around the Curtisville airport, he had loved watching planes landing and taking off, soaring like birds up from the wide Kansas prairies into a sky full of possibilities. He still felt a sense of awe and wonder at man's conquering of the heavens.

He knew that he would never pilot supersonic jets, nor would he be an astronaut. He liked nuts-and-bolts flying, where you could feel the engine vibrating in the metal of the plane, where you felt like part of the machine. No fancy equipment, just the basics, whether it be in a six-passenger Cessna charter or an AgTruck for spraying crops. If he was the owner, that kind of flying would be his way of life. He could think of nothing better.

"I want to do it, Haggerty," he said in a choked voice. Dimly he heard doors slamming behind him, locking him into this choice, but he felt a sense of exultation and relief. Never again would he have to wonder if he was deserting an elemental part of himself by giving up farming for good. He had found his place in life. It was here in Manitou. It was with Cricket. And it was owning his own flying service.

As though he was in a dream, Tim signed the papers. After he and Haggerty shared a celebratory glass of champagne from a bottle that Haggerty had been keeping in the trailer expressly for this purpose, Tim headed back into town, trying to shake off the bubble of unreality that seemed to surround him. Suddenly it was easy to make plans. He could see himself as a leading citizen of Manitou. He would be respected, just like Haggerty. Maybe someday he, too, would be asked to serve on the board of directors of the bank.

It was mind-boggling, but it was uplifting as well. He felt a surge of pride in himself. He had taken the big step. He perceived himself as well on the way to settling down.

The next thing to do was to reestablish his relationship with Cricket. That is, if she would have him. But then, why wouldn't she? They loved each other, didn't they? And he had finally stopped being what she had termed "wishy-washy."

He headed for the T-shirt shop near the college campus. He had a funny idea in mind, something that would make Cricket smile. After he did what he had to do, he would talk to her first thing tomorrow morning. It was a Saturday, and the weekend would be a good chance to move back in.

Chapter Eighteen

Cricket woke up on Saturday morning feeling sick to her stomach.
She lay in bed, becoming reacquainted with the different parts of
her body as sleep receded. She was loath to get up. She hoped
that what she was feeling wasn't morning sickness.

When she heard Jeremy calling, she tentatively stuck one foot
out from under the covers, then the other. Her upset stomach
didn't feel any better, but then, it didn't feel worse, either. She
crept about the house, getting herself and Jeremy ready to leave
on her route. Even Jeremy was subdued, taking his cue from her.

Because she had been so slow to get out of bed in the morning,
Cricket was over an hour late running her sandwich route. When
she returned, she double-checked her appointment card. Her doctor's appointment was at one o'clock.

But soon she knew that it would be useless to keep it. Her body
provided her with incontrovertible proof that she was not pregnant. Despite the positive home pregnancy-test, all her worry had
been for nothing. It had been a false alarm.

Cricket canceled her appointment. She sat at the dining room
window nursing cramps and drinking a cup of tea as she watched
Jeremy fitting small blocks into larger blocks on the floor. Across
the street, daffodils dipped their yellow-bonneted heads to a warm
spring wind. Cricket didn't know whether to be happy or sad that
she wasn't going to have Tim's baby. Seen through tears, the
daffodils wavered like a mirage.

THAT MORNING AT NINE O'CLOCK when Cricket should have been
through running her route, Tim stopped by the house. He knocked

on the door, but Cricket didn't answer. When he loped around to the back of her house, he saw that the old VW camper was gone.

He got in his car and drove to Main Street, hoping that she was out on a Saturday morning shopping jaunt and that he'd see her walking along the sidewalk. He saw no sign of her, but when a car in front of him pulled out of a convenient parking space, he whipped the Mustang into it. He got out and ambled along the sidewalk, going nowhere in particular. He drank a cup of coffee at the new snack shop, watching the window in case Cricket passed by.

When Cricket didn't appear, he paid his check at the snack shop and stopped by to see Trudy at the Card Boutique. He was filled with nervous energy, and he wanted to talk to someone.

"Hi, Tim," Trudy said casually, looking up from a stack of receipts.

"I came in to buy a card," he said. He hadn't, but that was of no consequence.

"For whom?" Trudy asked, lifting her head.

"For Cricket," he said.

"A card for Cricket," Trudy repeated, raising her eyebrows.

"Maybe something along the lines of, 'You've been such a good friend,'" Tim improvised.

Trudy's eyebrows flew even higher. "I have a clever new line of cards in the case along that wall," she said. Tim detected an ironic edge to her voice.

Tim headed in the direction she'd indicated, but then the sharp tone of Trudy's voice stopped him.

"On the other hand," she said carefully, "why don't you just tell her?"

"We're not seeing each other," Tim hedged. He wondered what Cricket had told Trudy about their falling-out.

"I know, but still."

He decided to be honest with Trudy. "I went by the house today, but she wasn't home. If I miss her when I go back, I'll write on the card asking her to call me and leave it under the storm door where she'll see it. I have to talk to her."

Trudy knew that Cricket was going to the doctor today, although she didn't know what time. She wasn't sure that Cricket would be in any shape to see Tim when she came home from her appointment.

"You wouldn't happen to know where she is, would you, Trudy?"

"Hmm," said Trudy, avoiding his eyes.

"If you do, I'd appreciate it if you'd let me know. It's really important for me to find her."

"Is it?" Trudy replied curiously.

Tim shifted his weight from one foot to the other. He had the feeling that Trudy was stalling him, so he opted to tell her his news in the hope that it might make a difference to her.

"I'm buying Haggerty's flying service," he said, breaking into a grin.

"Seriously?"

"As serious as I can be. Look, I've signed the papers," and he pulled the papers from his back pocket.

"So this means that you'll be staying here in Manitou," Trudy said.

"Yup. I wanted Cricket to know first, but now she's going to be second. I don't think she'll mind, do you?"

"Probably not," Trudy said. Her mind raced, trying to figure out what this would mean to Cricket.

"I'm hoping we can straighten things out. I'm going to try to talk her into marrying me."

"Wow," Trudy breathed.

"Yeah, that's what I think, too. Wow." Tim laughed, clearly delighted with himself.

"I think I know where Cricket is," Trudy said slowly. She had, after all, never really promised not to tell. And now that she was sure that Tim wasn't the enemy, that Tim would do Cricket no harm, she thought he ought to know.

"Where? Tell me," Tim said, and he smiled his most engaging smile.

"She's gone to the doctor, Tim. To find out if she's pregnant with your child."

Chapter Nineteen

It was the kind of news he had always flown away from before. But now it didn't even occur to him to put distance between himself and the problem. Instead he ran out of the Card Boutique and drove as fast as he could to the house he had once shared with Cricket. His heart pounded furiously as he ran up the front steps.

"Cricket!" he cried, slamming his fist on the door. The sounds reverberated inside his head. He thought he heard a short, animallike yelp, and this only made him hammer harder.

Cricket threw the door open, and tears streamed down her face.

He stepped into the foyer, and after one searching look, he started to sweep her into his arms. By this time, Cricket was sobbing, and he knew that what Trudy had told him must be true. She was going to bear his child.

"Crick—" he started to say, and then he saw the mousetrap dangling from her finger.

"My finger's stuck," she sobbed.

"I'll get it out," he said swiftly. He fumbled with the mechanism, swore, and snapped the trap open. It fell to the floor.

"Thank you," said Cricket. She managed to curtail her sobs.

"How did it happen?" he asked.

"I was resetting the mousetrap under the stairs, and the hammering on the door startled me. The trap went off, and my finger was in it."

"I'm sorry, Cricket. I didn't even know you were home."

"Then why were you pounding on the door?" she asked.

"I had to know if you were here because I came to ask you to marry me," he said.

Cricket swiped at a stray tear trickling down her cheek. "I think I should put some antibiotic on this finger," she said, moving toward the bathroom.

Tim peered at her through the sheer beige forest of panty hose while she stood at the sink digging through the medicine cabinet.

"Trudy told me this morning," he said quietly.

Cricket dropped the tube of antibiotic with a clatter. "Told you what this morning?"

"That you're pregnant."

"Oh, God," she whispered. It was a prayer.

"I want to get married," he said firmly.

"Because I'm pregnant? Great," she said.

"It's better than telling you I want a divorce, like the late, not-so-great Hugh Erling did when you informed him that Jeremy was on the way."

Cricket pushed her way past him. "If you think I'd marry somebody just because I was pregnant, you are mistaken. That's not a good enough reason to get married."

"How about this?" he said, unrolling a legal document of some kind right before her eyes.

"What is it?" Her finger smarted so much that she couldn't see straight.

"It's from the bank. It says that I'm approved for a loan to buy Haggerty's business. I've signed it, see, right here." Tim pointed to his signature on the bottom line.

"You're really going to buy it?" Cricket said. His words wouldn't sink in.

Tim nodded, watching her.

She still couldn't believe it.

At the door, Mungo meowed.

"I have to let the cat in," Cricket said irrelevantly.

"Cricket, don't you know what I'm saying? I'm going to stay in Manitou, and I want us to get married."

Cricket marched to the door and opened it slightly. Mungo squeezed through the small opening, his tail held high like a banner.

"Tim, pour some cat food in his dish, will you? I don't think I can with my finger hurting so much."

"I ask you to marry me and you tell me to feed the cat? Cricket, I don't believe this."

Cricket passed a weary hand over her eyes. "It's all happening too fast. I don't believe any of it. Besides, I'm not pregnant. False alarm.''

Tim shut his eyes and swallowed. ''Now it's all going too fast for me. I wish we could back up and start over.''

''I know the feeling,'' Cricket said.

''Are you going to marry me or not?'' he asked, his eyes wide open now.

''I'm not going to marry anyone who asks me because he thinks I'm pregnant,'' she said, turning away.

''I was going to ask you anyway,'' he said.

''Prove it,'' she challenged.

''Look,'' he said, and she turned around.

His T-shirt said: Marry Me, Cricket. It had yesterday's date imprinted at the bottom.

''Trudy only told me you were pregnant this morning,'' he said gently. ''I had this shirt printed last night.'' He pulled the receipt out of his pocket and handed it to her.

''You were going to ask me even before you thought I was pregnant?''

''That's right.''

She sank down on a kitchen chair and wiped her streaming eyes. ''I don't know what to say,'' she admitted.

He knelt beside her and took her hand, throbbing finger and all, into his.

''Say yes,'' he urged. He dipped his free hand into his coat pocket and took out the gold bracelet he had bought her when he was thinking of leaving Manitou. It was the closest thing he had to an engagement ring, and he clasped it around her wrist.

They looked at one another. He was very still. His eyes, blue and expectant, waited for her answer.

He'd thought she was pregnant, and he hadn't run the other way. To Cricket, that was proof enough that Tim had learned to face things that needed to be faced. She reached out and touched his cheek, and he started to smile.

''Yes,'' she breathed. ''Yes.''

He spread his arms, but not to fly away. Instead he enclosed her with them and brought her so close that their two hearts beat as one.

Epilogue

The roses were at the high tide of their June flowering when Cricket, Tim and Jeremy returned to Curtisville for their wedding.

Sarah cut heaps of roses to decorate her big farmhouse, where Cricket and Tim chose to be married.

"We're lucky you chose June because there are so many roses," said Sarah, climbing on a tall ladder to fasten a wedding bell fashioned entirely of white roses from the arch between living and dining rooms.

Cricket handed her a piece of tape. "It was the earliest we could be ready, what with my graduation from Manitou College and Tim's taking over the flying service," Cricket said.

"Mom, can I start winding the ivy around the banister?" Lucy called from the hall.

"Go ahead. And it's 'may I,' not 'can I.'"

"May I, can I, may I, can I," Lucy singsonged as she threaded ivy through the balusters.

"When is this wedding going to take place?" asked Cliff, coming in from outside.

"Three o'clock, I told you that," Sarah said, kissing him as she stepped down from the ladder.

"I'd better go get on my best bib and tucker," Cliff said as he hurried away.

"Bib and tucker, bib and tucker," Lucy sang.

"I should start getting dressed," Cricket said. She hadn't realized it was already so late.

She went into the downstairs room she shared with Jeremy and took Mina's latest creation, a confection of lace the color of pale lilacs, off its hanger. Mina had designed it especially for her.

Cricket took a leisurely bath, thinking about how beautifully everything was turning out.

When she returned from her honeymoon, her job at the mental health center in Manitou would be waiting, and she had found a young mother of one who would take care of Jeremy while Cricket worked. Tim was already chafing to get back to his business. She and Tim had rented a smaller house on the outskirts of Manitou. The main reason they had chosen it was that the owner swore that the house didn't have mice.

They had flown into Curtisville yesterday from Manitou in the six-passenger Cessna that Tim had bought with the business. Trudy had come with them, sharing space with a four-tier wedding cake baked by Gracie Haggerty.

"I'm going to be a nervous wreck by the time we get to Curtisville," Trudy had warned as she eyed the precarious cake. "If this cake doesn't survive this flight, you'll blame me."

The cake made it through the flight, and today Trudy was napping in the upstairs room she shared with Lucy.

Cricket dressed in the beautiful tea-length lilac dress and looked out the window into the sun-drenched June afternoon. Tim had arrived from his parents' trailer, looking happy and expectant. A boutonniere made of a single red rosebud wreathed in baby's breath adorned the lapel of his dark suit. He looked more handsome than ever.

Sarah peeked into Cricket's room.

"You look wonderful," she said admiringly.

"You look very nice, too," Cricket said, returning the compliment. She held the window curtain aside so that Sarah could see Tim.

"Don't you love the way Tim looks?" Sarah said.

Cricket laughed. "We think he looks like you," she said.

"People have always said so," Sarah said with a shrug.

She dropped the curtain and stood back from the mirror. "Tell me, Sarah, should I wear my hair brushed back? Or should I wear it forward like this?"

"How does Tim like it?"

"The way I usually wear it, I suppose," Cricket said, fiddling with a strand that wouldn't lie flat.

"Then wear it that way. Oh, here's our maid-of-honor," Sarah said, welcoming Trudy into the room.

Trudy yawned. "I almost overslept." She smoothed the pale pink dress she wore.

Sarah disappeared for a moment. "Here are your bouquets," she said. "Mina made them. She's a wonder with flowers."

A few cars nosed over the hill, stirring up a cloud of dust. "Our first guests are here. I'd better greet them," Sarah said.

"Where's Jeremy?"

"Mina's taking care of him. She loves that little fellow. Do you want me to tell Tim anything?"

"That I love him," Cricket said, her eyes sparkling.

Soon Sarah's mother Charlotte, who had volunteered, began to play the wedding march on the upright piano that stood in the hall. She played stiffly because of her arthritis, but the notes from the old piano were mellow and sweet. Cricket and Trudy waited by the door for their cue.

Cliff stopped by. "Are you sure you won't change your mind, Cricket, and let me give you away?"

Cricket smiled and shook her head. After Cliff had left, Cricket whispered to Trudy, "Everything I've got to give was given away long ago."

Trudy whispered back, "You have the capacity to go on giving and giving." Trudy's eyes shone with happy tears on her friend's behalf.

When Charlotte came down hard on the "Here Comes the Bride" refrain, Trudy preceded Cricket into the living room, and all eyes turned to watch Cricket as she walked slowly to meet Tim.

Their smiles lit up the room, and when she was at last standing beside him, he said, "I love you, Cricket," so that everyone in the room could hear.

Cricket and Tim tried not to grin like Cheshires through the whole ceremony, but they couldn't help it. It was a day for smiles, and for happiness, and for love.

"To have and to hold from this day forward," was all Cricket would remember the minister saying during the ceremony, although she knew that there had been other words before and after. "From this day forward" was a phrase of such promise and magnitude that she knew it would be engraved upon her heart forever.

At the end of the ceremony when the minister gently told them that they could kiss, Tim surprised everyone by declaring, "The first kiss is for Jeremy," and he swooped a surprised Jeremy from Mina's lap so that they could share their first kiss as a family of three. Then Cricket and Tim, still smiling, faced their friends and family as a married couple.

Whatever happened in the future, it would be all right. They had each other now, and they would face whatever needed to be faced. Together, and for a lifetime.

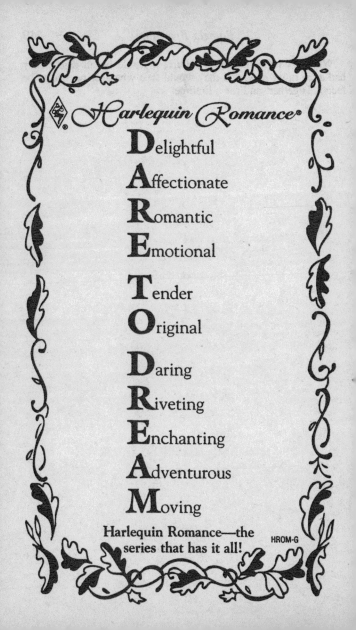

✦ *Harlequin Romance*®

Delightful
Affectionate
Romantic
Emotional
Tender
Original
Daring
Riveting
Enchanting
Adventurous
Moving

Harlequin Romance—the series that has it all!

HROM-G

HARLEQUIN  PRESENTS®

HARLEQUIN PRESENTS
men you won't be able to resist
falling in love with...

HARLEQUIN PRESENTS
women who have feelings
just like your own...

HARLEQUIN PRESENTS
powerful passion in
exotic international settings...

HARLEQUIN PRESENTS
intense, dramatic stories that will keep you
turning to the very last page...

HARLEQUIN PRESENTS
The world's bestselling romance series!

Harlequin® Historical

From rugged lawmen and
valiant knights to defiant heiresses
and spirited frontierswomen,
Harlequin Historicals will
capture your imagination with
their dramatic scope, passion
and adventure.

Harlequin Historicals...
they're too good to miss!

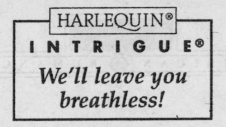

HARLEQUIN®
I N T R I G U E®
We'll leave you breathless!

If you've been looking for thrilling tales of
contemporary passion and sensuous love stories
with taut, edge-of-the-seat suspense—
then you'll *love* **Harlequin Intrigue!**

Every month, you'll meet four new heroes
who are guaranteed to make your spine tingle
and your pulse pound. With them you'll enter
into the exciting world of Harlequin Intrigue—
where your life is on the line
and so is your heart!

THAT'S INTRIGUE—DYNAMIC
ROMANCE AT ITS BEST!

HARLEQUIN®

I N T R I G U E®

INT-GENR

LOOK FOR OUR FOUR FABULOUS MEN!

Each month some of today's bestselling authors bring
four new fabulous men to Harlequin American Romance.
Whether they're rebel ranchers, millionaire power brokers
or sexy single dads, they're all gallant princes—and
they're all ready to sweep you into lighthearted fantasies
and contemporary fairy tales where anything is possible
and where all your dreams come true!

You don't even have to make a wish...
Harlequin American Romance will grant your every desire!

Look for Harlequin American Romance
wherever Harlequin books are sold!